THE COAL MINER'S SON

A Family Saga

Patricia M Osborne

White Wings Books

Published 2020 in United Kingdom
by White Wings Books

ISBN 978-0-9957107-1-9

British Cataloguing Publication data:
A catalogue record of this book is available from the British Library

This book is also available as an ebook.

In Memory of
my dearest mum,

Lila (1932-2014)

and Sister,

Heather (1956-2009)

Two courageous and inspiring women.

A light went out in my heart when you both left this world.

Part I

Chapter 1

George

Shuffling feet, giggles and chatter filled the school corridor. Ben pushed me into the cluttered coats making me land on my bum. Luckily for me Miss Jones wasn't around yet. We charged into the classroom and raced to our seats at the back. I won cos my legs were longer. Mam said I was like a stick. Eight of us sat round two tables squashed together as boy-girl-boy-girl. I shifted away from my neighbour, Susie Smith, a small girl with ginger frizzy hair and blotchy skin. Ben sat opposite her. Miss Jones strode into the room clapping her hands. Forty chairs scraped across the floor as everyone stood to attention and our rickety seats squeaked like mice when we sat back down.

Miss Jones wrote 11th June 1962 on the blackboard. 'Open your exercise books and practise the "Seven Times Table" in your heads. I shall test you after break.'

Paper rustled as pages turned. I got to four times seven when I heard the usual trickling. I bent down and found pee running close to my feet. Not again. I looked up towards Ben and rolled my eyes. He sniggered. I put up my hand.

'What is it, George?' Miss Jones said.

I signalled to Susie.

'Oh dear. Would you mind fetching the mop, George? Susan, you go too and find Nurse.'

I dragged my chair back to stand up and the whole class turned to watch as I strode out of the room with Smelly Susie wriggling behind me. Why hadn't she put up her hand to ask to go? No wonder no one wanted to play with her.

Humping the mop and bucket round to my table, I soaked up the puddle. The stink made me want to spew like when Mam asked me to put our Beth's smelly nappy in the bucket.

Miss Jones patted me on the shoulder. 'Thank you, George.'

I turned around and looked up into her light blue eyes. My heart banged like a drum. One day I was going to marry Miss Jones.

On my way back to the classroom the bell rang so I ran to catch up with Ben who was already nearly out of the door. We whispered and giggled.

'George, can you wait behind please?' asked Miss Jones.

She must've heard us laughing at Smelly Susie. Now Mam would find out, she'd tell Da and it'd be the slipper for me. But it wasn't fair, why didn't Ben have to stay behind too?

'Sit down, George.' Miss Jones pointed to the wooden chair next to her desk as she crossed her long legs. She looked like Marilyn Monroe with her blonde wavy hair. Da was always saying Marilyn Monroe was the most beautiful woman in the world, next to Mam and our Alice of course. I hadn't known what Marilyn Monroe looked like so Ben had showed me a picture in a magazine.

I crept towards the chair.

'Don't look so worried. I just want a quick word.' She flipped through the pages of my exercise book. 'Look at all these red ticks.'

I gawked at the pages.

'There's not one sum wrong,' she carried on. 'You're a bright boy. What would you like to be when you grow up?'

I shrugged my shoulders. Ben reckoned he was going to live with his aunty in America when he grew up. He wasn't going down the mine. It wasn't fair. 'Dunno, same as Da and his da, I s'pose.'

'That would be a waste. You could go to grammar school and get a good job. You're bright enough to do your eleven plus early. I could help.'

'But Miss, I'm only just nine.'

'Yes, George.' She smiled. 'But you're as bright as any ten-year-old. I'd like to speak to your mother. Is she home tomorrow morning?'

'Think so.'

'I also wanted to thank you for clearing up after Susan every day. You're a good boy, George Gilmore. I can't understand why Mr Mason complains about you.'

I shrugged my shoulders to pretend I didn't know why Sir used Percy Pump on me. I was never naughty for Miss Jones cos she was lovely and that's why I cleared up Susie's pee.

Miss Jones passed me the biscuit box that sometimes came out at break time. 'Take two.'

I sank my teeth into a melting chocolate finger, it was scrummy. I saved the other one for Ben.

*

'George Gilmore.' Mr Mason slashed a ruler down on my table. 'Dreaming again, boy? Stand up and spell Encyclopaedia.'

I nearly jumped off my chair and quickly covered my exercise book. I didn't want him to see the *George and Janet* heart I'd drawn on the back cover. I didn't know Miss Jones's first name but she looked like a Janet to me.

'Come on boy.' Mr Mason smirked.

He thought I didn't know how to spell it, but I did. The funny 'ae' in the middle helped me remember. I didn't want it to look too easy though as some of the lads already teased me cos I was clever and cos I helped Miss Jones. I took a deep breath. 'E N C err Y? C L O P E, oh no I mean A, E D A, sorry Sir I mean, I A.'

Sir's eyeballs bulged like frogs' eyes. He moved his speckled beard closer to my face. 'Excellent, Gilmore.' His sour breath made me gag. 'Does everyone else know how to spell it?' he asked, breathing all over me.

The class kept their heads down.

'Gilmore, write it on the blackboard. Class, watch carefully.'

Thank goodness, my chance to get away from the giant with bad breath. I stopped pretending I wasn't clever and bolted up to the blackboard. I picked up the white chalk and made it squeak as I wrote ENCYCLOPAEDIA in big letters under the date.

The bell rang. I escaped into fresh air.

Ben nudged me. 'Come on Brain Box.'

We skedaddled out to the playground pushing each other.

*

Mam was on the couch with her face hiding in Mrs Deane's chest. Why was *she* even here? She didn't even like Mam, she thought Mam was too posh. Our headmaster had sent everyone home early today because there'd been an accident at the mine. The road to the pit was blocked and bobbies were all over the place, dust flying everywhere. I tried to push through the barriers to find Da but the policeman wouldn't let me through, said it was off limits so I asked him about Jack Gilmore but he just told us to get on our way and 'straight home, mind.' Alice pestered me all the way back to our house, questions like, what's going on and is Daddy all right. 'Yes of course he's all right,' I told her. I hoped I was right.

Mrs Deane eased Mam away from her. 'Now that the bairns are home, Mrs Gilmore, I need to get next door to check on

Nancy. And that little one needs feeding.' She pointed to Beth lying in her cot. Mrs Deane stood up and patted Mam on the arm. On her way out she tapped me on the head. 'Look after your Mam, there's a good lad.' She waddled over to the door and closed it behind her.

'Mam, what's happened? I asked.

She covered her face with her hands.

'Is Da alright? Alice, get Mam a cup of water.' My chest started thumping.

Alice passed me a chipped mug. 'What's wrong with Mammy?'

'Here, Mam, drink this.'

Beth started howling so I strode over to the yellow carrycot and picked her up. She stopped crying when I rocked her in my arms. 'Mam, I think she's hungry.'

Mam took Beth, unbuttoned her blouse and stuck the baby on her bosom. Beth made smacking sounds as she sucked.

'What did Mrs Deane want?' I looked round, there was no pan on the stove. 'What's for tea? Da will be home soon.'

Mam just stared into space.

'Shall I peel some spuds?' If I got grub ready, Da would walk through the door. Mam always said he could smell food a mile off.

Mam's face was white. 'George, come and sit down, you too Alice.' She patted the couch next to her, still holding the baby. Alice and I snuggled up to Mam and Beth, making the springs ping. I placed my arm around Mam's neck. My throat closed up.

'How much did your headmaster tell you?'

'Something about an accident at the mine,' I said.

'You know your father loved us all very much, don't you?'

'Yeah.' My chest thumped faster.

'Your fa...' She sobbed making her body shake. 'Your fa...'

7

'No, not Da.' I squeezed my eyes.

'I'm sorry my darlings. I'm sorry but your fa.... A policewoman came around earlier to tell me that your father... he was in the mining accident.'

'But he's going to be all right, isn't he?' I clung to Mam.

'I'm sorry George, but no. No, he's not. I'm sorry but Dad's gone to Heaven. They said he wouldn't have been in pain. He didn't want to leave us. He couldn't help it.' She squeezed us both tight, so tight, I couldn't breathe. Her tears wet my cheeks.

'No, you're wrong. Daddy's coming home in a minute.' Alice broke away and shrieked, 'George said so.'

I wanted to believe Alice was right but I said under my breath, 'He's dead.'

Alice punched me. 'Stop it, stop saying things like that. I hate you.' She ran upstairs bawling.

I peered around the room. Da's best boots stood by the door. His clean white shirt hung from the pulley and his pipe lay in the ashtray.

Chapter 2

Elizabeth

I opened the solid oak wardrobe door and stared at the two dresses adjacent to each other. The first, a white lace gown with a broderie-anglaise bodice boasting tiny silk roses, and the second, an elegant black satin frock draped just below the knee. Neither reflected the right emotions.

It seemed a lifetime ago, much more than nine years, since I stepped into the wedding dress, experiencing only sadness, nerves and loneliness. I ran my fingers over it. If only things had been different, Grace would have been my bridesmaid. How we used to giggle as girls growing up together, chatting about our wedding days.

My mind slipped back to walking down the aisle at Loxhurst Cathedral, my arm hooked into Father's. Our feet paced in rhythm to Richard Wagner's bridal march, *Here Comes the Bride*. Faces I didn't recognise squinted their eyes to capture a view of me, the teenage bride, in my crisp silk-laced gown, trailing six-foot on the ground. I cuffed a bouquet of red roses dressed with gypsophila tightly between my fists. Strangers, daughters of Father's business acquaintances, tailed behind as bridesmaids in lemon, clasping baskets of mix-coloured chrysanthemums. I turned around to see the three-year-old twins, posing as pageboys, chasing behind in green plaid kilts. Martha, our housekeeper, her grey hair piled into a bun, pointed a stern finger at them. She mouthed towards me, *face the front*, where the large-framed man in his fifties, barely any hair on his round head, stood at the end of the first pew waiting eagerly for his prize.

I fingered the black, silky folds of the second dress. I flushed, remembering how I stood over his grave, in the pouring rain, with false tears, unable to mourn this man, my mind blank as the coffin was lowered. I'd shivered in the wet weather, and cringed as, one by one, I shook the hands of Father's and Gregory's business acquaintances while they offered their condolences.

How foolish I'd been to think my problems had been over. Two weeks after the funeral I was weeding the spring flowerbeds, enjoying the daffodils and red tulips dancing in the light breeze, when Winnie, the new maid, hurried into the garden. *Why had Gregory employed her?* His explanation *to take the burden off me*, somehow didn't ring true.

'It's the solicitor, Ma'am. He's waiting for you in the library.'

Finally, I was free. With renewed energy, I strode into the house.

'Mr Simpson.' I took his hand to shake. 'What's the news?'

He shook his head. 'It's not good, Lady Giles, I'm afraid there's very little left.'

'What do you mean?'

'Too many creditors, I'm afraid.'

I blacked out, opening my eyes to Winnie holding a glass of water under my nose. 'Here, Ma'am. Drink this.'

The solicitor was fidgeting with his hat. 'Are you all right, Lady Giles? Perhaps I should return another time?'

'No, no, I'm fine now. Please continue.'

'I'm sorry to be the bearer of such bad news.' The solicitor rustled his papers. 'Might it help if I notified Lord Granville, and filled him in with the details?'

As usual I'd need to rely on Father because I had no idea what to do. 'Thank you, Mr Simpson. Yes please if you don't mind.'

'Certainly, Lady Giles.' He shook my hand again. 'Good day to you.'

I clenched my fists, stormed out into the garden, knelt on the grass, and yanked a big bunch of buttercups, hidden under the crimson azaleas, from their roots. And then buried my face in my hands to weep.

Within a month, Father had taken over. Dealt with the death certificate, bribing the doctor and creditors. I begged him not to compromise the doctor but I didn't stand a chance.

'Elizabeth, the Granville reputation can't afford to let the Press get hold of your husband's drunken lifestyle. Myocardial infarction sits much better on the death certificate. I can't understand why you didn't come to me earlier.'

It was becoming clear why Grace left all those years ago. Father understood very little about me. His only interest was his reputation. I certainly wouldn't be wearing this dress again. I threw it on the bed in a heap along with the wedding dress.

Mother walked into the room. She didn't look any older than when I'd left the house nine years ago except her dark hair was now shorter and set in a wave just below her ears.

'How are you getting on? she asked. Are you sure you wouldn't like Martha or one of the girls to assist you?'

'I'm almost finished, Mother.'

'Elizabeth, what are these dresses doing here?' She picked up the wedding dress, cradling it in her arms. 'These beautiful gowns deserve to be treated with dignity.'

'I won't wear them again, Mother. We should give them away to a charitable cause.'

'Nonsense, dear child. This is all you have left. You need to hold on to your memories.' She draped the dresses over coathangers and hung them back in the wardrobe. 'Now let's not have any more talk about parting with them. Dinner is in fifteen minutes. If you can't sort this out' – she waved her hands around – 'I'll send one of the maids in to finish for you.'

'I'll do it, Mother. I'll be down in time.'

She left the room huffing and puffing. I pushed the bedroom door closed.

I slumped down onto the bed, in the same bedroom I'd slept in for my first sixteen years. Nothing had changed. And I was supposed to be grateful. Arching my back, I got up and smoothed down my straight skirt. Well I was no longer that naive young girl, but I needed to find strength to stand up to the great Lord Granville.

Chapter 3

George

After crawling out of bed I put on my Sunday best. I didn't want to wear these posh clothes and I didn't want to bury Da.

I took down the National Dried Milk from the shelf and scooped powder out of the blue and white drum, added boiling water and stood the bottle in cold water to cool. When it was ready I tipped it onto the back of my hand to test the temperature like Mam showed me. Warm milk trickled from the teat. Mam went to the baby clinic to get the powdered milk after she had to stop feeding Beth with her bosoms, and they gave her some bottles of thick orange juice and tasty rosehip syrup too. I picked Beth out of the cot and sat down on the couch to feed her. She guzzled, sucking on the teat. It was a good job the lads at school didn't see me, they'd have called me a cissy but I just wanted to help Mam cos she was sad. I didn't want to play footie now anyway and cuddling our Beth made me forget Da was dead. Mrs Deane would be here to take her soon.

'When's Mammy going to make breakfast?' asked Alice.

'Mam's getting ready. Stick a slice of bread under the grill and do one for me too.'

I lifted Beth towards my face. 'Pooh.' I laid her on the floor to change her nappy and managed to pin the new one together without stabbing her. Mam said I was a quick learner. I slipped a yellow frock that smelled of flowers over Beth's almost bald head. Mam said Beth was going to be blonde like me and Alice.

13

Beth wriggled making her silky skin slippery, so I put her down in the huge pram in case I dropped her.

Mam was still upstairs, crying. She was always crying since the accident, but I wasn't supposed to know. Alice was sitting on the floor staring at the telly as no one was there to say she shouldn't, and I couldn't be bothered. There was nothing on anyway, she was just staring at the test card that looked like a Ludo board.

Mrs Deane tapped on the back door before striding in. 'Morning lad, where's ya Mam?'

'Upstairs gettin ready. I'll tell her you're ere.' I tiptoed upstairs and found Mam just sitting, glaring into the mirror, holding her lippie.

'Mam, Mrs Deane's here.'

'Thank you, Sweetheart.' Mam smiled and brushed her wet face against my cheek before dropping a net veil from the black hat, hiding her eyes. I wished I had a veil to hide behind.

*

Mam clenched my hand tight. Her wedding ring dug into my fingers. Aunty Nancy, our neighbour, stepped out of her door as we were leaving. She stuck close to Mam and took Alice's hand. We walked sadly in the direction of the church. Ben went to Sunday school there every week, but Da said Sundays were for footie or picnics in the park. Red and yellow roses stood like soldiers as we passed by window boxes on the cobbled street. Crows flew on and off house roofs squawking. When we reached the church, Mam stopped and backed away. Nancy took her arm and led us into the dark building. We sat down in line on the hard, brown benches. The vicar opened his book and started to speak, his mouth moved but my ears had gone deaf. Mam stared into space, gripping my hand so tight it made my bones crunch. Alice's eyes were like pennies. She still thought Da was coming home. I tried to tell her he wasn't, but every time I did she threw a tantrum, punching me in the chest and belly, her long spiral curls buried into my chest.

Da's miner friends were dressed up in white shirts and dark suits. Six of them went up to the coffin and whispered. They moved around the coffin and then swapped over, still whispering between themselves. With three men on each side, they nodded, took a deep breath and heaved Da up onto their shoulders. One of the men sneezed, the coffin slipped. They were going to drop him.

Aunty Nancy leant over and patted my knee. 'It's all right, luvvie.'

The miners nodded again and started moving slowly out of church carrying Da. We followed behind while the other people carried on singing.

Aunty Nancy said the coloured flowers in the round shapes were called wreaths. She reached into her bag and passed a white rose to me and one to Alice. It made me sneeze like those in the boxes outside the houses. Why did Da get killed? Uncle John, Aunty Nancy's husband, got killed too, so there was no grown-up person left to play footie with Ben and me.

They put the wooden coffin down the huge hole. I didn't want them to put Da in the ground. The vicar waved his hand to tell us to throw in our flowers. Mam screamed, dropped to her knees on the grass and tried to climb in the hole with Da. I wanted to scream too but I didn't because big boys don't. Da said so. I wanted to run away and hide so I could blubber without anyone hearing. Mam was frightening me. She was frightening our Alice too.

Chapter 4

Elizabeth

Footsteps approached my room. I quickly gathered together the memorabilia scattered on my bed and hid it under the satin eiderdown.

'Miss Elizabeth.' Martha tapped on the door.

'Come in. What is it?'

'His Lordship has requested that you join him in the drawing room in fifteen minutes.'

'Thank you.'

As she left I returned to the bales of letters tied up in pink ribbon, all written in the same handwriting, from when Grace was at Greenemere. We wrote to each other almost every day. That was before she deserted me, chose the coal miner instead. I'd needed her these past few years but not one visit, letter or phone call. I held up a pair of red plaid trews that no longer fitted. These made me smile but also brought tears. Grace had put so much love into making them, yet she was able to walk away from me with ease. I screwed them up and threw them into the bin, just like I'd done numerous times before, but changed my mind. I couldn't do it. I pulled them out, smoothed out the creases and wrapped them back up in tissue, carefully placing them at the bottom of the box. If Father discovered them, he'd no doubt have them destroyed. They'd managed to survive the last twelve years so I certainly didn't want him finding them now.

What did Father want? Was he finally going to ask me to help run the estate? I'd hoped he was going to mention it at dinner last night, but instead, he made his apologies to leave on urgent business, leaving Mother and I, for the rest of the meal, sitting virtually in silence. Well if he was going to ask me, I was ready. Reading numerous commerce books had alleviated my boredom during the last three months at Cousin Victoria's.

At last he was ready to recognise me. I checked my watch. It was time. I brushed my fingers down the shiny bannister remembering the day Grace made me leap on behind her to slide down. Where were you Sister when I needed you? The double-door was ajar. I tapped.

'Come in,' Father said.

'Good morning, Father.'

'Good morning, Elizabeth. I trust you slept well.'

'Yes, thank you, Father.' Everything was the same. It was though I hadn't been absent, like the last nine years had never happened. How I wished that was so.

'Now, Elizabeth.' He was waving a letter around. 'I expect you're wondering why I asked you here?'

'Yes Father.' I tried to hide my smile while waiting for the words.

'Elizabeth. I'm speaking to you. Pay attention.'

'Sorry, Father.'

'I've received this letter from your sister.' The note in his hand rustled.

Grace. Why now?

'She too has become a widow but unlike you, has three children. She's asked for our help.'

'She's coming home?'

'Definitely not. Grace was told the day she left that all rights of being part of this family would be eliminated. The only reason I'm agreeing to help is I've discovered that her eldest child is a nine-year-old boy. My intention is to bring him to Granville Hall as my heir.'

Nausea crept up my stomach and into my throat. So now Grace's offspring would take my place. Why was I never good enough? 'And what does Grace say about that? Surely she won't hand over her child?'

'Don't worry about that. Grace will be more than happy to relinquish her rights once she's set up in a flat and shop with a lump sum to provide for her daughters. Your sister always did have a good business head on her shoulders.'

'You're going to buy him?' Grace would never give her firstborn away. Surely. Not for all the money in the world.

'Now, Elizabeth. I'd like you to turn this young lad into a gentleman and throw in a bit of schooling. Do you think you can manage that?'

'But Father, I thought perhaps you'd rather I was involved in the estate business? I've been reading up on commerce whilst in Devon.'

'What?' He tilted his head back and let out a roar of laughter. 'Dear child, whatever possessed you to think that? Grace, yes, but you…' He let out another roar.

Tears pricked my eyes but I forced myself to hold them in.

'My plan is for my grandson to take over matters of Granville Hall once he's old enough. Not you. You were never in the equation. Now are you able to deal with my request?'

'Yes, Father,' I managed to say.

'Very well, write down what you need, stationary, chalks, books etc. You're to use the old schoolroom at the top of the house. Do an inspection and get Martha to make the arrangements for whatever you need. That will be all.'

'Yes, Father.' I left the room briskly, went upstairs to my room, threw myself onto the bed and screamed into the bedding.

Chapter 5

George

There was no school today but I still got up early to lay the table and found it set. Mam was standing at the sink washing pots and pans so she must've been feeling better.

'Morning, sweetheart,' she said. 'Your grandmother's visiting today so you and Alice are to have a bath and put on your Sunday best.'

'Ah, Mam, do I ave to? I'll help you bring in the tinnie but do I ave to wear those clothes?'

'Yes, George, you do. And what have I told you about dropping your 'H's?'

'But those clothes make me think of Da getting buried.'

'Come here.' Mam cuddled me close, her dark wavy hair tickled my face. 'I know, sweetheart. You've been such a good boy, doing all those jobs and looking after Beth when you should've been playing outside with friends. Do this one more thing for me, please.'

'All right, Mam. Don't cry, I'll wear the clothes.'

'You're a good boy. Your father would be proud.'

Alice sloped downstairs and we sat down together at the table to eat jammy toast that was a little burnt around the edges.

'George, can you feed Beth while I bathe Alice, please?'

I wanted to say I was too tired but instead I said, 'Yes, Mam.' I wandered into the other room, lifted my sister out of the carrycot, sat down on the couch and picked up Beth's bottle from the table. She sucked hard at the teat. Everything was going to be all right. Mam had started doing the jobs again and

Grandma was coming to help us. I sat Beth up and patted her back. After she made a loud burp I put her down into the yellow carrycot and she went straight to sleep.

Mam peeped her head in. 'Your turn, George.'

I traipsed into the kitchen and shut the door behind me to strip off my clothes and splashed into the almost clean water. Alice didn't get dirty like me. Mam said I got filthy from wrestling around the yard with Ben. I wasn't filthy today though. I missed playing with Ben and I missed footie with Da and Uncle John. The funeral clothes hung across the chair. I didn't want to put them on but I'd promised Mam. I wanted Da to walk through the door and into the kitchen.

Using the sponge, I scrubbed under my arms and privates while wondering what Grandma was like. Would she look like Mam? I thought Mam was an orphan until yesterday when she told us that she had a Mam and Da who lived in a big mansion and they were called Lady and Lord Granville. She had a sister too, Elizabeth.

Mam tapped on the door. 'How are you getting on? Are you nearly finished?'

'Just comin.' I heaved myself up out of the bath and grabbed the towel. I buttoned up my best shirt and stepped into the dark-coloured shorts. Then, to surprise Mam, I dragged the tinnie outside and tipped the water out. A grey stream trickled down the yard, not black like when Da had his bath.

'Finished.' I dashed into the sitting room just as there was a click clack sound outside, then a knock on the front door.

'Now best behaviour, both of you,' Mam said.

A lady dressed in a tight suit with a small hat on her head stood at the door. Her high heels click-clacked on the blue patterned lino as she came into the house and peered all around the room with her nose up in the air.

I didn't like the look of her but still stretched out my hand to shake hers like Mam had taught me. 'I'm pleased to meet you, Grandma.'

'Grandmother,' she snapped.

'Sorry, Grandmother.'

Mam was busying around, putting the kettle on the stove and slicing Madeira cake.

'Mind the hat,' Grandma said to Alice.

Mam carried a tray of tea and cake and placed it on the coffee table. She'd used the best china that almost never came out of the cabinet.

'May we speak in private?' Grandma asked Mam.

'Yes of course. Children, yours is on the table.'

She didn't have to tell me twice, I was gone. I shovelled cake into my mouth but kept my ears pricked up. I couldn't catch what they were saying but Grandma was making Mam cry. I didn't like this grandma. She might look like Mam but she wasn't kind.

*

I wished Grandma wasn't coming back today because she wanted to take me away to Granville Hall. Mam promised she wouldn't let her take me but I still had to get strip washed.

Mam glanced at her watch. 'She'll be here in a minute, she's always punctual.'

I snatched back the nets and watched as a black shiny car drove up. Grandma stepped out of it and waved when she caught me staring out of the window.

'Good afternoon, Grace.' Grandma pecked Mam on the cheek before she click-clacked into the house wearing a different pair of high heels than yesterday. She took off her lampshade hat and passed it to Alice who managed to hide her face when trying it on.

Grandma laughed. 'And how old are you?'

'I'm six.' Alice walked around the room giggling like she was playing blind man's buff.

'Children, can you play upstairs in your room for a little while?' asked Mam.

I grabbed Alice's hand, and whispered, 'Come on, Mam's going to make Grandma let us all live in the big house.' I didn't want to go and live in the big house, I wanted to stay in our house and go to school with Ben, but Mam said we'd got no money to stay in our house now that Da was dead.

Alice passed Grandma her hat back and we stomped up the wooden stairs. I pushed toy cars and tractors around the bare floorboards and Alice brushed her doll's hair that looked like Smelly Susie's.

After a while, Mam shouted up, 'George, can you come down please?'

I dashed downstairs. 'Are we coming to live with you, Grandma? I mean, Grandmother.' I hoped she'd said no and just given Mam money to help us.

'Sit down, George.' Mam wiped her eyes. 'Grandmother would like you to go and live at Granville Hall.'

'Just me?'

'Yes, George.' Mam bowed her head.

'You said you wouldn't let her take me. Mam, you promised. I don't even want to live in her great big house.'

Grandma smiled. 'Now, George, this is a great opportunity and you'll be helping your mother and sisters too.'

'I'm helping Mam here. I'm man of the house now.'

Grandma flipped her head back. 'Oh dear, young man, you've such a lot to learn and Granville Hall will help you.'

'Mother, I'm not sure,' Mam said lifting her head.

22

Phew, she wasn't going to make me go. She was going to keep her promise. I hadn't been naughty, well not since Da died. I'd tried to be good, helping with Beth, washing the pans and I even made sausage and mash on the accident day. So why would Mam want to send me away?

'Stop it, Grace. Remember what I told you,' Grandma said, 'George, go upstairs and pack an overnight bag.'

I turned to Mam, she nodded yes but hid her face. What did Grandma mean by an overnight bag anyway? And what did Mam have to remember? 'I don't want to come. I'm only coming if Mam and me sisters come too.'

'I'm afraid that's not possible.'

'Why?'

'Because it's not,' Grandma answered.

'Well I'm not coming either. Mam, tell her.'

'Don't ask your mother.' Grandma's voice went softer. 'I'll tell you what, if you're not happy after a month you may return home.'

Mam's eyes twinkled. 'That's sounds like a good idea, George. A little holiday. What do you think?'

I'd never had a holiday. 'Can I go to a seaside, like this?' I picked up the jigsaw lid from the floor and passed her the picture of a seaside.

'That's Brighton. I recognise the West Pier. Yes, you can go to Brighton and lots of other places too,' Grandma said.

Mam turned her face away.

'Mam, what's up?'

Grandma interrupted, 'I'm sure you'd like to get to know your grandfather and aunt. And have new clothes?'

'Mam?'

Mam held my hands in hers. 'Why not go, just for a little while?'

'But I'll miss you and Beth, and our Alice.' I couldn't believe I was saying I'd miss Alice too but I knew I would.

'We'll miss you too. But you deserve a holiday. You're too young to take on so many responsibilities. I've been expecting far too much from you since your father died.'

I turned to Grandma. 'If I come for a few weeks do you promise to bring me back home?'

'Of course,' Grandma said, 'now be a good lad and go upstairs and pack a bag.'

'What should I pack, Mam?'

'Pyjamas for tonight and clean clothes for tomorrow,' answered Grandma. 'We'll buy new garments once we arrive at Granville Hall.'

'Mam?'

She nodded yes, so I ran upstairs and yanked Da's brown duffle bag out of the cupboard in Mam's room. He always carried it when we went on picnics in the park. Mam used to tell him off saying he needed a new one because he'd been using that one for years. Something was bulging in it so I dug my hands in and pulled out Da's black gloves. I sniffed them, they still smelled like Da. I wiped my eyes. *Stop being a cissy.* I flung out underpants, socks, shorts, a t-shirt, and pyjamas from the bottom two drawers in the tallboy and stuffed them into the bag and stuck Da's gloves back in.

'What you doing?' asked Alice.

She was standing in the doorway. I hoped she hadn't heard me boo. 'I'm going on holiday.'

'Can I come?'

'Grandma won't let you but when I get there I'll make Grandpa change her mind.'

I ran downstairs with Alice right behind me. Mam was crying again.

'Mam, what's wrong?' I asked.

24

'Nothing, George. I'm just being silly.'

'Have you got everything?' asked Grandma.

'I've changed my mind, I don't wanna go.'

'Grace,' Grandma said.

Mam hugged me tight then took a brass frame out of her pinny pocket. 'Take this with you.' She kissed me and made my face wet from her tears. 'Just remember, I'll always love you.'

Why was she saying that? And why was she crying? I'd told Grandma I wanted to come back home after a couple of weeks.

'Mam, I don't wanna go.'

'George, take no notice of me. Go and have a good time, you deserve it.' She kissed me again and nudged me to leave.

Grandma took my hand and hauled me out the house towards her big car. Mam started to blub again so I turned around to see her but Grandma pushed me into the back seat. 'Your mother will be fine. She's just upset because it's your first time away from home.'

The car smelled stuffy so I was glad Grandma asked the driver to open the windows to let in fresh air. My bare legs stuck to the red shiny seat.

'What's Aunty Elizabeth like?' I asked.

'You'll like her,' she said.

'What's Grandpa like?'

'It's Grandfather. Now close your eyes, we've a long journey ahead.'

'What's Granville Hall like? How many bedrooms has it got? Mam says it's got loads but how many?'

'That's enough questions, George.'

I didn't like this Grandma. I peered out of the back window watching Alice and Mam get smaller and smaller through the coal dust streaked glass. Something in my pocket dug into my leg, I pulled out the photo frame that always sat on the sideboard. Mam looked pretty in her special dress that trailed

25

on the ground and Da was doing that cheeky smile that used to make her say, 'You won't get around me, Jack Gilmore,' and then she'd smack a big kiss on his lips. His dark suit had a flower on it. He looked posh and he wasn't dead. I didn't want him to be dead. I wanted to bawl but didn't dare.

Chapter 6

Elizabeth

A car door slammed. I stood up and wandered over to the window. A young boy with blond curls hanging down from his cap climbed the steps. Dark grey shorts showed off his spindly legs. It seemed Grace had handed over her firstborn after all. I was sure that she wouldn't. Part of me wanted to go down and see this child but I still felt aggrieved that I was supposed to become no more than a governess and take care of him. The poor old aunt who couldn't bear any children of her own.

I sank down in the wicker chair, trying to shake away memories of that dreadful day, but as usual, images from my wedding night kept emerging, pressing me. The band had still been playing when he came up behind me and whispered in my ear, "It's time to go." His breath stunk of whisky. I'd no idea what it would be like to become a woman in that sense, no one to speak to about losing my virginity to the fat pompous man.

He sat close to me on the back seat of one of Father's limousines, his fingers inching my dress higher, to the top of my nylons, and touching my bare leg. Finally the torturous journey came to an end as we pulled into the drive of Ashburnham Lodge, his home and mine.

'We only have one servant in this house, Elizabeth,' he said, 'I expect you to muck in with the chores and get your hands dirty.'

'Yes of course, Gregory,' I said, feeling nauseous heading into the house.

'Hannah,' he called.

27

A short girl in the same type of uniform as the maids at Granville Hall rushed into the hallway. She looked about three years older than me, maybe the same age as Grace, but her skin was more weathered. Her blonde hair was pinned into a bun, small curls kissed her round face.

'Show Lady Giles to her room and take her bag.' He pointed to my small suitcase. In it were a few basics packed by Martha to keep me going until my trunk arrived from the Hall.

'Certainly, Sir,' she said picking up the small bag. 'Come along, Mistress. This way.'

I followed her up the straight stairway to the landing. She stopped at the third door on the right and swung it open. 'This is it, Miss.' She walked over to another door. 'And in here is your bathroom.'

At least I had my own bathroom, that was something. But this house was far from the mansion Gregory had portrayed to Father. I wondered what other lies this man had offered in exchange for me.

'Would you like me to pull back the bed, Miss?'

'Thank you.'

She dragged back the satin eiderdown revealing crisp cotton, white sheets. The thought of the bed, and what was to happen later, made me rush to the toilet, lean over and be sick.

'Are you all right, Miss?' Hannah looked concerned and was that pity in her eyes?

'I'm fine, thank you. The day has been a bit overwhelming, that's all. You can go now.'

'Very well, Miss.' She crept out of the room as Gregory took her place, drooling in the entrance.

'I'll be back up in fifteen minutes,' he said, 'that should give you time to get out of that thing.' He signalled to my wedding dress and was gone again.

This was it. I didn't know what to expect but I didn't for one moment anticipate it to be pleasurable with that letch. If only I had Grace to speak to, or a friend. But because of Grace, I had no chance to make a real friend. Father refused to let me have a roommate when I'd gone away to school at Greenemere, or allow anyone to get close to me. He said he didn't want the same thing happening again. The one friend I made got so fed up with my refusals to visit her home and not being invited to mine that we drifted apart once we finished school. So here I was alone and with no idea what to expect.

I struggled to unzip my dress but managed to step out of it, leaving it strewn across the floor. Nothing romantic about this gown. I unbuttoned the poppers on my suspenders and placed my nylons and the belt carefully across a chair. I fumbled through my suitcase and pulled out a full-length black silk nightdress with a red satin ribbon falling from the scoop neckline. Martha's idea of what a bride should wear on her wedding night, I presumed. Under different circumstances, if I was in love with the man that I was about to lie next to for the first time, I'd be shaking with excitement not repulsion. Leaving my white laced brassiere and matching knickers on, I lifted the nightdress over my head, smoothed it down and sat on the edge of the bed hugging a pillow, willing something or someone to stop whatever was about to happen.

He stormed in, banging the door with his massive frame, half a glassful of whisky swirling in his hand. 'What the fuck is this?'

I looked away to avoid his inebriated eyes.

He threw the tumbler across the room, shattering it into little pieces. The spray of whisky splatted my arms. 'What's the meaning of this lot?' He ripped off my nightdress and knickers before pushing me face down onto the bed.

'Gregory, don't, please …'

He was deaf to my screams. The pain was unbearable, I wanted it to stop. My insides seemed like they were being sliced in two. *Please God make him stop.* He just kept pushing and panting, faster and faster. I wanted to die. Finally, he groaned, slumped flat on top of me, and squashed me further into the mattress before rolling onto the other side of the bed and turning over to snore.

I limped to the bathroom, in-between my legs burned, my body trembled all over. Turning on the taps, I added soap flakes and sought comfort in the warm water.

Stop it, Elizabeth. I shuddered. That was the past and I couldn't turn the clock back. Mother and Father had forced me to marry Gregory and there wasn't anything I could do about it. It was time to move forward, bury that episode away and begin a new start by taking care of my nephew, George. Again, there was no choice in the matter, but to do what Father bade. I stood up, smoothed down my dress and was just about to go downstairs when a child screamed.

Martha was shouting. Part of me wanted to check the boy was all right, but I couldn't due to the resentment I held towards him. Goodness, what a racket. He certainly was making a lot of noise for a small lad. Poor little mite, torn away from his family, home, and what he knew.

Chapter 7

George

Martha wiped her hands down her pinny before hauling me up the winding staircase. Her grey wispy hair hung down from the white cap circling her crinkly face.

'Stop pulling,' I shouted.

She took no notice, just kept tugging and then pushed me into a large room with a big bath. It wasn't like our tinnie in the backyard that Mam had to drag into the kitchen every Sunday to fill with boiled water from the stove.

Martha turned on the gold coloured taps and water gushed into the sparkling white tub. It was like magic.

The room was bigger than our kitchen and it had a coloured window with yellow and green shapes like the ones in church at Da's funeral. Shiny dark green tiles on the walls went all the way up to the ceiling. Our Alice would love it because it was like a princess's palace but I'd have much rather been in our house with the flowery paper on the walls that Da put up before I was born.

Martha took a bottle of brown liquid off the shelf and poured it into the running water. It smelled like the mop I used to soak up Smelly Susie's wee.

Martha turned off the taps. 'Get undressed.'

'Not with you looking.'

'Do as you're told.'

I refused to budge so she pulled my clothes off, even my underpants. I put my hands over my privates and squeezed my eyes shut so she didn't see me cry.

'Get in. I haven't got all day.'

I climbed into the smelly warm water. Big boys shouldn't cry but I couldn't help it. I turned my head towards the door, a girl dressed like Martha stood in the doorway. She waved. I slithered down into the water and dipped my face so she couldn't see me cry. What would Ben have said if he'd known I was sitting in the nuddie with two women watching?

'Annie, don't stand there gawking.' Martha pointed. 'Pass the soap.'

She snatched the slab off the girl, grabbed me under my arms and started to scrub me like Mam scrubbed the floor. It smelled like the nurse's room at school. Martha's hands moved lower so I quickly covered up my willie but she wasn't having any of that, she shoved my hands out of the way and sunk hers down into the water.

'Stop it,' I said, 'you're hurting me.'

The girl gasped.

'What's your problem, Annie? Lady Granville wants him deloused. This is the best way.' Martha tutted. 'Make yourself useful, go and get his clean clothes.'

I looked up into the old hag's face. 'I don't have louses.'

Martha slapped my arm. 'Of course you do, all your lot do. Now shut bawling otherwise you'll have her Ladyship up here.'

'I don't, I don't. Mam checks me hair every week on bath night.' I pointed down in the water. 'I don't have any down there either.'

Annie dashed in and plonked my clothes on a stool.

Martha finally stopped scrubbing and turned to Annie. 'Pass that nit rake, will you?' She grabbed the metal comb and started tugging it through my hair. 'Go and get his room ready.'

The girl dashed out again.

Once the old hag was happy I didn't have louses, she threw a white towel on top of my clothes. 'Get out. I'll be back in five minutes.' She left the room huffing and puffing.

My skin was red like a lobster. Miss Jones had taught the class what happened to lobsters when they were cooked. She was going to speak to Mam about me going to grammar school. Mam said I'd be going for a holiday. This didn't seem like a holiday. Holidays were supposed to be fun. I drained the bath and the water whizzed down the plughole making a rude noise. Mam would like a bath like this instead of having to heave ours out into the yard to empty. Sometimes I'd helped since Da died. What was Mam going to do without me? Who'd help feed Beth and wash the pans? I wanted to go home.

'How could you do this to me, Mam?' I flung my clothes across the room and kicked the stool over. 'I hate you, Martha, and I hate you too, Grandma.' And I hated Mam for letting Grandma take me away. I kicked the stool again but when I heard footsteps coming I quickly scraped up my clothes and put the chair back in its right place. I wrapped the massive towel around my belly, it was soft on my sore skin. Martha and Annie wandered back in just as I'd climbed into my shorts.

'Good God, look at those rags,' Martha said, 'Miss Elizabeth had better sort something out quickly because he can't possibly meet his Lordship dressed like that.'

I lowered my head. There was nothing wrong with my clothes. Why did she say that? She sounded just like Grandma and I didn't want to meet his Lordship even if he was my grandpa.

'Is his room ready?' Martha added.

'Yes, I'll take him. Come along, ducky.' Annie smiled then marched along the landing making me run to keep up.

'This is your room and look, lots of space for toys. I'm sure Miss Elizabeth will buy you a few lorries and trains. And just for tonight you're allowed to eat dinner in here.'

I didn't care where I ate, I wasn't even hungry. I just wanted to go home. This room was big enough for Alice and the house was gigantic so I didn't know why Grandma said Mam and my sisters couldn't come too. Grandma was mean. I'd ask Grandpa tomorrow.

'It will give you time to adjust to your new surroundings,' Annie carried on, 'and I'm sure you must be very tired. Tomorrow you'll get a chance to meet Cook. She'll make a big fuss and make you a lovely breakfast. Cook loves children. She's got a nephew about your age. Martha's not that bad either once you get to know her. Chin up, chicken.' She tickled me under the chin.

She closed the door behind her and I sloped around the huge room, then ran my fingers over the silky blue cover on the bed. In the mirror of the tall wardrobe I gawped at the matching chest of drawers but then all I could see was Mam sitting at her dressing table putting her lippie on for Da's funeral. Just staring into the mirror. She didn't even know I was there.

I stomped over to the other side of the room to look out of the curvy window. Bumble bees hissed over purple flowers. Mam loved flowers. Maybe Grandma would let me pick some to take home to Mam. A pigeon plodded around on the grass hunting for worms. Da and I used to hunt for worms when we went to the park. Mam was too sick to come when she was expecting our Beth. I sank my fingers into the gold curtain. It felt different to the stripy orange ones Mam made for our bedroom on her sewing machine. Why hadn't she done sewing for the ladies in Bolton and Wigan like she used to before the sewing machine had broken? Then we could have stayed in our house. Grandma said we'd be evicted. Mam said that meant they wouldn't let us stay there anymore cos a new coal miner and his family would be living there instead. I brought the soft material up to my face and wiped my eyes.

The door opened. I quickly jumped away from the curtain. What was that horrid Martha going to do to me now? I shivered.

Chapter 8

Elizabeth

George jumped away from the window, his eyes flinching as I entered the room. My animosity seeped away as I moved closer. Tears stained his cheeks and I saw Grace in him.

'It's all right, George.' I moved towards him. 'I'm your Aunt Elizabeth.'

'I wanna go ome,' he said, 'that old hag, Martha, hurt me.'

'I'm quite sure Martha wouldn't do that.'

'She did. She hurt me. I promise.' George wiped his eyes using the back of his hand.

'It's all right, don't cry. I believe you and I'll make sure she never hurts you again.'

'I want my mam.'

'I'm sure you're missing your mother but you can't go home yet, you've only just got here. We haven't got to know each other, have we?'

A faint smile crossed his face and colour started to form back in his cheeks. He held out his hand. 'How do you do, Aunty Elizabeth?'

Well it looked like Grace had taught him some manners. 'I've come to measure you for new clothes.' I unravelled the tape measure from around my neck. 'Stand in front of me and we can get started. Look, I've got a notepad and pencil so you can help. You write down the figures when I call them out. I'm told you're good with numbers.'

George stood to attention, holding his shoulders back. 'I'm four-foot-eight. Mam says I'm tall for my age.'

'You are indeed,' I agreed, not knowing whether that was true or not. After all, I had no idea.

We were finishing off when there was a soft knock on the door. Annie wandered in with a tray of food. 'Cook's made scrambled egg on toast for the nipper.' She sat the tray down on the small table before leaving.

George's stomach rumbled in response. I wondered when he'd last eaten.

'Eat up,' I said, 'don't let it go cold, then get into your pyjamas and climb into bed. Tomorrow I'll organise the new clothes and you can meet Father.' I left George tucking into his food like Oliver Twist. I half expected a little voice to follow me asking for more.

*

I checked my watch, half-past-seven, that gave me half an hour before Mother and Father would be expecting me for dinner. Enough time to do a little embroidery. I rummaged through the dressing table drawers to find my sewing case. Carefully laid inside was a baby-nightgown. I unfolded it to see the little yellow teddy bears with big black eyes that I'd embroidered on the smock. It sent me back to the night when I'd received confirmation from the doctor about my first pregnancy. Gregory came to the bedroom as usual ready for his marital rights.

'I'm having a baby,' I told him, waiting for his reaction.

He just glared at me while continuing to unzip his trousers. I'd at least hoped he'd be happy that I was to give him a child.

'I thought perhaps we could not do this, you know, while I'm not feeling too well,' I managed to stutter, my hands shaking.

'You think that's going to stop me having my conjugals?' He slapped me onto the bed and thrust himself inside me, pushing and panting as I begged him, *no*.

Once he'd finished, I staggered to the bathroom coiled over with stomach cramps and agony in my back. The pain was much worse than my monthly. I ran a bath, immersed myself into the warm soapsuds and watched the water turn red.

Chapter 9

George

I climbed into the soft material. It was the first time I'd worn proper long trousers and they weren't itchy like my old shorts. I fastened up the buttons on the white shirt and knotted the striped tie like Mam showed me on the day of Da's funeral. I gazed into the mirror, I looked like Da when he got dressed up, only not so old.

Grandma opened the door. It was the first time I'd seen her since she brought me to Granville Hall. 'Good morning, George. Have you had breakfast?'

'Yes, thank you, Grandma, I mean Grandmother.'

'Good, I see you're wearing the new clothes.'

'I couldn't find mine.'

'I got Martha to burn them. Your grandfather's waiting to meet you.'

How dare she burn my clothes. I followed Grandma, amazed at how many huge pictures in gold frames hung on the walls down the staircase and along the hallway.

'He's in here.' Grandma pushed open the door and nudged me into a massive room. A tall man was standing at the fireplace puffing a pipe and Elizabeth sat on the couch reading.

'Come here, lad,' Grandpa said, 'you must be George.'

I moved closer. He blew smoke all round me. I didn't like the smell, it was different to Da's pipe, and I didn't like him gawking at me.

'I'd like to go home now please,' I said taking care not to drop my 'H.'

39

'Only speak when I ask you a question,' he said. 'And answer with Sir.'

So, this was Mam's da. A stupid man in a red jacket and a bow round his neck. Didn't he know only girls wear bows?

'Do you understand?' he said.

A large painting in a frame hung above the fireplace. It was a man who looked like Grandpa only with white hair. I wondered if he was Grandpa's da. He was puffing a pipe too.

'George, do you understand?'

'Yes,' I answered.

'Yes Sir, remember.'

'Yes Sir.'

'He's a bit lanky, Margaret,' he said to Grandma.

'Don't worry, I'll get Cook to fatten him up. He's probably been starved,' Grandma said.

I wanted to yell that I wasn't starved but instead I asked, 'Please can I go home, Sir?'

'What did I tell you, George? Only speak when you're spoken to. However, in answer to your question, this is your home now and your Aunt Elizabeth is going to teach you how to behave like a young gentleman.'

I stamped my feet. 'Grandma promised to take me back if I wasn't happy and I don't like it ere, so I wanna go ome.'

'Good God, it's worse than I thought.' He touched his belt. 'This will be going across your bottom if you insist on stamping your feet and speaking to me that way. Do you understand?'

'Yes Sir,' I managed to stutter squeezing my eyes shut.

'Elizabeth, I need you to ship this boy into shape. If we're going to send him to Sandalwood as arranged then something must be done. Apart from showing up the Granville name, it'll be like sending cattle to slaughter.'

'I'll do my best Father,' Elizabeth said. 'Mother, George mentioned you promised him a trip to Brighton?'

40

'That's true, Charles.' Grandma faced Grandpa. 'I did say that. Perhaps Elizabeth can take him?'

'Very well, a promise is a promise and we must keep our promises. George, I've a proposition for you. If you work hard on your speech and behaviour with Elizabeth over the next couple of weeks and I notice a difference, then as a reward I will allow your aunt to take you to Brighton. Do we have a deal?'

He wasn't going to let me go home yet. Mam said I'd be back home in a few weeks and Grandpa said a promise is a promise and Grandma promised so he has to let me go home then. 'Yes Sir,' I answered.

'Very well, go with your aunt.'

'Yes Sir.' I'd stay until I'd been to Brighton and then go home.

Chapter 10

Elizabeth

It was hard spending most of my time upstairs in my bedroom after being mistress in my own house. I fidgeted in the ivory wicker chair by the window trying to read Jane Austen's *Emma*, but to no avail. I kept reading the first page over and over. I stood up to stretch, arched my back and rolled my shoulders. Glancing out the window I noticed Harry, the gardener, tending to the dahlias and chrysanthemums. Gosh, he was only a teenager when Grace and I were children and Father offered him a position as an apprentice. Sometimes when our parents weren't around, Grace would grab my arm and say, 'Let's go and chat to Harry.' He taught us about flowers, and what we could expect to bloom each season. I learned all about gardening from him. How I miss the sowing of seeds and planting bulbs. My one solace during the time I lived at Ashburnham was working in the flower borders. Perhaps a project like George was just what I needed. Transforming him may help bury my black thoughts, after all, Doctor Chambers said he was only discharging me on the understanding that I found a new focus. On my last visit to him he'd said, 'So, Lady Giles I think it may be time to let you fly your wings. What do you think?'

My eyes had searched the consulting room stopping at the soft-grey, draylon-covered couch by the window. The couch, where I'd lain twice a week, those past three months, unravelling my internal thoughts out loud. I stared down towards my feet. My black stiletto heels dug into the mosaic-patterned rug, where shadowed light from the cream lamp on the desk glowed various shades of orange. The black and white photograph in a gilt frame showing off the doctor's family caused my throat to tighten, alerting me to what I was missing.

'Elizabeth, what do you say? Do you think you're ready?'

'Sorry, Doctor.' I coughed. 'Yes, I think I am.'

'And you have a plan for a new venture?'

'I'm going to work for Father. I've been studying commerce since you mentioned me learning a skill. I'm ready.' My clasped hands sat in my lap.

He passed me his card. 'Any problems just call me. Night or day.'

Well I hadn't called him so I supposed that meant I must be much better, though today it didn't feel like it. Thoughts of Gregory kept intruding. I was just about to sit back down on the wicker chair when the scrape of metal against concrete proved too much for my curiosity. I stared back out of the window. Harry was digging a flowerbed, in this heat too. He propped the spade against the fence, brushed his hair back from his forehead, and unfastened his white shirt, slipping it off his brown bare shoulders, before tossing it onto the nearby fence. His slim physique and tanned muscles stirred butterflies in my stomach. How old was he? Around thirty-five? Twenty years Gregory's junior, at least. Six o'clock, this temperature wasn't letting up. I drew my window up to its maximum, craving for a breeze. Harry looked up and waved. I offered a delicate wave in return, sensing my face flush at having been caught watching him. Doctor Chambers was right, I needed a focus. If only Victoria was closer, I missed her friendship. She gave me strength and helped me work things out.

That day, after I'd left Doctor Chambers' rooms, I'd taken a taxi back to Victoria's cottage. She was leaning over a window box, watering the flowers, when the driver dropped me. Sweet

William and stocks filled the container with shades of pink and white, while purple lobelia hung down its side. Victoria turned her head and walked towards me. 'How did you get on?'

'He's discharged me.'

'I'm so pleased, Elizabeth. I'd like you to stay here but your father has requested you return to Granville Hall, we don't want to argue with him, do we? He said he needs you home.'

'It's all right, Victoria, I imagine he wants me to start learning the business. I wrote and told him I'd been studying.'

Victoria patted my shoulder. 'I've grown quite attached to your company, I'm going to miss you.'

'I'll miss you too, but I can visit, and you can always come and stay at Gerrard's Cross.'

'I don't think so, dear. I never feel comfortable there.'

Looking around at her quaint little cottage with its picture-box garden, I understood why.

Harry had returned to his digging. I should write to Victoria. I grabbed my Basildon Bond white-papered notepad, sat down at my desk and wrote.

Dear Victoria…

It was no use, I put the pen down. Although, after Gregory died I'd felt relief, I couldn't rid myself of images of that night when he collapsed in the bedroom.

Unbuttoning his shirt, unzipping his fly, his yellowed eyes had followed me as he staggered towards me, pushing me onto the bed. Suddenly, he vomited a spurt of reddish-brown liquid and collapsed onto the floor at the bottom of the bed. My ivory nightdress turned a ground coffee colour.

'Gregory.' I rushed to his side. The doctor had been warning him for months to stop drinking but he'd ignored the advice.

'Get the doctor.' His hand stretched out towards mine.

I stared motionless.

'Doctor, get the doctor,' he stuttered.

I darted to the telephone to dial the doctor's number. Within minutes Doctor Green was at the door, the same doctor that had confirmed my last three miscarriages. An ambulance screamed its siren as it sped up the drive but by that time Gregory was unconscious.

'He was speaking a minute ago?' I said.

'His pulse is very weak.' The doctor released Gregory's wrist. 'I'm afraid you need to prepare yourself for the worse, Elizabeth.'

I put my hands to my face. 'Oh God, is he going to die?'

The uniformed ambulance men lifted Gregory onto the stretcher, fastening a strap, before raising him up and out of the door.

Doctor Green took my arm. 'Come on, I'll drive you to the hospital.'

It was the last time I saw Gregory alive. *Stop it Elizabeth. It wasn't your fault.* I snatched myself back to today and picked up the pen to continue the letter when voices and giggles from outside drove me to the window. Harry was packing up his tools while chatting to Annie who'd brought him refreshments. A glass of Cook's elderflower cordial most likely and a huge slice of fruit cake. My stomach rumbled at the thought. I'd missed lunch and afternoon tea. There was another hour at least before supper. I clenched my teeth. Annie was chinning up to Harry, but why should I care?

It's just loneliness, Elizabeth. Returning to my desk I continued to write to Victoria but the words on the page blurred as I recalled that Monday afternoon when Hannah had barged into my room. Again, I stopped writing. Her girth appeared rounder, her hair uncombed and scraped up into a bun, strands straggling down towards her pointed chin. She seemed older, lines ran under her eyes, across her ashen face, almost witchlike.

45

The new maid, Winnie, tried to pull her away. 'Don't, Hannah, don't.'

'What's going on?' I asked.

'You need to get that posh daddy of yours back here and tell him I want payin.' Hannah stood with her hands firmly on her hips.

'How dare you speak to me in that tone, Hannah, or about my father. I'll let it pass on this occasion because you're upset after Sir Gregory's death. Of course, both you and Winnie will be paid in full, Lord Granville will see to that, and be generous. He's already assured me.' Why was she behaving like this? And what had happened to her appearance? I hadn't seen her for a few weeks, there was always an excuse whenever I asked Winnie about her. What had happened to that sweet girl that stroked my shoulders when I was being sick and held me in her arms after my miscarriages, telling me it would be all right next time?

'I don't mean me wages. I mean for this.' Unravelling the top layer of clothing, she revealed a full belly.

'Oh. I see.' She was expecting, and a fair way along by the look of it too. I lightly touched my stomach, I was ten weeks, hoping this time I'd carry to term. 'But why should Lord Granville pay you? What's it got to do with him?'

'Don't, Hannah, don't,' Winnie said again.

'Did Sir Gregory know?' I asked still waiting for an answer to my previous question.

'Of course he bloody knew. He promised to look after me and the bairn.'

So that explained why he employed Winnie to make sure Hannah didn't have the heavy chores. But why was I not told? And why was she asking for payment? I was totally confused.

'I'm sorry, Hannah, but you're going to have to help me here. What has you having a baby got to do with me, Lord Granville or Sir Gregory?'

'Are you really that bloody stupid that you don't know? It's his, Gregory's. That's why.'

'Is this a joke?' I let out a nervous laugh. Surely it couldn't be true. How could it be when he was in my room every night and most mornings?

'Ask er if you don't believe me.' Hannah pointed to Winnie.

'I'm sorry Ma'am but it's true.'

I shook my head. No one must find out. I mustn't let this get out, Father would never forgive me. 'You're lying,' I said, 'why would he go to you?'

'Why wouldn't he when he was married to a frigid bitch like you? You couldn't satisfy him like I did.' Hannah hugged her big belly. It wasn't fair, she must be at least seven months, I'd never gone further than three.

She carried on talking but I tried not to listen, how he went to her room each night, and how they were in love, and how she and the baby would never want for anything.

I reached to my mouth to stop gagging. It was bad enough he'd forced himself on me, but sleeping with her at the same time? He was nothing more than an animal. I was glad he was dead.

'Now what are you going to do about it?' Hannah asked. 'Are you going to sort it out with Posh Daddy, or am I? And you can tell im I want five hundred quid.'

I gulped, coughed, and pulled myself together. 'You'll get your money.' I raised my hand. 'Winnie, get her out of here, before...'

'I'm going,' said Hannah. 'I've ad enough of slaving over the likes of you.' She stormed out of the room.

47

I walked over to the phone, picked up the handpiece and dialled Granville Hall.

'Winnie, find out where she wants the money sent. And I'm trusting you.'

'I won't let you down, Ma'am. I didn't agree with what they did. I wanted to tell you, but the master would ave had me out on me ear. And then where'd I be?'

'It's not your fault. I promise you'll receive a good settlement before you leave.'

Winnie had found the information, the money had been sent, and I'd made sure Winnie was looked after.

A crack of thunder made me jolt. The curtains blew up at the open window. I checked my watch. Gosh, it had gone eight o'clock. I'd lost complete track of the time. Thank heavens the weather was about to break. I pushed away the half empty page.

There was a knock on my bedroom door. 'Miss Elizabeth, Lady and Lord Granville are wondering what's happened to you,' Annie said. 'They're waiting to dine.'

'Tell them I'm coming straight down.'

I charged into the bathroom to swill water on my face and pull a comb through my hair before making my way downstairs to the dining room.

'I'm sorry, Mother and Father, I got caught up in a book I was reading.'

'Well you're here now,' Father said, 'but remember Elizabeth, in this house we run disciplined times for meals.'

'Yes, Father, it won't happen again.'

Martha and Annie paraded into the dining room carrying silverware. They served carrots, cauliflower and roast potatoes as Father carved the rack of lamb.

'You're looking peaky, Elizabeth,' Mother said, 'Are you ill?'

'I'm fine, Mother.'

'Grief is hard, but it will get better,' she said.

I hoped so as I mourned for my lost babies, the babies that I'd never made to term. The babies I hadn't held on to for more than fourteen weeks. But I especially mourned my final pregnancy which ended at Victoria's. I'd been confident that one would be different and I'd hold a baby in my arms because Gregory wasn't there to interfere with me.

How wrong I was.

The clatter of dishes jogged me back to the dinner table. 'Have you finished, Miss Elizabeth,' Annie asked.

'Sorry, yes.' Silent tears seeped softly onto my cheeks. I bent my head downwards to hide my face.

Mother surprised me by squeezing my hand. 'It will get better, dear.'

Chapter 11

Elizabeth

My small suitcase packed, I wandered downstairs to the drawing room. Mother was sitting by the fire with a book in her hand and Father's head was buried in the Financial Times.

'Mother, Father, I'd like to visit Cousin Victoria for the weekend.'

'You're not having a relapse, are you?' Father asked.

'I thought being around your nephew was helping?' Mother said.

'No, I'm not and yes, it is, but I think Victoria could do with the company. I wondered if there's a car available to take me this morning. I'll be back by tomorrow night.'

'I don't have a problem. What do you think, Margaret?'

'I was just writing to Victoria. Perhaps if Elizabeth is insistent on going she can hand deliver it for me?'

'I can do that for you, Mother, but do you have a problem with me going?'

'Margaret?' Father looked to Mother.

'No, of course not.'

'That's settled then,' Father said. 'I'll organise the car and we'll expect you back in time for dinner tomorrow evening.'

'Thank you, Mother and Father.' I let out a breath once outside the double doors. Well that had been easier than expected. I marched down the corridor towards the kitchen.

'Cook, I'm taking a little trip to Devon. Would you mind keeping an eye on Master George while I'm away please?'

'No problem, Miss Elizabeth.' Cook stirred a big pan of steaming oats. 'He's a dear little chappie.'

'That porridge smells nice. Is that for him?'

'It is, he loves porridge. There's plenty spare if you'd like a bowl?'

'Go on then, thank you.' I'd missed breakfast this morning and there'd be a short wait before the car was ready.

'Sit yourself down and I'll set another place.' Cook waddled over to the cutlery box, pulled out a dessert spoon and placed it onto the table. 'Here's our young man now.'

George yawned as he sloped in. 'Good morning, Aunt Elizabeth.' He squinted. 'Are you having breakfast with me?'

'Yes I am. I couldn't resist the smell of Cook's delightful porridge. Come and sit down.' I patted the chair next to me. 'I need to speak with you.'

'Have I done something wrong?' he asked.

Cook scooped out the porridge and placed a steaming bowl in front of George and one in front of me.

'No, not at all. I wanted to let you know that I'm going to visit my cousin in Devon, but I'll be back tomorrow evening.'

'I've never been to Devon. May I come too?' George picked up the jug of cold milk and poured some onto his porridge then sprinkled sugar on it.

'I'll take you to meet Cousin Victoria another time but not today.'

After finishing my oatmeal, I said, 'Right I must find the car.' I pecked George on the cheek. 'Be a good boy.' I wandered back up the hallway, out of the front door and down the steps towards the silver Rolls-Royce.

*

Victoria was curled up on the couch when I let myself in with the spare key from under the flowerpot. She half lifted a cup to her lips. A book sat opened on her lap.

'Elizabeth.' She placed the cup on a saucer and stood up. 'It's good to see you my friend. I've been lonely. Pacifying myself with a good read.'

'What is it you're reading?'

She held up Harper Lee's, *To Kill a Mocking Bird*. 'Have you read it yet?'

'No, I haven't. Do you recommend it?'

'Definitely, my dear. You can borrow my copy once I've finished. The tea in the pot's fresh. Grab yourself a cup and then come and sit down. I'll pop to the kitchen to get us a packet of Digestives.' Victoria left the room.

I walked over to the sideboard and poured myself a cup from the bone china teapot. My hand shook, and hot tea burned my palm. I cried out. *No, please.* I was back to that night in June, bent over with stomach cramps before blacking out. Victoria had found me collapsed on the bathroom floor, covered in blood.

I woke to a bright beam shining in my eyes. 'Ambulance is on its way, Lady Giles,' said the doctor. 'It's a good job Victoria found you when she did.'

The uniformed men lifted me onto a stretcher. It was just like with Gregory. *Was I going to die?*

'Don't worry.' The younger man patted my hand and smiled.

The ambulance drove away fast. Victoria sat at my side holding my hand. I looked up at the ceiling praying that I hadn't lost my baby. *Not again.*

Voices chattered around me, someone was removing my clothes and dressing me in a hospital gown. Nausea churned inside me as I was wheeled into an operating theatre.

'Count down from ten,' said the anaesthetist.

'Ten, nine, eight…

A needle dug into my arm. I opened my eyes. Was it over? I turned to the side, following the tubing from the cannula in my arm. A sachet containing blood hung from a stand. 'What's this?'

The nurse pressed my hand. 'Now dear, don't try to move. Doctor ordered a transfusion because you'd lost a lot of blood. He did speak to you about it after the operation. Don't you remember? You gave your consent.'

'No, I don't remember. My baby?' I asked.

'I'm sorry, dear. It's gone. The surgeon carried out a scrape.'

'A scrape?'

'D and C to make sure everything's gone.'

'Everything's gone?'

'Everything's gone, dear. I'm very sorry. You can try again once you recover. Get some rest now.'

I was nudged back to the present with Victoria pressing a wet cloth to my palm. 'Elizabeth, I'm speaking to you.'

'Sorry, Victoria. I don't know what happened there. I spilled tea, and then the next thing I found myself…' I tried to hold back the tears.

'Don't worry, darling, but why are you here? No letter and then a phone call telling me you're on your way.'

I let her cool the burn. 'Sorry, I did try to write but the letter always ended up in the bin. I missed talking to you.'

She smoothed my hand and led me to the couch. 'I've missed you too. How are you getting on with the mighty Lord Granville's business?'

I gave a small laugh. Victoria never ceased to amaze me, speaking as she wished. Clutching the wet cloth, I eased myself down next to my cousin. 'Father didn't want me to help in the business. Instead he's brought Grace's son to the house and

I'm supposed to prepare him as the Granville heir. Can you believe it? Grace sold her boy and I'm the one that's supposed to take him under my wing. How is that fair?'

'What do you mean, Grace sold him?'

'Grace became a widow a similar time to me and was left penniless. She contacted Mother and Father and they took George in exchange for paying her off with a lump sum. She sold him, Victoria.'

'Don't you like the boy?'

'Oh, I do. He's lovely but…'

'But what?'

'It's just Grace does what she likes and I'm left to pick up the pieces.'

'Now, Elizabeth, where's your Christian charity? Perhaps your sister was in a bad way? She'd lost her husband and was left with a child…'

'Not one, but three.'

'So, Grace is left with three children and your father offered to take the boy?'

'Yes. George. And I'm the one that's got to ship him into shape. How's that fair?'

'Was Grace happily married?'

'I don't know but she chose to marry the coal miner, didn't she? She gave up everything for him and from what I gather he was caught in a collapse of the mine.'

'Your poor sister.' Victoria took a Woodbine cigarette out of the packet, dabbed the end on the box and struck a match. She took a puff and inhaled. 'Ah that's better.'

She sat there curled up on the couch, her greying hair piled into a hairnet and puffing on the cigarette.

'My poor sister? What about poor me?'

'Elizabeth, think about it. Yes, you had an awful time with that Gregory but you were given medical help afterwards.

54

Who's been there to help Grace? It sounds to me like your sister may have been desperate when handing over her son.'

'I hadn't thought about it like that.'

'No, because you've been brainwashed by those parents of yours. Grace had guts. She stood up to your parents and chose to marry for love. You need to make some friends, girl, and learn to think for yourself.'

'It's Grace's fault I have no friends. It's because of her guts that Father made sure no one ever got close to me.'

'Enough of this self-pity. You can't blame everything on Grace.'

I laid down the cloth, rubbed the red patch on my palm, and took out a handkerchief from my bag. 'Who then?'

'No one, dear. You make your own destiny. Now back to your nephew. Do you like him?'

'Yes, I said so before. He's lovely.'

'Then you owe it to your sister to take care of him. He needs you and one day Grace will thank you.'

'You're right of course. How did you get to be so wise?'

'Old age my dear, old age.'

'You're not that old.'

She got up and passed me a fresh cup of tea. 'I'm sixty next month.'

'Not that old then. Do you regret not marrying?'

'Dah.' She placed her cup down onto the saucer making the china ring and brushed her hand into mid-air. 'I'm my own person, I didn't want a man telling me what to do. I was lucky that my father left me this cottage, unlike your poor mother who was destined for an arranged marriage.'

'Like me?'

'Yes, like you. She too couldn't stand up to her father. Thankfully mine was quite different. You'd have liked him. Such a shame he died before you and Grace were born.

55

Influenza.' She gazed wistfully up to the ceiling. 'Took my mother too.'

'But don't you wish you'd had children?'

'No, dear.' She smiled. 'You and Grace came to stay when you were children, that was enough for me. I loved you girls like my own. And that's why I say that you should let George into your heart. He'll be enough for you too.'

'I wish I could talk to Mother like this.'

Victoria squeezed my hand. 'Your mother gave up her spirit the day she married your father. Why do you think she never comes to see me? She's frightened Lord Granville will object.'

'What was she like as a child?'

'She was very like Grace but once she married his lordship, well you know what she's like now.' Victoria stood up, picked up her book from the arm of the couch and settled it onto the lamp table. 'How long do I have the pleasure of your company?'

'Until tomorrow afternoon. I need to be home in time for dinner.'

'Talking about dinner, I've a casserole in the oven. Let's eat and then you can take these curlers out of my hair.'

'Yes, of course.'

I followed her through to the kitchen. My mouth watered from the aroma. The more I got to know the real Victoria the more I liked her.

Chapter 12

George

My eyes popped out of my head when the curtains opened.

It was Grandpa's idea that Elizabeth took me to see *My Fair Lady*. Maybe he wasn't such a bad man after all? The journey was fun. Elizabeth and I huddled up together on the back seat as she pointed out Tower Bridge, Buckingham Palace, and St Paul's Cathedral on our way to Drury Lane Theatre.

The show was all about a poor little flower girl and Professor Higgins was teaching her to speak properly. Elizabeth said it's the same as she was doing with me. The flower girl recited *The Rain in Spain* as it came to an end.

'Now that's the right way,' whispered Elizabeth, 'we'll do that in our lessons.'

Everyone clapped as the curtains closed. The curtains opened again and the cast came out to bow. It went on forever, curtains closing, curtains opening, more clapping making my hands sting. The lights came on. Elizabeth led us out of the theatre into the sunshine.

'Let's wander around the sights,' she said.

I twisted and turned trying not to miss any of the enormous buildings.

She stopped on a huge bridge. 'This is The Thames, and this is Hungerford Bridge. Would you like to go for a ride on a boat?'

'Yes please.' I'd never been on a boat.

'Come along then.'

After a short stroll, we joined a queue of people. A steamboat pulled in. Its name was written on the side.

'*Majestic,* that sounds like majesty.'

Elizabeth squeezed my arm. 'You're such a sweetheart.' She smelled like flowers. We climbed onto the boat and as we moved along the river, I breathed in the air and copied Elizabeth singing, *The Rain in Spain*, like Henry Higgins.

'You're a quick learner.'

'Mam says that.' That was the first time I'd thought of Mam all day. I couldn't wait to tell her and Alice about the theatre and the boat and The Thames and everything.

Elizabeth pointed out The Houses of Parliament as we drifted by. The boat drew up at Victoria Embankment marking the end of the tour. Everyone clambered off. I wished we didn't have to get off but Elizabeth took my hand and we made our way to a bench overlooking the water. I thought about yanking my hand away but changed my mind as no one knew me and I quite liked holding her hand. Some ducks swam by, stopping to dip their heads in the muddy water.

Elizabeth took a deep breath. 'Mother mentioned your father died. What was he like?'

'He was the best. We used to play footie together all the time and he'd give me a penny for polishing his boots.'

'You must miss him?'

'I do.' I turned away.

'Let it out,' she said.

I wasn't sure what she meant. Let what out? I tried not to cry as I thought about Da and Mam and my sisters.

'It's all right to cry, George.'

I didn't want everyone to think I was a cissy but I couldn't help it. Once I started crying, I couldn't stop. Elizabeth pulled me towards her chest.

'It must be hard with your mother sending you away?'

'Mam'll come and get me soon.'

Elizabeth shrugged her shoulders. 'We'll see. But remember we're your family now.'

I had an aunty and grandparents that I never knew about. Grandpa was nice letting me go to the theatre. Tomorrow I'd ask him if Mam and my sisters could come and live with us too.

'Come on.' Elizabeth looked up at the sky. 'We'd best make our way back to the car. Those clouds look like rain. How fast can you run?'

'Very fast.' I felt better after crying. I clasped Elizabeth's hand and sprinted along the riverside at Southbank's in piddling rain.

Elizabeth looked down at my splashed legs. 'Don't worry,' she said, 'we'll clean you up in the car.'

I hoped so cos I didn't want to upset Grandpa and Grandma, otherwise they wouldn't let Mam, Alice and Beth come to stay.

Chapter 13

George

Elizabeth went downstairs to get us something to eat. I was supposed to carry on doing fractions but instead I dribbled my new football along the floorboards. I wished I could go in the garden but it was teeming down. I dragged the wooden chair back and sat down at Mam's old-fashioned desk with an inkwell. Before Elizabeth returned, I lifted the lid, took out a pencil and wrote, *George Gilmore sat here*. I rooted inside and pulled out sheets of paper marked Grace Granville. Elizabeth told me her and Mam used to study in here until they went to boarding school.

'Here we are.' Elizabeth pushed through the door carrying a tray. 'High tea.'

I chomped on salmon and cucumber sandwiches, and jam sponge cake just like Mam used to make, while Elizabeth taught me what not to say.

'Don't say Mam, say Mother. Don't say me, say my. Don't drop your 'H's, it's house.'

Mam was always telling me off for dropping my 'H's too.

'George,' Elizabeth said, 'don't rush your food, eat slowly.'

There was nothing wrong with the way I ate. Our Alice ate slower, perhaps she should've come to Granville Hall instead of me.

'George.' Elizabeth waved her hands in front of my eyes. 'Pay attention, you're daydreaming.'

'Sorry, I was thinkin about Mam and me sisters.'

'Thinking, George. And remember it's my, not me and Mother, not Mam. I need to go and speak to Father for a few minutes so be a good boy and finish that sheet of fractions and remember, no playing football in the house.'

'Yes, Aunt Elizabeth.' Once she left the room I jumped up to dribble the football around the floor again.

The big brass bell on the front door dinged. I wondered who it was. Delivery men always went to the back door and the posh people didn't usually arrive until the evening. I could hear loud voices. One sounded like Mam. I charged over to the window. Yes, hooray, it was Mam. She'd come to get me. I knew she would. I banged on the glass and shouted, 'Mam, Mam.'

'What's all the noise about?' Martha came up behind me and snatched me away. 'Sit down and get on with your sums until Miss Elizabeth returns.'

'No, it's Mam. She's come to get me. She's come to take me ome.'

Martha pushed me into the chair. 'Stay sat there.'

'You can't tell me what to do. I'm goin ome.' I shoved her away and charged back to the window. 'Mam, Mam.'

Martha dragged me away again.

'Get off me you old hag. I'm gonna tell Mam of you.' I kicked her but she was too strong.

'You little... How dare...?' She picked up a wooden ruler and smacked the back of my legs. 'Now let that be a lesson to you.' She yanked me up and dragged me down the landing, pushing me inside my bedroom. My legs burned. The key in the lock turned. I tried to open the door but it was locked. The old hag had locked me in. I banged on the door with my fists and kicked it but no one came. The window looked out on to the back garden which meant I couldn't see Mam. I curled up on the

61

floor, screaming and then cried quietly. I didn't care if big boys shouldn't cry.

*

There was a tap on the door. The key turned in the lock. I climbed off the bed and picked up the duffle bag. If it was that Martha coming to bash me again, I was ready.

'Good morning, George,' Elizabeth said. 'Whatever happened yesterday? I wanted to come to see you but Mother and Father forbade it.'

My tummy rumbled. Last night's dinner sat on the dressing table.

'George.' Elizabeth touched my arm. 'Why didn't you eat your dinner?'

'I don't wanna talk to you.'

'It's want, remember?'

'I don't care. I wanna go ome. Mam came to get me and that old hag wouldn't let me see her. She belted me with a ruler.'

Elizabeth flinched. 'I didn't know about that. Martha said you were behaving like an animal.'

'You can't keep me ere like a prisoner. I'm goin ome and no one's gonna stop me. And I'm gonna set the NSPCC on to that Martha.'

'Calm down, George. You must be hungry and thirsty after all that screaming? Father was going to let me take you to Brighton today but I'm afraid following your behaviour he's forbidden it and given instructions that you must stay in here until you calm down. I'll arrange for breakfast to be brought up to you.'

'I thought you were my friend but you're just horrid just like the rest of them. I don't care if I'm hungry or thirsty, and if that old hag comes near me again…' I put my fists up. 'I'm gonna punch her.'

Elizabeth tutted and shook her head. 'Very well, George, if that's your attitude.' She headed towards the door.

'Aunt Elizabeth, help me, please. I want my mam.'

She walked back over to me and took my hands. 'George, darling, your mother didn't come to take you home. She came for money.'

'You're lying. Mam wouldn't. She was shouting for me. I heard her.'

'She was shouting because Mother wouldn't give her money.'

'I don't believe you.'

Elizabeth shrugged her shoulders and left the room but didn't lock the door.

Chapter 14

Elizabeth

Remembering what Victoria had said to me, I stomped down the stairs and pushed past Martha towards Father's study. 'Is Lord Granville in there?'

'Yes, Miss, but he's busy.'

'I don't care if he's busy and I shall be speaking to you later.' I pulled open the double doors and marched into the room making a confident entrance.

'Father, how could you let that woman hurt that poor boy?'

Father lifted his head and dropped his pen onto the desk. 'What on earth has got into you, girl? And what are you talking about?'

'I'm not that naive sixteen-year-old that you married off anymore. I've been running my own household for the last nine years and I deserve an opinion.'

'Yes, you're quite right, Elizabeth, but remember I am your father and deserve respect.'

'I'm sorry, Father.' I bent my head down and then remembered why I was there. 'But Father, how could you let Martha thrash George? You say you brought him to Granville Hall to be your heir yet you allowed a servant to do that to him? The poor little mite needs love not aggression. He's lost his father, mother and sisters. Is it any wonder he played up?'

'I had no knowledge of this. I shall speak to the woman and make sure it doesn't happen again.'

'And I need a responsible job to work towards. That's what the doctor in Devon said. How am I to get well just sitting around the house without a challenge?'

'I am pleased to see you've developed some spirit, I thought only your sister was blessed with that. You will have sole charge of George including punishment where necessary. If anyone has a problem with him they should come to you. You can begin by reprimanding the housekeeper. Does that satisfy you?' He half-smiled and picked up his black fountain pen. He looked up at me and frowned. 'Is there something else, Elizabeth?'

'Yes, Father, there is. What about George? We should do more to help him settle in.'

'What do you suggest?'

'I was wondering about riding lessons.'

'That's not a bad idea, but first he needs to learn about the horses. Get him started by mucking out the stables. Maybe we should consider buying him a pony. Fix up a meeting with those equestrians, the Anson boys, see what advice they can offer. But don't tell George, it will be a surprise, a bonus if he behaves himself. Now…' He bent his head towards his ledger, gripping the pen before looking up. 'Is that it?'

'Yes, Father. Thank you.'

On my way out of the room I smiled. I did it. I stood up to Father and what's more he seemed to respect me for doing so.

Martha was nowhere to be seen so I trundled down to the kitchen to find Cook.

She was stirring the contents of a huge pan with a wooden spoon. The flavour of hotpot found its way to my nose. 'That lamb smells good, Cook.'

'Ah Miss Elizabeth, I didn't see you there. Thank you.'

'Cook, you mentioned once that you had a young nephew. How old is he?'

'Little Jimmy? Ah he's ten now Miss. A sweet little thing.'

'Why not invite him over to come and play with George.'

'Are you sure, Miss? Jimmy would love that. But what about the Master?'

'Leave him to me. Does Jimmy ride?'

'No, Miss. His mam and dad don't have that sort of money.'

'Well George is to learn so it will be a good opportunity for Jimmy to learn at the same time. A bit of competition never hurt anyone. They'll start at the bottom though, mucking out the stables and learning about horses.'

'A great opportunity. When shall I invite him to come?'

'I'll get back to you on that. Now the other reason I came in here was in search of Martha. Have you seen her?'

'I do believe she was attending to the drawing room fires. Annie, poor little love, is sick this morning so it's down to Martha. Not very happy about it either if I do say.' She gave a little snort which made me smile.

'Thank you, Cook.' This was turning out to be a good day. Respect from Father, a chance to do business with the Anson twins and best of all, Martha had to lay the fires. I charged back up the hall and stopped at the drawing room. The door was wide open and I could see Martha bent down raking out the ashes. I stopped to compose myself. Lifted my shoulders back and marched inside.

'Martha, I need to speak to you.'

She shuffled her hands together to dispel the ash and turned towards me. I had to force myself not to laugh as I noticed the black smudge across her cheeks. And I was about to make her feel more miserable.

'How dare you lift a finger to Master George? Who do you think you are?'

'Sorry, Miss, I'm not sure what you mean.'

'Did you or did you not slap a ruler across his legs. Terrorising him?'

'But Miss…'

'No 'but's.' Did you or did you not?'

'Yes, Miss, but he was out of control. I'm sure the Master will agree with me.'

'Well the Master doesn't agree with you. So, listen carefully, don't you dare lay a hand on the Heir of Granville ever again. Do you understand?'

'Yes, Miss.'

'And what's more I expect you to apologise to Master George.'

'You can't be serious.'

'I am and if you don't comply then there's the door. I'm sure there are plenty of women who would love your job.'

'Very well, Miss Elizabeth.'

Respect at last. I marched towards the door but took a peep over my shoulder as Martha knelt back down towards the hearth. Was that a sob? I didn't feel pleased with myself, instead I felt a little ugly inside. I wasn't a bully, yet I'd behaved no better than one the way I spoke to Martha, but I was standing up for George.

Chapter 15

George

It had been three weeks since Mam came to the house and Martha locked me up. I hadn't seen Grandma or Grandpa since.

Elizabeth popped her head around my door. 'Good morning, George. Have you eaten breakfast?'

'Yes, thank you. I had porridge and orange juice.'

'Good boy. Now remember, keep up the nice manners when you speak to Father.'

'Has there been a letter for me?'

'I'm afraid not.'

'But it's been ages.'

'Yes, I know.'

Why hadn't Mam answered my letters? And why hadn't she come back to get me? Was Elizabeth right and she only came for money? But Mam wouldn't do that. Mam loved me. 'Don't ever forget I love you,' that's what she'd said.

Elizabeth tried to cheer me up. 'Father's making his decision about Brighton this morning.'

I followed her downstairs into the massive room where Grandpa was standing by the fireplace just like last time. He puffed on his pipe and took it out of his mouth to blow smoke. It made me think of Da. I wondered what had happened to his pipe. I hoped Mam hadn't given it away as it should be mine for when I'm older.

'Good morning, young George,' Grandpa said.

'Good morning, Grandfather.' I remembered what Elizabeth told me.

He turned to Elizabeth. 'It looks like you've done a good job.'

'Thank you, Father. He's a quick learner.'

Grandma came through into the drawing room and sat by the fireplace. 'You know, Charles, I think he looks a bit like you.'

Elizabeth agreed and Grandpa chuckled.

'Now, young man,' he said, 'I believe you were promised an outing to Brighton. He looked at his watch. 'Half-past eleven. It's a little late to go today but how about tomorrow?'

'Yes please, Sir.'

'I'll organise a driver. Cook can make up a picnic basket. Pop along to the schoolroom now and do some sums or writing with your aunt.' He patted me on the head.

I wanted to ask when I could go home but I didn't want to make him cross. I'd ask him after Brighton.

*

Elizabeth was taking me to the seaside. I skipped into the kitchen to find Cook.

'Good morning Master George.' She ruffled my hair. 'I suppose you'd like some breakfast.'

'Yes please.' I dragged the chair from under the table to sit down. It made a scraping noise, a bit like home. I missed Mam, Alice and Beth. And Da too of course, but I was never going to see him again because he was dead.

I was careful to say 'my' and not 'me' when I spoke, otherwise Grandpa would get cross and wouldn't let me go to Brighton and most likely he'd belt my legs like Martha did.

'Come on, lad, stop daydreaming and get this down you.' Cook tossed a fried egg and two sausages onto a plate with a slice of toast.

'Ta, Cook.'

She shook her head and waved a finger at me. 'Tut tut, that isn't the way to speak, is it?'

'Sorry, Cook. Thank you.'

'That's better, now eat up, otherwise Miss Elizabeth will be down here looking for you.' Cook placed little parcels covered in greaseproof paper into a wicker basket with a red and white checked tablecloth inside. 'This is a picnic for you and Miss Elizabeth to take with you on your adventure. Are you excited?'

I nodded my head frantically as I'd got a mouthful of gooey egg with toast.

'Yummy.' I rubbed my tum after mopping up the last bit of egg yolk.

Cook laughed. 'Don't let your grandfather see you doing that but I do like to see a young lad appreciative of my cooking. Here, take this.' She thrust the picnic basket into my hands. 'It's half-past ten and I know Miss Elizabeth wants to leave by eleven.'

'Bye then, Cook.'

'Goodbye, Master George. Have a lovely day.'

I ran into the hall swinging the basket. Elizabeth walked towards me after leaving the drawing room.

'Good morning, George. I see you've got the picnic.'

'Good morning Aunt Elizabeth. Yes, Cook gave it to me. Are we going on the train?'

'Not this time. Father prefers that we drive down.'

'All right.' The train would have been a lot more fun than the posh car but at least I was going to the seaside.

Elizabeth took my hand and led me outside where a driver was standing next to a silver Rolls-Royce. I bounced down the steps, Elizabeth yanked me back to walk at her speed, which was slow. She took the basket off me, passed it to the driver and eased me gently into the back of the car onto the leather seat. It smelled hot.

The driver started up the car. It was a long drive but Elizabeth chatted to me, unlike my trip to Granville Hall when Grandma ignored me.

'Let's practise your lessons,' Elizabeth said. 'Introduce yourself.'

'I'm George.'

'Not like that. Remember how I taught you. How do you do, my name is George Granville.'

'But I'm not George Granville, I'm George Gilmore.'

'You're George Granville now. Introduce yourself like a young gentleman.'

'How do you do?' I took Elizabeth's hand to shake. 'My name's George Granville.' Saying it made my stomach curdle but Elizabeth smiled.

'Well done, George.'

For the rest of the journey she tested me on different things. What did I like to eat? Where was I from? I wasn't allowed to say from Wintermore, but instead, Gerrard's Cross.

'I can see the sea. Can I go for a paddle?'

'How should you ask?'

'I mean, may I go for a paddle? Please, Aunt Elizabeth.'

'I don't see why not.'

The driver stopped the car, climbed out and opened the back door. We stepped out onto the pavement. He rushed to the boot and took out the picnic basket. 'Here you are Master George.'

'Thank you,' I said, 'what's your name?'

'We don't ask drivers their names,' Elizabeth said. 'They're all called Driver.'

Driver smiled at me when Elizabeth wasn't looking and I smiled back.

We strolled towards the sea, well maybe Elizabeth strolled, I skipped and for once she didn't stop me. I let the wicker basket swing backwards and forwards and counted one hundred before reaching the water. Elizabeth sat down onto a stripy deckchair, I dropped the basket, ripped off my socks and shoes and ran towards the shore. I jumped the waves, not once but over and over getting splashed.

'George,' Elizabeth called. She held up a towel in her hand that was flying like a kite.

I didn't want to get out of the water but I did as I was told, tiptoeing across the stones so I didn't hurt the soles of my feet too much.

'Here, dry yourself and then we'll have a bite to eat before doing something else.' She threw the towel and I caught it. My PE teacher reckoned I was a good catcher.

'Are you not having a paddle, Elizabeth?'

'It's not very ladylike and Aunt Elizabeth, remember?'

'Yeah, I mean, yes, sorry Aunt Elizabeth.' Gawd it was hard work trying to say the right thing all the time.

'George. Stop daydreaming. I'm speaking to you,' Elizabeth said.

'Sorry.'

'Come and sit down to eat.' She opened the basket and passed me a chicken drumstick.

I tucked into the chicken and circled it around my mouth. 'What else have we got?'

'Eat some salad, and a hard-boiled egg.'

I laughed. 'Mam, sorry Mother, calls these picnic eggs.'

Elizabeth smiled. 'You're learning well, George. You'll settle into your new school nicely.'

'But why do I have to go to a new school? I'm going home soon and back to my old school and teacher. Miss Jones, my teacher, has lovely blue eyes. One day I'm going to marry her.'

'Are you now? Well I'm afraid you won't be going back to Wintermore, because your mother's no longer there, she's in London. And you're the new heir to Granville so you belong with your grandfather. I'm sure your mother will contact you in due course. I'll speak to Father about enrolling you in a local school so you don't have to go away.'

What was she talking about? Mam's left our house? What about my stuff? What had she done with it and why hadn't she told me we'd moved? I didn't even get a chance to say goodbye to Ben or Miss Jones.

'Here.' Elizabeth passed me a beaker of orange juice.

I drank the drink and wiped my hand across my forehead to cool down. 'Cor, I needed that.'

'Language, remember.'

I giggled. It really was a fun day and Elizabeth wasn't being too strict either. I gazed around the beach and spotted a man with an ice cream wheelbarrow. 'May I have an ice cream, please?' We had an ice cream man that used to come down our road playing music and Mam would let me buy one with pennies I'd saved up that Da gave me for doing jobs. Thinking about Da made me sniffle.

'Yes, you can.' Elizabeth opened her purse and took out ten bob and passed it to me.

'Would you like one?'

'Yes, why not? I'll have a ninety-nine.'

'What's that?'

'It's an ice cream cornet with a chocolate flake.'

'Wow. May I have one too?'

'Of course. Run along now and don't drop them on your way back.'

I slipped on my socks and shoes and ran across stony pebbles to the ice cream man and stood in the queue. There were four kids in front of me. The first was a girl a bit older than me, the next was another girl, but with Shirley Temple hair that reminded me of our Alice. Then a small boy with his big sister, holding his hand. I should have been standing with Alice, and holding our Beth, and it should be Mam sitting in that deckchair waiting for ice cream. It wasn't fair.

The ice cream man's forehead was wet. He must've been hot from walking around the beach all day. I wondered why he didn't eat one of his lollies to cool himself down.

'Two ninety-nines please.'

He took a wafer cone and added the block of ice cream then dug in the chocolate flake. 'Would you like chocolate sauce?'

'Hmm, yep please.' I handed him the note. He passed me two ice cream cornets and change. I headed towards Elizabeth but started licking my ninety-nine cos it was dripping onto my hands, so I licked them too.

'Sorry it's dripping.' I passed Elizabeth hers and ice cream dripped onto her dress. Now I was for it, but she surprised me by taking out her hankie and wiping the cream away before licking her ninety-nine.

'I haven't eaten an ice cream for years. We're both having an adventure today.'

'Did Grandmother and Grandfather bring you and Mother to the beach?'

'No, they didn't take us anywhere. Nanny brought us down a few times but she never allowed us close to the water.'

'Have you never paddled then?'

'No, I haven't.'

'Why don't we go in together once we've finished eating these?' I signalled to our ice creams with my elbow.

'You know what? Let's.' She gave a huge smile before taking another lick.

'That was yum.' I circled my hand on my tum.

'Yes, it was.' She giggled like Mam. 'Come on, let's go.' She flicked off her shoes and held her dress above her knees and ran towards the water.

'Wait for me, Aunty.' I tossed off my socks and shoes and bounded behind her.

We splashed, giggled and jumped the waves and as I was standing with my back to the sea I noticed a little train stop on the prom. 'Aunt Elizabeth, may we go on that little train?'

'Yes, let's get dry quickly and make our way up there.' She threw the towel into my face. It was just like being at home with Mam.

'Race you.' Aunt Elizabeth grabbed the picnic basket off the ground.

I charged behind her but deliberately let her win. She was puffing and panting by the time we reached the driver.

'Does this train go anywhere in particular?' she asked him.

'It has lots of stops, but the most popular is Peter Pan's Playground. I'm sure the young lad will enjoy it there. Hop on.'

'Thank you.' Elizabeth handed him the fare. We squeezed onto the seat together, she wrapped her arm around me and pecked a kiss on my cheek. 'You're a lovely boy, George. Grace did well.'

'What was Mam, Mother like, when you were growing up?'

'Your mam, oops, I'm being a rebel today, she was always up to mischief when Mother and Father weren't around. One day she made us both a pair of trousers. It wasn't acceptable then for ladies to wear trousers and Father went berserk. Your mother was always giving him grief. I was a good girl. Of course not today George Granville, you're a bad influence.' She tossed her head back as she laughed.

75

The train came to a halt. 'Peter Pan's Playground,' shouted the driver.

'Come on,' Elizabeth said, 'this is our stop.'

Wow, it was full of fab rides. Swing boats, merry-go-rounds, helter-skelters and more. I stood gobsmacked until Elizabeth gave me a gentle shove to make me go in.

I ran from one ride to another and stopped at the swing boats. 'May I have a go?'

'Yes,' Elizabeth said, 'but I think we have to get tickets first.'

We found the ticket office and she bought enough tokens for ten rides. I couldn't wait to tell Alice.

In the queue, I stood behind a girl with pigtails and red cheeks. She was probably about eight or nine like me. Her mam was chatting to Elizabeth, but Elizabeth didn't look interested.

'Does your boy fancy a go on the boat with my girl?' The woman asked.

'Oh, I'm not sure.'

'Please, Aunt Elizabeth, may I?' I held my hands in prayer mode.

'Go on, Liz. Our Tina would love that.'

'Please, Aunt Elizabeth.' I winked at Tina like Da used to wink at Mam.

'One ride, George.' Elizabeth frowned.

The swing boats stopped and the previous swingers clambered out. I let Tina climb up first and then took my place. It was a good job she didn't know that I could see her knickers when she sat like that. I moved my eyes away cos Mam told me boys shouldn't try and look at girls' knickers. We tugged on the ropes and made ourselves go high, backwards and forwards, it was fun. I counted five hundred swings before the man made us stop.

'I'm going on the merry-go-round next.' Tina said, 'Comin?'

I turned to Elizabeth but she scowled and answered, 'No, we need to go now. It was nice meeting you both.' She took my hand and dragged me away from Tina and her mam.

'But Aunt Elizabeth, I liked Tina.' I tried to pull back.

'Don't start, George.'

'But I want to stay and play with Tina.'

'I know you do but we need to go.'

'That's not fair. I've still got tickets.'

'We'll come back another day.'

'Just tell me why? And why are you so angry?'

'Stop throwing a tantrum otherwise this will be the last visit you get. The car's over there, now get moving unless you want me to speak to Father.'

She'd turned mean just like Grandma and Grandpa. I hated them all. I wanted Mam. I squeezed my eyes closed so Elizabeth couldn't see my tears.

Elizabeth pushed me lightly onto the back seat. The driver started up the engine and we drove back to Granville Hall in silence.

Chapter 16

Elizabeth

After finishing the letter to Victoria I sat the pen down on my desk. I'd written to her about George and how I was taking her advice to treat him like my own. He was a little gem. How my sister could have given him up, no matter how desperate, I just didn't know. He melted my heart when he peered up at me with those blue-grey eyes.

It might have been a lovely day at Brighton if it hadn't been for that girl's mother at the playground. I'd never heard such strong language from a woman. Poor George, he was so upset when I'd made us leave, but I couldn't risk him hearing those undesirable words from her mouth.

Jane Benezra was arriving today. Father had agreed it was in George's interest for me to hire a live-in governess until he'd learned enough etiquette for us to consider sending him to the local private school. He certainly wasn't ready to board and I intended to fight that decision if Father went back on his word.

I'd studied Jane Benezra's papers closely and was impressed by her education in English, Mathematics, General Science, and languages including French and German. The reference from her previous position at a private school had been impeccable. She seemed a good fit for George.

There was a tap on my study door. Father had even allowed me to have an office.

'Come in,' I said.

Annie entered the room. 'Miss Benezra has arrived.'

'Thank you. Can you show her to the schoolroom please and I'll be along in a minute?' I shuffled around some documents and sifted through to find the paperwork to take upstairs with me.

As I stepped upstairs, footsteps moved around in the room ahead as if someone was pacing up and down.

'Miss Benezra.' I offered my hand. She was in her early twenties, plain but had a nice smile. 'As you can see this is the school room. You should have everything you need and if not then just let me know and I'll organise it.'

After shaking my hand, she paced up and down looking around the small room. Her nose turned up slightly. 'It's a bit out-of-date, isn't it?'

I laughed. 'I suppose it is. My sister and I studied in here when we were children. These were our desks.' I raised the lid of the one on the right-hand side. 'This was mine. Seems like a lifetime ago now but they're still in perfectly good condition.' I pointed to the blackboard. 'And I'm sure you'll find that works well too. Do take a seat.'

She eased herself down onto one of the small chairs and I joined her. 'Remind me, why did you say you left your last position?' I rustled through the communication trying to find the relevant correspondence.

'As I mentioned in my letter I was in a relationship with one of the male teachers and unfortunately that fell apart. I found it impossible to work alongside him.'

'Yes, I can understand that. I trust that you don't let relationships get in the way of working?'

'No Ma'am, that's why I felt it was the right thing to move on. The pupil will be my priority. What's the lad's name?'

'George. And a very bright young gentleman he is, as you'll soon discover. His previous teacher wanted him to take his eleven plus this year.' I shuffled the paperwork. 'Well I must say everything looks in order and I think you'll make a grand governess for Master George. When are you able to start?'

'I can start immediately, Ma'am, but I'll need to arrange transport for my trunk.'

'How about tomorrow? I see you have a small suitcase with you. Why don't I get the housekeeper to show you around and to your room?' I rang the bell. 'One of our drivers can collect your luggage, just let them have the details.'

'Thank you, Ma'am. You won't regret it.' She shook my hand.

'There are a few rules. You must eat in the kitchen with the other staff and address me as Miss Elizabeth and your pupil as Master George. Any questions?'

'No, that all seems quite clear. Thank you.' She smiled.

'Oh just one more thing. There will be a three-month probation period. That gives us all the chance to find out if you're the right candidate for George and for you to ensure that you're happy to work with him.'

'Thank you,' she said.

'Ah, here's Martha, our housekeeper. Martha this is Jane Benezra, Master George's new governess. Please can you show Miss Benezra where her room is and give her a tour of the house so she knows where to go for meals etc. She also needs to speak to one of the drivers about collecting her things.' I turned to the governess. 'I'll see you in here at nine-o'clock sharp tomorrow morning.' I shook her hand. 'Welcome to Granville Hall, Miss Benezra.'

'Come along.' Martha shuffled out of the room with Miss Benezra following smartly behind her.

Chapter 17

George

Elizabeth had arranged for a teacher to come to the house and work with me in that dull schoolroom. I hoped that this teacher could teach better than Elizabeth.

I looked at my watch which showed the date and time. Five-to-nine, September 4th. Ben and Miss Jones would be wondering where I was. Had Mam even told anyone that I wasn't going to be there? I still hoped that she'd come and get me so I could go back to my old school.

I stomped along the landing to the schoolroom and through the open door. Elizabeth was already in there talking to some woman.

'Ah, George, meet Miss Benezra, your new teacher.'

Yuk, she looked horrid. Her hair was scraped away from her face and stuck in a bun. Not pretty like Miss Jones. I held out my hand to shake. 'How do you do, Miss Benezra?'

'Very well, thank you. And you, Master George?'

I wasn't sure I liked being called Master but nodded and the teacher smiled. Not a smile like Miss Jones or even Elizabeth. More like a pretend smile. I didn't like her.

'I'll leave you two to get acquainted. Have fun.' Elizabeth left me in the room with the ugly teacher.

Miss Benezra opened her bag, pulled out a bundle of papers and long thin books. 'I thought we should start off with some tests to assess how much you know. Now what would you like to do first, arithmetic or spelling?'

The room looked different. Miss Benezra had a new large desk, close to the blackboard, with one of Mam's and Elizabeth's desks facing. I lifted the lid and was pleased to see it was Mam's old desk.

'Master George, pay attention, I asked you a question.'

I shrugged my shoulders.

'That's not an answer now, is it?' She raised her voice.

I checked my watch. Not even quarter-past-nine and already she was cross with me.

'Very well, I'll decide.' She placed two books in front of me. One red-coloured, titled Mental Arithmetic, and a blue one with Spelling written across it. 'We will work from these. I'll ask the question and you write down the answer in your exercise book. Do you understand?'

'Yes,' I said. Of course, I understood.

She turned to the clock on the wall with Roman numerals and wrote down the time before starting to speak,

'18 x 4

6 x 9

50 + 124…'

The sums were easy-peasy. After question 100 she stopped.

'Spelling next. Use a clean sheet of paper. Rainbow, Caterpillar, Sardines, Encyclopaedia…'

I'm sure she grinned when she said Encyclopaedia. Probably thought she'd catch me out just like Mr Mason at my old school. Ha ha.

'Final question. Number 100. Spell *vein*. Right that's it. Now I'd like you to write about yourself. Just one side of the paper so we can get to know each other.' Again, she pretended to smile.

I wrote: *My name is George Gilmore*, then crossed out Gilmore. *My name is George, I'm nine years old. My birthday was in May…*

It was twelve o'clock and my tummy started to rumble. I put my hand on it. 'Shh.'

Miss Benezra started to laugh. 'Are you hungry, Master George?'

'Yes I am. Sorry,' I said.

'What time is it?'

I lifted my wrist to check my watch.

'No, don't look at your watch. What time is it on the Roman Numeral clock?'

I looked up at the wall. 'Twenty-past twelve.'

'Then I think it's time we stopped for something to eat. Pop down to the kitchen and see what Cook's prepared for us. Tell her I'll be down shortly, I want to finish marking your work first so I can assess where you're at.'

She didn't have to tell me twice. I longed to escape and see Cook's cheerful face. I ran downstairs taking two at a time and charged into the kitchen.

'Hello, Cook.' I skipped to her side.

'Master George. Good afternoon.'

The sausages spat in the frying pan and Cook pounded the potatoes with the masher.

'My favourite.' A tear dripped on my cheek as I remembered cooking sausage and mash on the day Da died. I wiped my sleeve across my eye.

'Has Miss Elizabeth mentioned that Jimmy, my nephew, is to come to the Hall at the weekend?'

'Yeah, she did. How old is he?'

'Same as you and don't let the Master or Miss Elizabeth hear you speak like that. My Jimmy'll get the blame.'

'Sorry, Cook. Miss Benezra said she'll be down in a minute...' Before I'd finished speaking the teacher walked into the room.

'Sit yourself down opposite Master George, Miss Benezra, the others will be along later, so just the two of you for now.' Cook scooped the mash onto the plates and prodded the sausages with a fork. 'Vegetables with gravy or baked beans?'

'Beans please, Cook. I love beans. Are they Heinz?' My tummy rumbled.

'Vegetables for me please,' Miss Benezra said.

Cook served sliced carrot and gravy onto the teacher's plate and baked beans onto mine. 'How's this young man doing with his work?'

'Well his tests certainly lived up to what I'd been told. Full marks for his mental arithmetic and spelling, and a well written piece of work too.'

I faced Cook and beamed before ramming a sausage into my mouth.

'Goodness, Master George. Where are your manners? I was under the impression I was teaching gentry not riff-raff.' The teacher huffed.

'Sorry.' I forced myself to eat slower even though my stomach was screaming for food fast.

Chapter 18

Elizabeth

I'd spent far too long with the new governess and had to hurry or I'd be late for my very first business meeting. I rummaged through my wardrobe, finally picking out a green tweed suit. It would be just the thing with a white shirt. I stepped into the skirt to check it still fitted as I hadn't worn it since my marriage. Fastening the zip and button, I glanced in the mirror. A perfect fit accentuating my small waist. I looked the part for the Anson twins to take me seriously.

I walked down the steps to the Rolls and climbed into the back. The driver started the engine and pulled away, driving along lanes lined with trees that had started to turn orange. We reached the equestrian gate, the driver slowed as we drove into Ashland's Farm. Two men who looked alike, but not identical, stood waiting. The one with blond hair winked.

'Good Morning, you must be Lady Elizabeth? I think the last time we met you were nothing more than a schoolgirl.'

'And you are?'

'Simon, and this is Richard, my brother.' He signalled to the mousy haired man standing next to him.

'Nice to meet you both.' I offered my hand.

Simon took my hand and alarmed me by lifting it to his mouth and brushing his lips against my skin.

'So how come Lord Granville has sent a woman to do his business?' Richard's hands stayed tucked in his jacket pocket. 'Shouldn't you be at home sewing or something?'

I took a deep breath. 'We don't all live in the dark ages, Mr Anson.'

'Well I'll leave you in my brother's capable hands. I've got real work to do.' He marched off towards a black Daimler, got in, started it up, and drove away with speed.

Thank goodness I wasn't going to have to deal with a chauvinist like him. 'Is your brother always so unpleasant?' I asked Simon.

'I'm sorry about that. Unfortunately, he is. I feel sorry for his poor wife.' Simon's eyes sparkled when he smiled.

A quiver stirred in my stomach. 'Down to business.' I tried to compose myself. 'Shall we?'

'Certainly, the stables are this way.' He peered down at my black stilettos. 'Are your boots in the car?'

How could I have been so foolish not to think about footwear? I was glad Richard had gone, he'd have had a condescending comment to make, but Simon wasn't like that at all.

'Don't worry, I've got a spare pair in the barn. Give me a minute.' He strode over to the nearby building and returned holding a pair of green wellington boots that matched the ones he was wearing.

'Thank you.' I inspected them and found them to be clean. In fact they looked brand new. I sat down on the nearby bench to step out of my shoes.

'Here, let me.' Simon eased my foot into the boot. 'The stables are around the corner. We have four thoroughbreds but I'm expecting more later in the week if you can't find one to your liking.'

When I stood up my feet slipped around in the boots but they'd have to do as I hadn't brought any socks with me. 'I'm looking for a pony suitable for a nine-year-old boy.'

'I reckon I have just the one. Come with me.'

We padded across the soggy grass and came to a stable. Simon opened the door. 'This is Alfie. He's a lovely 15.3 gelding.'

I stroked his silky chestnut coat.

'He's good with kids too. His last owner's young lad learned to ride on him.' We moved to the next stall.

'This one's Bella, a Bay mare. She's a polo pony so used to jumping. She's not silly like some ponies.'

'She's a beauty.' I ran my fingers across her black shiny coat.

'No good for your boy though as she needs a confident rider.'

'And finally, Zena, a 14.2 Connemara gelding. I think she could be just what you're looking for. She's four-years-old and finished her schooling.' He patted the pony's back. 'She's perfect for a young lad, aren't you, girl?'

'Marvellous.' Zena's marble coat with honey tones took my breath away. George would love her. 'I'd like a veterinary's report. If that's suitable and we can agree on a price then you have yourself a deal.'

'Excellent. I'll get on to the vet later today and we should be good to sign the paperwork in around a month.'

'Sounds fabulous. Now let me get rid of these boots.'

'Have you time for tea?'

I was enjoying Simon's company. Too much perhaps as my heart pumped faster whenever he smiled and his big brown eyes glistened. I checked my watch. 'I have half an hour to spare so yes, thank you.'

Chapter 19

George

Rubbing my eyes I climbed out of bed. The sun blinded me as I drew open the curtains. I wandered out onto the landing and into the bathroom to wash my face and brush my teeth. It was Saturday and today I was allowed down the paddock to muck out the stables and meet Jimmy, Cook's nephew. It was eight o'clock. Elizabeth told me to be ready by ten.

I skipped back to my bedroom, pulled on a pair of trousers and tossed a blue-striped jumper over my head. I took the stairs two at a time to go down for breakfast. Elizabeth told me that Mam used to slide down the bannister and encourage Elizabeth to tag on behind. I decided that next time Grandma and Grandpa were out of the house that I was going to slide down the shiny snake too.

I raced towards the kitchen to find Cook.

'Bacon and egg, Master George?' she asked.

'Yes please. When's Jimmy arriving?'

'I'm sorry, Master George, but he's not coming. His mam's just rung me and poor Jimmy's been up all night running to the toilet.'

'I was looking forward to playing with someone.'

'Never mind, Pet, I'm sure you'll still have a good time at the stables with the horses.' She patted me on my head.

The horses would be fun I suppose but not quite the same as running around playing footie with someone. I missed Ben so much.

'Get stuck into this.' Cook placed a plate down in front of me. 'You need energy for manual work.' She poured tea into my cup.

Elizabeth walked into the room. 'Hasn't Jimmy arrived yet?'

'I'm awfully sorry, Miss Elizabeth, but his mam rang earlier to say he's poorly. She was very apologetic and little Jimmy's heartbroken.'

'It can't be helped. Don't worry.' Elizabeth stroked her lips. 'I suppose you should get something for your efforts, George. How does sixpence sound?'

'Yes please.' I wondered where I'd spend it.

'Right, George, if you've finished breakfast get your wellies.' Elizabeth moved towards the kitchen back door and I followed, pushed my feet into the wellies and yanked my blue anorak off the coat hook.

We strode into the garden and out through a gate leading into the paddock. I squidged my wellies into the soggy ground and splashed in puddles. As we reached the stables a lad with long ginger hair backed out of the bay.

'Hi,' he said, 'I'm Andy. I understand you've come to learn how to muck out.' He looked around. 'I thought there was going to be two of you?'

'Jimmy's sick,' I answered.

'Andy, this is Master George. I'll leave him in your care and pick him up around four o'clock, before it gets dark.' Elizabeth turned to me. 'Work hard now or no wages. And have fun. Oh and I nearly forgot.' She passed a basket to me. 'Cook's made up a flask of chicken soup and bread rolls. There's enough for you too, Andy.'

'Thank you, Miss Elizabeth,' he said.

Elizabeth plodded off across the paddock.

'Can I see the horses?' I asked.

'Yeah sure. Come on.' He led me into the first stall. 'This is Jupiter, he's a stallion. You need to be careful with him. He's a strong one and has a mind of his own. So you mustn't come in here without me. Is that clear?'

'Yes,' I said. 'Wow, he's jet black. Can I stroke him. Please.'

'Yes, all right. But gently as he may decide to kick back.'

I stroked Jupiter's silky skin. 'I love him.' The only horse I'd ever seen before was the rag and bone man's shire horse that pulled the cart along the cobbled street while he shouted, 'Rag and bone – any old iron', and our Alice would be nagging Mam for rags so she could get a balloon.

'Are you all right, Master George?' Andy asked.

'Oh yes, sorry. I was just thinking how beautiful Jupiter is. He's like King of Horses.'

'Well you haven't seen them all yet. Come along now.' Andy hurried to the next unit. 'This is Cookie. He's called that because his coat is a biscuit colour. He's quite a gem. There's no way Lord Granville will let you ride him though because he's far too strong.'

Andy rushed to the next stall. 'And this one's Ayasha,' he said, 'she's a little gentler but you still need to be an experienced rider. She's happy to be petted though. There's a couple more horses but they're out with the groom for exercise. I believe Lord Granville's contemplating expanding so I'm sure I'll have more horses to introduce you to before long.'

I patted Ayasha. 'She looks like coffee and cream.'

'She does, doesn't she?' Andy replied. 'Now it's time we got down to cleaning her home.'

The smell of wee in the stall made me think of Susie Smith in the classroom.

'It usually takes me about twenty minutes to do this but if I miss a day then it takes longer. However, with your help today I reckon we'll do it in half the time.' Andy guided Ayasha out

90

into the pasture. 'George can you pick up the feed tubs, toys and water buckets to give us a clear space.'

I rushed around the stall gathering up the items and popping them outside. 'What's next, Andy?'

'Grab that fork I just brought in and I'll fetch the wheelbarrow from around the corner.' He disappeared but was back in a couple of minutes and pushed the barrow into the middle of the floor. 'I'll sweep up the straw and you pile it into the barrow using the fork and half way we'll swap over. Does that sound like a plan?'

'Yes,' I said, 'I know what to do.' I picked up the fork. It was heavier than I was expecting but I didn't let on. Instead I started singing.

'Let's clear up the hay, hay, hay,
by the end of the day, day, day,
I'll have a new bed for Ayasha
made from hay, hay, hay.'

'You're doing a grand job there?' Andy said.

'We're nearly done,' I said. 'What's next?'

'Follow me.' Andy rushed across to a barn and grabbed a bale of hay. 'Can you manage to bring one too?'

'Sure.' I lugged the bale into my arms and started sneezing. When we got back to Ayasha's bay we broke up the hay to make her a new bed. 'It's not smelly in here now,' I said.

Andy laughed.

We finished off the next stall and the one after that. It was tiring work. I wiped my forehead. 'Is it time for a rest yet?' I was certainly earning my sixpence. Maybe I could send it home to Mam.

'Yes, I think we should have something to eat now. There's a tap outside the barn so we can wash our hands.' I followed Andy across to the barn. He swilled his hands under the running water and I copied.

'It's a bit cold.' I shook my hands.

'The hot soup will warm us up. Sit in the barn ready and I'll get the picnic.'

I looked around the barn for something to sit on but there was nothing so I sat on a bale of straw and within seconds started sneezing again. Andy returned carrying the basket.

'Oh dear, do you suffer from hay fever?'

I shrugged my shoulders. I didn't even know what hay fever was. Andy took the flask from the picnic basket and poured steaming chicken soup into two mugs.

'Yummy,' I said, as the hot liquid warmed me. I tore off a piece of bread and dipped it into my mug.

'So how do you like living at Granville Hall?' Andy sipped his soup.

'I miss my mam. I mean Mother. And my sisters and friends. It's lonely without anyone to play with.'

'Must be tough. How old are you?'

'Nine.'

'Do you like footie?'

'Yeah, love it.'

'Fancy a kick-about after we've finished?'

'Really?'

'Yes. I'll go gentle with you though because I play in my spare time with some mates.'

'I used to play for my school team but now I don't even go to school. Instead I have a horrid old governess to teach me. I hate her. She's not like my teacher, Miss Jones, from my old school. I wish I was back there.'

'Your grandfather's a great guy, you know?'

'He is?'

'Yeah, he looks after his staff really well. Much better than any other employer around here. Pays us well too. You know you can always come down and chat to me if you get lonely.

You have a good excuse now that you're learning to muck out the stables.' He slurped the last of his soup and put his mug down. 'And anything you say – stops here.' He placed his hand onto his chest. 'You understand?'

'Sure thing.' I smiled, and dipped the last of my bread roll in the soup before slapping my mug down on the ground like Andy did. Maybe it wasn't going to be so bad here after all.

'Right, time for footie.' Andy rushed to the back of the barn and grabbed a ball. 'Come on then.'

I flung my anorak onto the ground to use for goal. Andy kicked the ball.

Chapter 20

Elizabeth

'Mother,' I said, sitting down next to her on the chaise longue. 'I'm planning on taking a trip to Devon for a couple of days to see Victoria. Why don't you come with me?'

'Indeed not. And what about George if you're disappearing?'

'George will be fine with the new governess and he can always pop down to the stables if he's looking for something to do. Victoria would love to see you. She said you'd changed since you married.'

'I've no idea what she's talking about. And it's Cousin Victoria, you're being far too familiar. You've spent so much time down there that she's having a bad influence on you. I'm not sure about this visit.'

'I wasn't asking permission.'

Mother shook her head and pursed her lips. 'It seems you've made up your mind no matter what I say. When will you return?'

'In time for dinner tomorrow. I'll pop into the school room and let George know I'm off. Do you know if there's a car free?'

'Check with the head chauffeur.' She stood up, smoothed her skirt down and paraded out of the drawing room.

I followed her out and made my way upstairs to the school room. I positioned my ear towards the door before opening. George sounded at ease.

'Sorry to interrupt, Miss Benezra, but may I have a few moments with my nephew please?'

'Certainly, Miss Elizabeth.' She placed the white piece of chalk onto the blackboard ledge. 'I'll give you some privacy.'

'Thank you.' George would be fine with the governess while I was gone.

George looked up at me, waiting.

'Nothing to worry about,' I said, 'I wanted to let you know that I won't be around until tomorrow evening because I'm going to visit my cousin in Devon.'

'Can't I come?'

'Not this time.'

'That's what you said last time. You promised to take me one day.'

'And I will, but not today. You have school.'

'Will Mam, I mean my mother, be there?'

'No, she won't George. Now be a good boy while I'm gone.' I pecked a kiss on his cheek. 'Now sit back down and do some work while you're waiting for Miss Benezra to return. She won't be long.' I waited until he sat at his desk, picked up a pencil, and began writing in the opened exercise book.

*

Red and brown crusted leaves were falling like snowflakes when I arrived at Victoria's cottage. Feeling liberated, I watched the car glide away knowing I was free until tomorrow afternoon. I bent down towards the flowerpot, housing a pink geranium, tilted the pot and retrieved the hidden key. Unlocking the front door, I let myself in.

'It's only me,' I called.

'Elizabeth, how wonderful to see you again. Sit by the fire.' Tall golden flames crackled as the wood burned. 'I've got a lentil soup cooking.' She pulled her cardigan tighter and padded towards the kitchen in her furry slippers.

I stood by the fire and rubbed my hands. Garlic spices reached my nose and my stomach gurgled in acknowledgement.

Victoria came back in with two steaming mugs in her hands. 'Here, get that down you, girl. That'll warm you up.' She handed me one of the large mugs and sat down on the cream draylon, Queen Anne, chair. I made my way to the comfy couch.

I sipped the thick yellow liquid, licking my lips. 'This is glorious, Cousin Victoria.' What would Mother and Father say if they saw me drinking from a working man's mug?

'Drop the cousin, remember. Now tell me what's been happening?'

'Do you remember the Anson twins?'

'Aren't they suitors that your father chose for Grace. Middle-aged men, I seem to remember.'

'Yes, that's them. But they're nowhere near as old as Gregory was.' I felt my face flush.

'You're blushing dear.'

'Am I?' I turned away. 'Father's put me in charge of buying a pony for George and sent me to Ashland's Farm, the Anson's own it. Richard, Simon's brother, is a horrid man. He was so rude but Simon, Simon's really nice.'

Victoria frowned. 'Isn't he married?'

'He's a widower. We had tea together while talking business and he kissed my cheek as I was leaving. It sent shivers down my spine.'

'In what way? Did it make you think back to Gregory?'

'No, it was nothing like that. It was kind of nice.'

'Hmm. Now tell me about George. How's he settling in?'

'He's a dear little thing but I feel sorry for him.'

'Why?'

'Well, you remember you mentioned that George must be lonely and needed young company?'

'That's right.'

'Well I'd arranged for the cook's nephew to help muck out the stables. Father said George had to learn to muck out before he learns to ride and so I thought a playmate to help him may make it more fun.'

'So why feel sorry for George?'

'Well young Jimmy didn't show. Cook said the boy was poorly but later when George wasn't around she revealed that the boy is scared of horses. I mean, why didn't she say that in the first place?'

'Maybe she didn't know then?'

'Hmm, possibly but then she added that he was a very shy child and apparently had been having nightmares at the idea of coming up to Granville Hall.'

'I can understand that.'

'I suppose so.'

'It's a shame but I'm sure George will get over it. The main thing is, did he enjoy being at the stables?' She placed her mug down onto the coffee table.

'Yes I think so. He had a big smile on his face when I picked him up. Seemed to get on with Andy too. This soup's tasty.'

'You should bring him here for a weekend. And are you planning on seeing this Anson chap again?'

'Well yes of course. I need Simon's help to get the right pony for George. They breed thoroughbreds. And yes, I like being around Simon.'

'As long as you realise it's far too soon to contemplate dating and you need much more time before considering marriage again. Just keep it to business.'

'Of course. I don't think he's interested in me that way. anyway.' *Unfortunately for me.* 'He's still grieving for his wife.'

'That's just as well.' Victoria stood up, lifted the mugs from the table and wandered out into the kitchen.

Chapter 21

George

It had been a long eleven weeks since Miss Benezra became my teacher. I climbed the stairs to the schoolroom but she wasn't there. I knew that meant *outdoor learning* again. Not that I ever learnt anything when she left me on my own studying wild flowers or newts in the pond while she went off with that dark-haired driver.

'Master George,' she yelled, 'down here. We're working outside today.'

I sloped downstairs and shuffled into the kitchen. 'Do we 'ave to? I'd rather do arithmetic in the warm.'

'Don't be a cissy and stop dropping those 'H's or I'll have to report you to your aunt.' She opened the back door letting in the cold air. 'Hurry up, get your coat and wellingtons.'

After grabbing my duffle coat off the hook and picking up my wellies from the corner, I sat on the back step and sank my feet into the boots. 'Bye Cook,' I said, fastening the pegs on my coat up to the top.

'Bye, Master George. Have a good day.'

Have a good day, I knew it was going to be a bad day. 'Can we take a football?' I asked Miss Benezra. At least if I had something to kick about I could try and stay warm.

'No, it's science today.' She thrust a fishing net into my hands. 'I don't want your aunt sacking me for letting you play around.'

I wondered what Elizabeth would make of me being left on my own while she went off with the chauffeur.

'Here. Carry this.' She shoved a picnic basket into my hands. We plodded through the paddock. I waved to Andy who was leading out Jupiter, and we carried on past the lake and over the hill.

She stopped when we got to the brook. 'Now I want you to write down what you catch from the stream. Once we get back to the schoolroom you can look up the creatures in your encyclopaedia and find out more about them. I shall be about half an hour. So no slacking.'

'Are you leaving me on my own again?'

'Don't be insolent. That's no way to speak to your teacher or your elders. Do you understand? Remember there's a cane back in the schoolroom, don't make me use it.' She waltzed off up another hill and left me shivering in the cold.

I swished the net in the water and managed to scoop up a newt but otherwise there was nothing but leaves. She was going to bash me with that cane if I didn't come up with something. I started to write down stuff I hadn't seen but she wouldn't know. Frogs, a toad, another newt…

It started to rain. I was cold and wet. I looked at the Timex watch Elizabeth had bought me. Twenty-five past twelve, my stomach was rumbling and Miss Benezra had taken the picnic basket. I trekked up the hill to look for a place to shelter and came across an outhouse. Maybe there was straw to keep me warm.

Groaning came from inside. I pushed open the door and found Miss Benezra with the driver pulling up his trousers. What were they doing?

'What the fuckin 'ell?' He shouted. 'I'm not losing me bloody job for anyone. I'm out of 'ere.' He stumbled out of the barn.

My teacher buttoned up her blouse. She grabbed hold of me. 'What the hell are you doing here? You're supposed to be fishing in the stream. How dare you spy on me?'

'I wasn't. It's raining so I came looking for somewhere dry. I didn't know you were here, I promise.' I shivered. Starving, I glanced around for the picnic basket. It was on the floor in the corner. I rushed over to get a sandwich but all the food had gone.

She smoothed her skirt down. 'It's not raining now so come along, let's get you back to the schoolroom before it starts again. And don't you dare speak of this to anyone. Do you understand?' She grabbed me. 'I said, do you understand?'

'Yes,' I said.

'Yes, Miss Benezra.' She pressed her fingers into my arm. *Ouch, that hurts.* 'Answer me.'

'Yes, Miss Benezra.'

Chapter 22

Elizabeth

The school room was empty again for the third time this week. Where was the governess? Why wasn't she tutoring George and where was he?

I hurried downstairs to find Martha. 'Do you know where Miss Benezra is?'

'She left the house before nine o'clock with George, and a hamper swinging on her hip.'

'Did she say where she was going?'

'No, but why not ask Cook? Maybe she mentioned it to her when organising the picnic.'

'Thank you, I'll do that.' I made my way down the hall. The tap of my high-heeled shoes echoed throughout the quiet space. The kitchen door was ajar, I pushed it open. Cook kneaded a lump of floured dough, punching it viciously with her large fists.

'Ah, good morning, Miss Elizabeth. What can I do for you?'

'I understand from Martha that you made up a hamper for Miss Benezra and Master George this morning. Did she say where she was taking him?'

'Outdoor learning, apparently. To be honest I thought it was a bit parky out there for the little lad, especially as it looked like rain. But Madam threw me a mouthful of abuse when I tried to say as much.' Cook continued to punch the dough. 'Oh, and by the way, Andy, the stable lad, was out exercising the pony the other day and he said he'd spotted them down by the glade heading towards the old barn. He approached her, but she basically told him to clear off and mind his own business. I thought that was a bit strange.'

It certainly did seem out of the ordinary. What would she be doing all the way out there with George? 'Thank you, Cook.'

*

A door slammed. George charged upstairs with his hands over his eyes. I went in search for his governess and found her in the kitchen ridiculing him.

'That blasted lad. You can tell he's not gentry.'

'How dare you speak about Master George in that way. And where've you been?' I asked.

'Out and about. Exploring for science. But the boy was disobedient.'

'Have you been shouting at him? He seemed very upset.'

'I disciplined him. The child has no spine.'

'I won't have you speaking about him that way. It's wet and cold out there and you've kept him outside for hours. It's almost four o'clock and you left the house before nine.' I clenched my fists and stood firm although my legs were shaking. 'I'm going to find Master George. I'll deal with you later.'

I made my way upstairs and tapped on George's bedroom door before pushing it open. He was lying on his bed sobbing.

'Whatever is it?' I held him in my arms. He pushed his face against my chest, his cries muffled. 'George?' I lifted his wet face towards me. 'Whatever's happened?'

'She said not to tell.'

I knew only too well who 'she' was. 'Don't take any notice. I want to hear your story. Were you badly behaved? Did she strike you?'

'No. You won't believe me.'

'Try me. Come on wipe your tears.' I passed him my handkerchief. 'It's all right, it's clean.'

'She, she… she left me by the brook. Said I had to catch creatures and write them down in me notebook.'

This woman was certainly having a bad effect on him. However, the task she'd set him seemed perfectly reasonable. 'What was wrong with what she asked you to do?'

'It started to rain and she hadn't come back. I was cold and wet so I went looking for shelter over the hill and found a barn.'

'That was a long way. What happened then. Did you find her?'

'She'd taken the picnic basket. I was hungry. When I pushed the barn door open, I heard voices.'

'Someone was in there?'

'I can't tell you.'

'What do you mean?'

'I can't.' He bent his head down in-between his legs hugging his knees.

'George, I want you to tell me what happened. I promise no one will hurt you.'

'It was…'

'It's all right. Tell me.'

'She was with one of the drivers.'

'What was he doing in there?'

'I can't tell you. I promised.'

'George, you can tell me. I don't care what you promised, I want you to tell me what happened. Did he do something to you?'

George shook his head.

'Then what? Tell me.'

'He shouted at me.'

'Why did he do that? Did you do something wrong?'

'No. But I'm not allowed to tell you.'

103

I stroked his arm. 'Tell me, George.' *Good God what have they done to him.* My imagination ran riot.

'They were …' George sobbed.

'What were they doing?' Did they do something to you?'

'No. He… His trousers were down around his ankles…'

Oh my God. 'It's important, George, that you tell me if he did something to you.'

'No, he didn't.'

'You can tell me.'

'Nothing, I promise. He was with her. Miss Benezra. Her blouse was unbuttoned and she started shouting at me too. She said I was spying on her. But I wasn't. I promise. I was just looking for somewhere to get dry. And I was hungry. She said if I told you, she'd beat me with a cane. Now she's going to thrash me.' He started sobbing again.

'There, there.' I rocked him in my arms, holding him close. 'No one's going to beat you. She'll be getting her marching orders. There's no need for you to see her again. Let's get Cook to make you some of her special cocoa. In the meantime, don't worry, I'll sort that woman out.'

I gritted my teeth, stomped downstairs and made my way to the kitchen where the woman was still disparaging George to Cook and Annie.

'Miss Benezra. My office now.'

She rolled her eyes at Cook thinking I couldn't see. 'Yes, Miss Elizabeth. Do you mind if I finish my cuppa first?'

'I mind very much. My office immediately.' I marched to my office and sat behind the desk. On opening the cashbox, I took out a five-pound note. This was more than the woman deserved.

She knocked on the door and walked straight in. 'What appears to be the problem, Miss Elizabeth?'

'I've spoken to George and I'm appalled by your behaviour. And I know all about the driver you were with.'

'Driver? I'm not sure what you're getting at, Miss?'

'George has told me the full story. You were obviously up to no good in the barn. While getting paid to tutor my ward I might add.'

She folded her arms. 'He's lying.'

'No, you're the one who's lying and there will be no more discussion. You're fired, Benezra. And don't expect a reference.' I stood up from behind the desk and shoved the five pound note into her hand. 'And that's more than generous.' I moved over to the window and looked outside, taking a deep breath before turning back around. 'Pack your bags, I want you off the property.' I rang the bell.

After a few moments Martha stood in the doorway. 'Yes, Miss Elizabeth?'

'Please can you pack up Miss Benezra's belongings and escort her off the premises. She's no longer an employee here with immediate effect.'

'You won't get away with this?' Benezra said, her voice shaky.

*

'Now you know the whole story,' I said to Father.

He puffed on his pipe. 'And you say you checked her references?'

'Yes, Father, they were excellent.'

'The question is what are we going to do now? Is the boy on his way down?'

'Yes, he is.'

'Well we have three options. One is to get another governess but that's going to take time and by the sounds of this escapade

105

not a very good idea. Number two is we send him to Oakleaf Prep and thirdly to board at Sandalwood.'

'Don't send him away, Father. I think he's lost too many people already in his short life.'

'Very well, let's see what George would like to do. Check if he's coming, I don't have all day.'

I walked out of the door into the hall as George was trampling downstairs. 'Hurry, Father's waiting. There's nothing to be frightened of.'

We drifted into Father's study together. He was away from his desk and standing by the fireplace, tapping ash out of his pipe into the grate.

'George, I hear you've been having a bit of a hard time with the governess?'

'Yes, Sir.'

'What do you suggest we do about your schooling now?'

'I don't know, Sir.'

I've been speaking to your aunt and we've concluded that there are only two real options as getting another governess seems out of the question. Therefore, do we send you to the local private school, Oakleaf Prep, or to board at Sandalwood? Which would you prefer? Do you think you're ready to go away to school?'

'No, Sir. I don't want to go away.'

'Very well, your aunt will enrol you in Oakleaf and you can start next week. Elizabeth, does that give you enough time to organise the uniform?'

'Yes, Father.'

'That will be all.' He strode towards his desk, sat down and immersed himself in his papers.

George and I left the room and shut the door quietly behind us.

'You'll like Oakleaf,' I said.

Chapter 23

George

A bell signalled school was finished for the day. I strolled out of the classroom in no rush to get back to Granville Hall. If Ben were here we'd have charged out to the playground, scrambling about on the ground, but I had no special friend here. I was just about to go outside when a group of lads circled me.

'Not so fast, Granville.'

They shoved me through a heavy wooden door into the boys' bogs. Two lads grabbed me, one either side. I searched the watchers' faces for help but only saw smirks when I was pushed into a cubicle. Someone pressed me down, pinching my shoulders, another pushed my head in the bog, both of them holding me firm, dipping me lower. I squeezed my eyes shut and clenched my mouth. I wouldn't cry or let them think I was a cissy. My knees stung from the damp concrete floor.

'Say your prayers, namby-pamby,' said one lad as he pulled the chain on me.

Da's voice popped into my head. *The only way to deal with bullies, George, is a strong right hook.*

I shoved hard on the pan, pushing myself up with all my strength, bowled into the lad on the right, and elbowed the other in the chest. We scuttled, slipped and spilled out of the cubicle. Our arms and legs tangled until we landed flat on our arses. The pillocks stared wide-eyed in silence. I was ready for them.

Everyone started laughing as the lads hauled themselves up. One grabbed my arm, heaved me up with a grin and surprised me by patting me on the back before leaving. The other lads in the room did the same, cackling and chatting as they pushed their way through the door.

I was shaking my soggy hair when through the mirror I noticed a figure behind me. A ginger haired boy with freckles was watching me.

He passed me a couple of paper towels before adjusting his round rimmed glasses. I rubbed the towels over my hair and face, dabbing my blazer where it had got splashed.

'Pendlebury, Neil.' He passed my schoolbag.

'Thanks. Gilmore, I mean Granville – George.' We shook hands. His confident grip shocked me. I searched the room for a bin.

'Behind the door.' Neil pointed. 'We can walk out together if you like?'

I chucked away the towels, slung my satchel over my shoulders and walked outside with Neil. A couple of lads from in the bog were waiting.

'So, you think you're a big guy,' the lanky one said.

'I don't want any more trouble.' I wasn't up to another fight.

'Over here.' Neil led me towards the playground.

'Not so fast.' The fat one pushed me.

Don't let them see any fear. Da's voice popped into my head. 'You're asking for it, mate.' I raised my fists.

They ran off as the Head wandered across. 'Is there a problem here?'

'No,' I said.

'Good. We don't tolerate fighting in this school, Granville.'

'No, Sir.'

The lads had gone so we ran across the tarmac.

Neil clambered onto a three-foot stone wall that faced the road. 'We can wait here.' What time's your lift?'

I glanced at my watch. 'It's supposed to be here now. Maybe he got fed up waiting.' How would I get home if he didn't come? Only it wasn't my home, my home was in Wintermore.

A maroon and grey Zephyr pulled up by the kerb and tooted.

'That's my ride.' Neil slapped his palm against mine. 'I'll see you tomorrow.' He piled himself into the front seat and the car drove off but not before I noticed the woman's long dark hair reminding me of Mam. It had been weeks since she'd been to Granville Hall.

The wind started to pick up. Brown leaves flipped in the air. I shivered, pulling my blazer tighter and noticed there was a button missing. That would give Martha something else to yell about. It must've fallen off when those lads grabbed me. How I wished I was home and still at my old school with Ben. No one ever dunked someone's head down the bog like that. I felt sick, I jumped off the wall and spewed my guts out into the gutter. I thought I was a goner with my face staring into the bottom of that lav but that's when I sensed Da standing over me, telling me to sort them out. The taste of vomit was still sitting in my throat and I couldn't stop shaking. Good job Da taught me to box and wrestle. Mam never liked it. *Leave him be, Jack*, she'd say but he'd answer, *there's nothing of the lad. He needs to learn to take care of himself.* Well today I did. Da's voice popped into my head again. *I'm proud of you son.*

That Neil seemed all right but he wasn't Ben. When there was a new person at our school, Miss Jones always asked for two volunteers in the class to become buddies for at least a week but there was none of that at this school, all I got was a gangly Mr Ellis pointing to the front desk, and a *sit there, lad.*

109

The Rolls still wasn't here. I was sure Grandpa told the driver to be at least fifteen minutes early and to wait for me. It started to drizzle, I hoped it wouldn't come down hard. I paced up and down glancing at my watch. Ten-to-five. My knees had gone goosey, I fastened the blazer tighter to stop me shivering. 'Where are you, Driver?'

It was almost dark, pelting rain ran down my nose and lips as I paced up and down. My new black shoes squeaked and squelched. Martha would be screaming at me about them too.

A motor finally pulled up close to the kerb but it was silver and it wasn't a Rolls. I stepped back towards the wall blowing on my hands. The driver got out of the car. I couldn't see his face because it was covered by a black balaclava. He crept closer. I ran down the pavement, away from the car, puffing and panting but I wasn't fast enough.

A sweet-smelling cloth clamped my nose and mouth.

*

It was pitch black. My eyes were opened wide but I still couldn't see. *Where am I?* It smelled sooty. The ground was scratchy and soggy. Water dripped onto my face. My blazer and trousers were soaked from the pouring rain. *Why was I here?*

I checked my watch, the green-lit hands showed it was half-past-ten. I put it up to my ear, it was still ticking, but was it half-past-ten in the night or the next morning? *How long have I been stuck down this black hole? Am I going to die? Is this how Da felt when the mine collapsed?* But Mam said he didn't feel anything. I opened my mouth and yelled as loud as I could. 'Help, someone, help me please. Help.' But no one came.

Where was my schoolbag? Using my hands, I rooted around the hard, damp shingle floor, and managed to find my satchel to use as a pillow.

Suddenly there was a noise. A bang. Light blinded me. Footsteps. Heavy and soft footsteps.

'Help,' I yelled again.

They moved towards me. The ground crunched under their feet. Someone waved a lamp and someone else, shorter, shone a torch into my face. It was a woman with big bosoms, and a man stood just behind her. They both had black balaclavas over their faces. The man placed the oil lamp down on the ground and it lit up the inside of the hole. He was taller than the woman and his huge belly hung over his trousers.

What was this place? A tunnel, a cave of some sort? It was a lot bigger than I'd expected. *Could I make a run for it?* But it was too dark to see the way out.

'Why have you brought me here?' I asked. *Are they going to kill me?*

They didn't answer.

'What are you going to do with me?'

He smudged his finger under my eye smearing my tears.

I punched his chest. 'Let me out of here. Me mam'll set the bobbies on you.'

He grabbed my wrists, tied them behind my back before shoving a sack over my head. The ropey smell made me gag and the rough material made me itch. 'Why are you doing this to me?' I wrestled to free my hands.

I was hauled outside and pushed into a car on a hot leather seat. The vehicle drove off fast, rocking me from side to side as it hurled around corners. *I'm going to be sick.* Eventually it slowed down to a stop. Someone grabbed me, pulled me out and dragged me across boggy ground then pushed me inside somewhere. *A house?* Someone removed the sack so I could see and breathe. It was light so must be daytime. The man and woman's faces were still hidden. The man hauled me across a

111

small room, flung me down onto a wooden chair and cut the rope setting my hands free.

'Why are you doing this?'

He threw a pencil and notebook into my lap and shoved a card into my face that read, *Write to Lord Granville and tell him to pay £500 if he wants to see you again.*

I just glared at him. He came up behind me and nudged something into my back. *Was it a gun?* Shaking, I started to write. *Dear Grandfather... Suppose he didn't pay. What would happen to me?* I got to the end of the note and signed it 'George' but wasn't sure whether I should write Gilmore or Granville so decided to just leave it as George.

The man snatched the pad off me. He dug into a duffle bag like Da's and pulled out a small bottle and thrust it into my hands. I flicked off the silver lid and gulped the milk down. It was warm and moistened my throat. The man snatched the empty bottle, then tied my wrists with rope. It dug into my skin, stinging me. The woman unhooked a strap attached to a big box camera from around her neck. She put it up towards her face and pushed the button. The camera went click.

'Why am I here?'

None of them answered. The man waved the photograph backwards and forwards. I wasn't sure why he was waving it around but as I watched a picture appeared like magic. It was me sitting on the chair with a dirty face and my wrists tied up. The woman dragged me off the chair and flung me onto the floor in the corner of the room on top of a hairy grey blanket like the one on my bed at home in Wintermore. She threw a brown package wrapped in greaseproof paper like Cook used into my lap. It rustled as I struggled to unwrap it with my hands tied. Starving I tucked into a spam sandwich.

'What are you going to do to me?' I asked, stuffing bread into my mouth.

They left the room without speaking and locked the door. My wrists burned. I couldn't stop shaking. I didn't know whether it was because I was cold or because I was frightened or both. At least now I wasn't in the dark. If I ever did get out of here, Martha or Grandpa would probably belt me for ruining the new uniform because my coat and trousers were both torn.

I peered around the small room, it wasn't much bigger than a cupboard. It had a tiny window high up towards the ceiling. A tin bucket stood in another corner with a note on the wall. *Toilet.* I was desperate. It was difficult to stand up and unzip my trousers with my hands tied but I managed and peed in the container breathing a sigh of relief.

I lay down and closed my eyes for a while but when I woke up it was getting dark. I looked at my watch. Four o'clock. That meant I'd not been home for over a day. Surely someone was searching for me. Using my elbows, I managed to stumble to my feet and stamp towards the door. I tried pulling it but the lock was too strong to force open so I lay back down and curled up in the hairy blanket, using my satchel as a pillow. It was lumpy but better than the floor. *Mam, come and find me.* I cried so much that I made the blanket wet.

Chapter 24

Elizabeth

Father had called an urgent meeting. I ran into the drawing room, pushing open the double doors and found him standing in his usual pose by the fireplace puffing his pipe.

'Have they found him? Is there any news?' I shouted.

'Calm down, Elizabeth. That's no way for a young lady to behave.'

'But Father, where is he? What's happened to him?'

'I suppose there's always the possibility that he could have gone looking for Grace,' Mother said, 'or maybe she's snatched him?'

'That seems unlikely now, Margaret. Foul play is suspected because the chauffeur was attacked and I really don't think Grace is capable of that.'

'Do you think the driver could be in on it?' I asked.

'No, I don't. Simmonds is one of my most trusted drivers, he's worked for me since he was a boy. He didn't alert us straight away because he was knocked unconscious from a cosh on the head. As soon as he came to, he notified the Head Driver. I spoke to Chief Inspector Bennett a couple of hours ago to get an update on the case. He said that the search party last night was fruitless but he's positive there will be some news for us shortly.' Father puffed on his pipe. 'I've told him though, I want this kept out of the press. The last thing I want is Grace turning up here.'

Martha tapped on the open drawing room, pushing it wider. 'Sir, it's the police.'

'Come in, Bennett,' Father said to the chief inspector. 'You have news?'

'I'm afraid not but in view of your driver's statement it's looking more like a kidnap.'

'Poor George.' I started to cry into my hands.

'Get a grip, Elizabeth. The chief inspector has some questions he wants to ask, I'm sure.' Father squeezed his upper lip, using his thumb and finger as he always did when there was a problem.

The inspector stroked his greyish beard. 'Have you received a ransom phone call or letter?'

'No, nothing.' Father tapped ash into the marble ashtray. 'But how would they know the boy was anything to do with me? It's not like we've made an announcement.'

'Agreed, Sir. That's why I consider it to be an inside job. Has anyone recently left your household, perhaps with a grudge?'

'Father.' I wiped my eyes. 'The governess and that driver we sacked,' I stuttered, 'they were both very upset and shouting threats. If anyone's going to have a grudge, it's them.'

The chief inspector took his notebook and pen from his top pocket. 'May I take their full names?'

'I'll just get them for you.' Father rang the bell.

Martha hurried in. 'Yes, Sir?'

'Can you get the head chauffer up here immediately, please?'

'Certainly, Lord Granville. I believe he's in the kitchen.'

'Elizabeth, what was the governess's full name?' Mother asked.

'Jane Benezra. I know she let us down but she did have excellent references. Surely, she can't be responsible for kidnapping George?'

There was a heavy knock on the door.

'Come,' Father said.

The head chauffeur strode in. 'You wanted to see me, Lord Granville?'

'That driver you fired the other day, what was his name?'

'That was Kierney, Sir. Douglas Kierney.'

'Does he own a car?' The chief inspector asked as he scribbled the name down in his notebook.

'Yes, he does. A white Capri, I believe.'

'And the number plate?' Father asked.

'The chauffeur tapped his index finger onto his lip, pursing them as he spoke. 'Err, hmm, let me see. I believe it does begin with an 'A' and it has the numbers 136. Does that help?'

'At this stage, any lead helps. I'll put out a *lookout alert*, straight away.' The chief inspector stepped outside of the room, his Walkie Talkie crackled.

'Father, the head gardener said he'd seen Kierney looking suspicious the other day so he followed him through the glade. Apparently, he was hanging around the old war bunker. You don't think…?'

'Bennett,' Father called. 'I think we may have a lead. Get your men up at the old war bunker beyond the glade.'

The chief inspector stepped back in. 'I'll get right on it, Sir.'

'I'm coming too. Martha, get my coat.' Father dabbed out his pipe and left it in the ashtray.

'I don't think so, Lord Granville. You need to stay here in case they telephone or a ransom note arrives.'

'Very well but let me know as soon as you know anything.'

Chapter 25

George

I huddled in the corner trying to keep warm. It was light so it must be morning. Thank goodness I was out of that dark cave which really scared me cos of what happened to Da. And at least here I didn't have to worry about rats. I checked my watch. The fingers sat at ten-past-three, which was the same time it read ages ago. I put it up to my ear, it was silent. I'd forgotten to wind it up. *How could I have been so stupid?* Now I didn't know what time it was. My tummy rumbled. I wondered if Grandpa had received the photograph and ransom letter yet.

I heard a click and thumping noise. Soft footsteps crept outside the door. The woman opened it, she was on her own but still wearing the black balaclava over her face. She threw a package at me.

'Thank you.' I unravelled the greaseproof paper and bit into a stale spam sandwich, my stomach gurgling as I swallowed. She knelt on the floor next to me and flicked the lid off a small bottle of milk and pushed it to my lips. I took a swig. It was warm, but I didn't care, I was hungry and thirsty. I gulped the whole lot.

'When will you let me go?' I asked with a mouth full of food. She didn't answer.

'How long will you keep me here? What's the time?' She leant close to me. I thought she was going to speak but instead she slapped my hand, and stood up, but not before I managed to spot half-past-eight on her watch.

She left the room without speaking, locking the door behind her.

I quickly set my watch to the correct time and wound it up. At least I could keep track of time. *Hurry up Grandpa.*

Chapter 26

Elizabeth

Martha tapped on the door before she walked in. 'I'm sorry to interrupt, Lord Granville, but I think you'll want to see this.' She passed a brown envelope to Father. 'A young lad from the village said a man gave him threepence to deliver it.'

Father took the packet from Martha and ripped it open.

I moved closer to peer over Father's shoulder. 'It's a photograph of George. He can't be underground then for them to have taken this.'

'They could have taken this first then stuck him in the bunker. What's keeping that inspector?' Father paced up and down the room.

'If George is down there he must be freezing cold and terrified.' Mother took the picture from Father's hand.

'This is your doing, Elizabeth. You should have checked that governess's references properly. I gave you some responsibility and you've proven that you can't be trusted.' Father rummaged into the package pulling out a note.

Oh my God, was it my fault?

Father read out loud. 'Dear Grandfather, please pay the money and don't call the police. They said they'll hurt me if you do. Please don't let them kill me.'

Heavy footfalls reached the room. After a loud knock on the drawing room door the chief inspector entered.

'Have you found him?' Father asked.

'No, Sir. No sign but it does look like he may have been there for a time. The area's been disturbed, so your theory could be right.'

Father passed the note and photograph to the chief inspector. 'These just arrived.'

'Hmm…' The inspector studied the unlined paper and Polaroid photograph.

'Bennett,' Father said, 'I suggest you set up a search party sharpish for Kierney and Benezra. Elizabeth will describe the governess to you and the head driver will help with Kierney's description.'

'Very well, Sir. I'm onto it.'

'But, Father, George said don't call the police. They might kill him.'

'Nonsense, be quiet, child. Haven't you done enough? These are amateurs. Now remember, Bennett, I'm relying on you to keep the press out of this. I don't care what it costs me in a donation to the Police Benevolent Fund, but we must keep this quiet. Understand?'

'I understand, Sir.'

The inspector and I left the room together.

Chapter 27

George

There was nothing for me to do. I'd managed to sleep for a while but woke up shivering from the freezing cold. My wrists hurt from being tied. They were red and sore with specks of blood from where I'd tried to pull off the rope. I checked my watch. Half-past-five. *Is this my third day?* My stomach rumbled. I tightened the blanket across my chest and leant my head against the wall trying not to cry again.

'Woof, woof.' A whistle.

I jumped up off the floor holding my ear. A dog? Bobbies? Someone's out there. Are they searching for me? 'Help, help,' I yelled in my loudest voice.

The key turned in the lock with a squeak and a clunk. *They've found me.* The door flung open but it was the fat man with a black balaclava over his head.

He threw the usual package at me and flipped the silver lid on the milk, putting it to my mouth for me to drink. I took a bite of the spam sandwich. The bread was stale like last time. Muffled voices came from outside. *Was someone looking for me?* The man didn't seem bothered. He didn't speak but dropped a new pile of cut newspaper next to the bucket before leaving and turning the key in the lock.

The bucket was starting to smell like Beth's nappies. I hated using it. *What choice did I have?* I could still hear voices from outside. 'I'm here, I'm here,' I shouted. I stood on the chair and tried to reach the window waving my arms but no one came to rescue me.

Chapter 28

Elizabeth

George had been missing for three days. *Why did Mother and Father blame me?* Yes, I'd recruited the governess, but I'd checked and checked her references to make sure they were good. And it wasn't me that employed Kierney. But that didn't matter in Father's eyes.

He stepped into the drawing room.

'Has there been any news?' I asked him.

'The chief inspector is on his way now. Let's hope he has something for us.'

There was a tap on the door. Bennett popped his head around the door.

'Lord Granville, they told me to come straight through.'

'Come in, Inspector. Please tell me you have good news.'

'I'm afraid not, Sir. We managed to track down Kierney and Benezra but it seems they had no part in this.'

'They must have,' Father said.

'No, Sir, they both have alibis. We believe this to be someone bigger, I'm afraid.'

'It's amateurs,' Father said, 'I still believe this to be an inside job. No one else knew of the boy.'

'Possibly someone at the school?' The chief inspector took a handkerchief from his trouser pocket and blew his nose. 'I'll check with the Headmaster to see if he's employed any new staff.'

'Good idea,' Father said, 'but check all the staff not just new. It could be any of them.'

'One more thing, Sir. I know you want this kept out of the press but how about we make a television announcement that we're searching for a young lad. It might help if we have people on the lookout.'

Father thumped the table. 'I thought I made it clear that the press is to be kept out.'

'I understand that, Lord Granville, but I'll make sure there's no connection to you.'

'Please, Father. We have to try. George must be so frightened.'

'Very well but there's to be no mention that he's my grandson or anything about Granville Hall. Understand?'

'Yes, Sir. I'll get onto the school straight away.' The chief inspector left the room.

'Do you think George is going to be all right, Father?'

'I'm sure he will be, but let me make myself quite clear, in future you're to come to me before authorising anything. Is that understood?'

It wasn't fair that Father was blaming me. It wasn't even the governess so why was I still getting the blame? I wanted to run away and stay with Victoria but I couldn't leave not knowing what had happened to George.

*

'What are the police doing about it, Father? I asked, 'He's been gone for five days. Suppose he's dead because you couldn't part with £500.'

'Stop being so melodramatic, Elizabeth. The police are searching across the local farms for him now and it's being broadcast on BBC television. Hopefully a witness will come forward.'

123

'How can you stay so calm? He's your grandson. You took him from Grace and he's not even been here six months and already look what's happened. Perhaps you should send him home to Grace once he's found.'

'Getting hysterical doesn't help anybody and suggesting George goes back to your sister is out of the question. George is my heir and stays with me.'

The grandfather clock in the hall chimed.

'Six o'clock. Switch on the television set,' Father said.

'Does Chief Inspector Bennett think it's someone from the school?'

'No, he's ruled out all the staff. It's either a random kidnap and they've discovered later that he's my grandson or it must be an inside job. Possibly a delivery driver. Quiet now. Margaret, it's on,' Father shouted.

Mother rushed into the room and sank into the chaise longue.

The screen showed Police with dogs trudging across farmland. A reporter kicked in. 'A nine-year-old boy is missing and believed to have been kidnapped. The child is around four-foot-ten tall, thin with blond curly hair. If anybody has seen anyone suspicious hanging around unused farmhouses or barns please ring this number.' A number jumped up on the bottom of the screen.

I gripped my hands together and put them to my mouth. *Please let them find him.*

Chapter 29

George

The stink from the almost full bucket was unbearable. A key in the lock squeaked and clunked before the door flew open. The fat man with the balaclava on his face stood at the entrance, he brought his hand to his mouth and heaved. I looked the other way. He kept his hand across his mouth and moved towards me pointing to the smelly bucket. Digging in my back he mimed me to pick it up.

'I can't. My hands are tied.' I lifted them up to show him.

The man pulled a penknife from his pocket and sawed through the rope. My hands were free. He dug something in my back again to tell me to pick up the bucket. I was guided outside the door and down a corridor. He shoved me into a small room with a proper toilet. The man stayed outside gagging. This was my chance but I had to be careful because he had that knife and a gun.

I listened to see if anyone else was around but the man was on his own. He was so fat he wouldn't be able to run fast and the woman didn't seem to be with him. As the man paced up and down I came up with a plan. I peeped out of the toilet cubicle and when the fat man's back was turned, I threw the bucket at his head.

He screamed and gagged at the smell. 'You little bastard.'

I ran down the corridor as fast as I could and found a back door, turned the key and rushed outside. It was pouring with rain but I didn't care. I'd escaped but now I must keep running and find a hiding place.

I could hear the man shouting, 'Get back here you little bastard.' He'd come out of the house but I was a good runner and ran fast over the hill and hid in some prickly bushes so he couldn't shoot me. I was cold but I didn't dare move in case he was out there looking for me so I stayed buried in the bushes. My watch had stopped so I couldn't see what time it was but my stomach rumbling reminded me that I hadn't eaten. The normal spam sandwich was probably still in that cottage but I wasn't going back for that. I pressed my stomach. 'Shut-up stomach. We're alive. Once we get back to Granville Hall I can feed you.' I just needed to wait until it was dark and then the fat man was less likely to see me moving.

Daylight started to fade. It must have been over two hours since I first slid into the bushes. I started to creep out but heard rustlings in the grass. I quickly returned to my hiding place. I was shivering. It started to rain again. *Why can't I be at home in Wintermore? Why did Mam send me away?*

Woof woof. Dogs were barking and men shouting. What were they shouting?

'George.'

My name. It was my name they were shouting. They were looking for me. But it might be the kidnapper man, and he had got more people to help him. I sunk deeper into the grass. A dog ran towards me. Whistles blew. 'George, George.'

'Down here, Sarge,' someone said.

Lots of lights shone in my eyes. Police bobbies gathered around me. An older man, not in a uniform, and with a funny curly moustache, leaned towards me and wrapped a blanket around me. 'You're all right, lad, you're all right now. Do you know where the men are that took you?'

I started sobbing and couldn't stop. 'I escaped... I ran away... A fat man chased me from a house over the hill so I ran faster and managed to hide. There was a woman too.' I sniffled. 'But I don't know where she was today.'

'Don't worry, George. We'll catch them.' He patted me on the shoulder. 'Come on boys, get this lad into the car.'

One of them lifted me up and headed across the field. 'We'll soon have you home.'

*

The car drove fast. I wanted it to go faster. I wanted to be home. Mam would be there. I just knew it. I couldn't wait to get into the bath and wash away the smell of sweat and grunge as I hadn't washed for days. The road was empty except when headlights shone from odd vehicles driving the other way. We reached the big gates at Granville Hall. The man without a uniform got out of the car and pressed a button. The iron gates opened and the car drove up the drive and stopped outside the mansion.

'Stay here,' he said to the police bobby. The man picked me up, climbed the steps and knocked on the lion shaped, brass door knocker.

Martha opened the door. 'Thank God, bring him in. I'll let the Master know.' I'd never seen her run so fast.

'You're safe, now.' The man put me down.

'George, thank God.' Grandpa held me in his arms. 'You've given us all a fright. Are you all right?'

I nodded but started crying.

'Sit yourself down.' Grandfather guided me to a bench seat by the door.

Elizabeth ran down the hall. 'George, George. Oh my God, thank God you're safe.' She hugged me. 'Martha, ring the doctor and tell him to come quickly.'

'George, thank God,' Grandmother said.

'I'm taking him upstairs to give him a bath,' Elizabeth said.

'A good idea. I'll come and see you later, George.' Grandpa patted my head.

*

The first day I'd come to Granville Hall, Martha had forced me into the bath and I was terrified. Today was different. Today the bath was filled with bubbles and I couldn't wait to strip off my shabby, smelly clothes and step into the warm suds.

'I'm sorry, Aunt Elizabeth,' I said, 'but my clothes got ripped and mucky.'

'Don't worry about them, George. New clothes may be bought. The main thing is that you're safe. We've been so worried.'

I let the bubbles surround me. And then I couldn't help it, I started to blub and tears ran down my cheeks and into my mouth. This time there was no Martha coming in and shouting but instead gentle Elizabeth knelt beside me and wrapped her arms around my slippery shoulders.

'It's going to be all right, now, George.'

'How long was I gone?'

'A week. We've been looking everywhere for you.'

'I thought they were going to kill me.' I wheezed. 'They tied me up.' I lifted my wrists to show.'

'My poor boy. The doctor will prescribe some cream for them. I'm so sorry that you've had to go through this.'

'I made a plan and managed to escape. And I ran and ran really fast. I was so scared because the fat man had a knife and a gun, but I knew I had to try and escape or they were going to kill me.' I panted. 'Is Mam here?'

'No, she's not, George, but don't worry, I'll look after you.'

I cried again because Mam hadn't come. She mustn't love me anymore.

'Did Grandfather really hug me?'

'Yes, he did. He was very worried.'

'But he's never hugged me before.'

'That's because he thought he'd lost you and realised how much he loves you.'

And I thought, yes, he does. He sent the police to look for me but where was Mam? If Mam didn't want me anymore then I didn't want her either. I had my new family that wanted me. Really wanted me and Grandpa had sent the men to rescue me.

After tapping on the door Martha walked in. 'Some pyjamas for Master George.'

Elizabeth passed me a big white fluffy towel and popped the striped pyjamas on the stool. 'Time to get out. The doctor's waiting in your room.' She patted my arm.

'Good to have you home, Master George.' Martha smiled.

Once both women left the room, I pulled out the plug to drain the water, fixed the towel around me, and stepped out of the bath. My legs felt like jelly. All I wanted was to climb into clean sheets and sleep. I rubbed myself dry, slipped on my pyjamas and tottered out onto the landing to find my bed. I heard men's voices as I got closer.

'This is Doctor Jennings,' said Grandpa. 'He needs to check you over.'

'Sit down on the bed,' the doctor said. He pulled out a stethoscope from his black bag. 'Take deep breaths, lad. Let's just listen at the back. There's a bit of a crackle,' he said to Grandpa, 'I'll prescribe Penicillin and keep a close eye. We don't want him developing pneumonia after being in that damp place for so long. I'll call back tomorrow. But in the meantime, any problems, just give me a ring.'

'Thank you, Doctor.' Grandpa shook the doctor's hand and Martha led him out of the door as Annie wandered in with a tray.

'Cook has made a ham sandwich and hot chocolate for Master George.' She set the tray down on the bedside cabinet and left the room.

'Of course, you must be hungry. Eat up, young man and no more frights like that please.' Grandpa gripped my arm. He was being a nice grandpa. 'Get some rest.' He left the room leaving me with Elizabeth.

'Eat up, sweetheart,' she said, 'then you can get some rest.'

I nibbled on the sandwich and took a swig of the warm liquid. I placed the cup back on the tray. 'I think I just need to go to sleep.'

'Of course. You've had quite an ordeal. Let's get you inside the covers.' Elizabeth smoothed the clean sheet over me. It smelled of fresh flowers. 'Now try and get some sleep.' She kissed me on the cheek, picked up the tray, turned off the light, and shut the door behind her.

Chapter 30

George

I was being buried alive, someone was hammering nails into the coffin. My eyes were wide open but I couldn't see. I opened my mouth to scream but nothing came out. I tried to move but stayed still. I shivered yet I was sweating all over. My head was burning hot.

'Sip this,' said a gentle voice. 'You've been having a bad dream.' She passed me a glass of water and placed a cool flannel onto my forehead. 'Take this.' She handed me a tablet. 'You're a very poorly boy.'

'Who are you?' *Was she an angel?* Maybe I hadn't woken up but I was dead.

'I'm your nurse. Your grandfather employed me to take care of you. You're quite a poorly boy after your ordeal. Do you remember what happened to you?'

'Yes, I was kidnapped but I don't know where they took me.'

'To an old war bunker on your grandfather's estate first of all. I believe he's closing it up so nothing like that can happen again and then later they held you at the cottage nearby where the police found you.'

'What time is it?'

'It's the morning. Ten-past-seven. I expect you're still very tired as you've had a wrestled sleep.'

My stomach gurgled. 'I think I'm hungry.'

'Well that's a good sign. I'll organise some breakfast.'

'I'll get up for it.' I tried to climb out of the bed but my jellied legs gave way.

'Come on, young man, back into bed.'

She was right. I fell back into the sheets and rested my head onto the pillow. I was so tired. 'Am I going to die?'

'No, you'll be fine in a few days. You have a chest infection.' She rang a bell and Annie came hurrying in.

'Please can you organise breakfast for this young man. He's feeling hungry.'

'What would you like, Master George? Boiled egg with soldiers?' She gave a big smile.

'Yes, thank you.'

As Annie left the room I heard Elizabeth's voice.

'Good morning, you're looking a bit better than last night,' she said. 'How are you feeling?'

'Hungry. I went to climb out of bed but my legs collapsed.'

'He's still got a way to go,' the nurse said. 'He's fighting a nasty infection but the fact that his stomach is calling for food is a good sign. Doctor will be back later to check on him.'

'I've brought you some comics,' Elizabeth said.

'Thank you.' I dragged myself up but fell back down again.

'He needs to rest,' the nurse said.

'I'll pop these here for when you're up to reading them.' Elizabeth placed the comics at the bottom of my bed.

Heavy footsteps got closer and someone knocked loudly on the door, pushed it open, and walked in. 'How are you this morning, young George?' Grandpa said.

Before I could answer the nurse interrupted. 'He's going to be very tired at this rate with all these visitors.'

Doesn't she know who he is?

'Quite right, I won't stay, I just wanted to make sure he was on the mend. I'll come back tomorrow. Now, George, make sure you do everything that Nurse tells you to do. Elizabeth, come along, let the patient rest.' Grandpa left the room.

Elizabeth kissed me on my cheek. 'I'll be back later. I'm so pleased that we have you back home.'

It seemed that Granville Hall wasn't such a bad place after all. I wondered why Grandma hadn't been to see me, perhaps she'd come later. Maybe I should forget about Mam, she wasn't coming back and this family loved me. *Welcome to Granville Hall, George*, although I wasn't sure about losing my Gilmore name.

Nurse picked up the comics from the bed.

'Please can I just have a quick peep.' I'd never seen so many comics, well except on the shelf in the newspaper shop. And these were all mine.

'Plenty of time for that. You need to rest.'

I closed my eyes and forgot all about breakfast.

Chapter 31

Elizabeth

I headed towards the drawing room, shaking, still not recovered from George's kidnapping.

Mother and Father were already inside with the chief inspector.

On pushing the door open, I asked, 'Have you caught them?'

'They're on their way to the cells now.' The inspector stroked his beard. 'A couple of amateurs so they didn't stand a chance in getting away. They'll be locked up for a very long time.'

'Don't forget, Bennett, no Press.' Father puffed on his pipe. 'You must keep them out at all costs. I don't want anyone else getting ideas. Understand?'

'I understand, Sir. I've managed to keep the story from them and the Force have been warned that there will be serious repercussions if anyone lets this leak.'

'I appreciate that,' Father said, 'but before you go, I'm still not sure how these culprits found out about George's relationship with me. It doesn't quite add up. Are you able to throw any light on that?'

'Ah, yes, Sir, I can. Your initial suspicions about the governess and your driver appear not to have been unfounded.'

'But I thought you said…' I said.

'Let me explain.' The inspector hunched over and moved towards a chair. 'May I?'

'Certainly but get on with it, man.' Father tapped his pipe chamber into the ashtray, emptying out the contents before refilling.

'It seems Kierney and Benezra were shouting off about Lord Granville's spoiled grandson in the pub. The kidnappers were in the vicinity and offered money to your ex-employees to supply further information.'

'Have they been charged too?' Father struck a match and puffed on his pipe.

'They will be. My officers are picking them up as we speak and as they are accessories before the act they will be charged with aiding and abetting by supplying information for financial gain.' The inspector stood up. 'Now if that's all, Lord Granville, I'll bid you good day.' He shook Father's hand and left the room.

*

We moved to the drawing room for coffee following dinner. Mother sat down on the chaise longue and I eased myself down next to her. Father stood by the fire tipping the contents from his pipe into an ashtray on the mantelpiece. 'I'll speak to George tomorrow to see what he wants to do about school. He may prefer to go away than go back to the local one after this, but he can choose. I quite like the idea of keeping the little chap around the Hall for longer. And let's get him riding.' Father packed the pipe chamber with fresh tobacco, struck a match, and puffed slowly on his pipe.

'Would you like me to organise that, Father?' I asked. George had only been here a few months yet already Father appeared to be softening. In fact I was surprised when he'd hugged George. I didn't remember one moment in my life when Mother or Father had given either Grace or me that kind of affection. Strangely enough, I didn't feel resentful towards George but glad he was now part of our family and Father had trusted me to be George's main protector. Maybe it was fate that Grace and I became widows at a similar time and that it was the right thing for George to come to Granville Hall.

Mother shocked me by shouting and waving her finger at me. 'It would have been your fault, Elizabeth, if something had happened to him.'

'No, it wouldn't. Why am I getting the blame?'

'Your mother is quite right, Elizabeth. After serious consideration I made you sole carer to George and it was your responsibility to keep him safe but like most things you do, you failed, and you failed your nephew. You've proven that you can't be trusted. In future you must come to me before making any final decisions.'

'That's just not fair, Father.' They were right though. Maybe it was my fault because I'd employed the governess, but the driver had been nothing to do with me, so I didn't see why I should be taking all the blame.

'Stop arguing, girl, and accept that you failed. Be responsible for once.'

I fought the tears long enough to get out of the door and run upstairs to my room. I'd had enough. I needed to get away. I pulled a couple of dresses out of my wardrobe, underwear from the chest of drawers, grabbed a small suitcase and packed my clothes into it before creeping downstairs and outside to find one of Father's drivers.

A driver in his thirties I didn't recognise was sitting in the garage drinking a cup of something. Tea I imagined.

'Hello,' I said, 'are you on duty?'

'Officially no, Miss. I've just knocked off and was having a cuppa before I make my way home. I've been on duty since early this morning.'

136

'Are there any available drivers?'

He looked at his watch. 'None back until morning I'm afraid.'

I sighed. I didn't want to wait until morning. I needed to get away now before anyone noticed I was missing.

'Where did you want to go?'

'Devon.'

'That's quite a trip, although...'

'I'll make it worth your while.' I opened my purse and pulled out a wad of notes. 'Fifty pounds. It's yours if you agree to drive me and wait a while.' I needed to make sure Victoria agreed to me staying. 'And one more thing, this is between you and me.'

The driver's eyes bulged. Clearly, he was taken aback. I could have probably offered him half that. 'Sure, Miss, I'll take you and no one need know because I'm due to take the car home with me.' He pointed to the silver Rolls sitting outside the garage. 'Are you ready to go now?'

'Yes, I am.'

'Just give me two minutes to use the facilities.' He wandered into a small room off the garage.

As I made my way towards the vehicle I considered phoning Victoria before leaving but decided against it in case she tried to talk me out of coming. Instead I slipped into the back seat and hoped no one had seen me.

*

It was gone midnight by the time we pulled up outside Victoria's. We'd been lucky and had a clear run with barely any traffic on the road.

'Wait here. I'll get my cousin to rustle up a cup of tea and a sandwich for you before you go.' I lifted the barren flowerpot, felt for the key in the dark, and knocked before struggling to place the key in the lock. As I opened the door I called out, 'It's only me.' I switched on the hallway light revealing Victoria in a hairnet and red-plaid dressing gown, creeping downstairs brandishing a brass candlestick. 'My God, Elizabeth, it's you.' She held her hand on the left side of her chest. 'What are you trying to do, give me a heart attack? Why didn't you phone first?'

'I'm sorry, I didn't think.'

'Obviously not. Well what the hell are you doing here? Is George all right?'

'Yes, yes, he's tucked up in bed.'

'Then why aren't you with him?'

I began to cry and once the tears started they wouldn't stop. I took a handkerchief from my handbag and blew my nose.

'And why have you brought a suitcase?'

'I've moved out. I'm coming to live with you. That's all right, isn't it?'

She just stared at me.

'Isn't it?'

Victoria frowned and gritted her teeth. 'No, it's bloody not. Look you'd better come in for a while and get warm, you look frozen. I'll see if the fire is still alight.' I followed her into the living room. She switched on the standard lamp and rushed around clearing up a used mug and plate from the coffee table, and a large-cupped white bra flung over the couch. 'As you can see, I wasn't expecting company. I'll just get rid of these.' She wasn't gone long and on return picked up the poker from the hearth and prodded the fire forcing a spark before adding two pieces of coal. 'Sit down.' Victoria sat down on an armchair by the fire pulling her dressing gown closer as she shivered. I sat close by on the couch.

'I'm sorry, I should have phoned. But I don't understand. Why can't I stay?'

'Yes you should have, Elizabeth. That's your problem, you just don't think. And I can't believe you've left your nephew. Your nephew that's just gone through an awful ordeal and you've left him there alone.'

'But he has Mother and Father.'

'He trusts you. First, he loses his mother, and then you walk out on him, just when he needs you most. You owe this to George and to Grace.'

'Grace again. Why's it my responsibility yet not Grace's?'

'We've been through this. You're acting like a spoiled child. That boy needs you. Imagine how you'd feel if you were kidnapped. Stuck down a hole and not knowing whether you'll get out alive or not. Imagine losing your father to a coal mining accident and then you lose your mother and sisters and then waking up to find you've lost your aunt too.' She sighed.

'I never thought about it like that.' I sat down on the couch. 'Mother and Father were ganging up on me. They said it was my fault. And it was in a way because I employed the governess but the driver was nothing to do with me. So I didn't see why I should get all the blame. I had to get away. I couldn't bear it any longer.' I wiped my eyes.

Victoria stood up from her chair and sat down beside me. She patted my hand and spoke softly. 'I know, dear, but that boy needs his aunt and I believe you need him too.'

I nodded my head. 'But I can stay tonight?'

'No, you can't. You need to get back before George realises you've gone. You don't want him to think you've abandoned him, do you?'

'No, no. You're right of course. I'm sorry.'

'Your job is to take care of that child and stand up to your parents. You're not a child anymore, you're a grown woman. A widow. You've seen life so don't let them treat you like a

139

sixteen-year-old girl. I'll make you a sandwich and a cuppa and then on your way you go.'

'Thank you. Oh, I forgot, I promised the driver something to eat and a cup of tea.'

'It's perishing out there. That wind is ferocious. Poor fellow must be freezing outside in the car. Give him a yell at once to come in and I'll make you both a quick snack.' Victoria shuffled into the kitchen and I followed her to the back door and picked up a torch. When I opened the door the wind almost blew me away. I positioned the torch to beckon the driver and called, 'Come in and get warm.'

He climbed out of the car.

'Hurry. The wind's going to have the door off its hinges.'

He locked the car, raced up the footpath, and wiped his feet on the mat before stepping inside. The back door banged shut.

'Sit down, lad.' Victoria placed a mug of tea and a corned beef sandwich down on the wooden table.'

'Thank you, Ma'am.'

'And take that coat off otherwise you won't benefit when you go back out into the cold.' Victoria pointed. 'You'll soon warm up in here from the stove. She lifted the lid, stoked the boiler and added a shovel of coal.'

He slipped off his reefer jacket and hung it over the ladder-back chair before wrapping his hands around the hot cup.

'And you,' she turned to me, 'you can eat in there. Then back to Gerrard's Cross before the weather turns really nasty as they're predicting gale force winds.'

I followed her back into the living room and sat down by the fire. After finishing the refreshments, Victoria glanced at the clock and said, 'It's gone half past one, you should think about leaving and I need to get back to my bed.'

'Of course.' I called out to the driver. 'Are you ready?'

'Yes Miss. I'll wait in the car. Would you like me to take your bag?'

'No, that's fine, you go ahead and get the car running. I'll be two minutes.'

'You're doing the right thing.' Victoria hugged me. 'You should be back in time for some sleep tonight and see George in the morning. He needn't be any the wiser. I'm proud of you, Elizabeth. I know it's tough but you can do it.'

I held back tears. 'Thank you, Victoria.'

'And come back soon when you're not running away and preferably in daylight. And make sure you phone first.'

I strode towards the front door. 'Don't come out.' I stepped outside and the wind nearly blew me away.

The driver opened the boot ready for my bag. I eased myself onto the back seat and knew that I'd gained renewed strength. *I can do this*. We'd be home before light and George would never know I'd been gone.

Chapter 32

George

'It's all right, Master George, it's just a nightmare. You're quite safe now.' The nurse bathed my forehead with a flannel.

'What time is it?'

'Just gone midnight. Try and get back off to sleep.'

'I want Aunt Elizabeth?'

'Rest now, you can see your aunt in the morning.'

'I want to see her now.' I started to cry.

'Don't upset yourself. I'll get someone to fetch her.' Nurse rang the bell.

Martha appeared a few minutes later. She yawned. 'What is it, Nurse? You do realise what time it is?'

'Yes, I do but Master George is getting rather distressed and would like to see his aunt.'

'Get her please,' I said.

Martha left the room.

'She's been gone ages,' I managed to splutter.

'Shh, she'll be here in a minute. Look, Martha's back now.'

Martha whispered to the nurse.

'She's out it seems,' Nurse said. 'Go back to sleep and you can see her in the morning.'

'I don't want to wait until the morning. I want to see her now.' I screamed.

'What's going on?' Grandpa was outside the room.

'He's a little hysterical,' the nurse said.

'What have you done to him?' Grandpa rushed to my side.

'It's all right, George, you're safe now. You're at Granville Hall.'

'Where's Aunt Elizabeth gone?' I asked Grandpa.

'I imagine she's in bed, although how anyone could manage to sleep with the racket you're making, I just don't know.'

'She's not,' the nurse whispered, but I could still hear, 'Martha said one of the staff saw her leaving with a suitcase.'

'There must be some mistake. I'll go and speak to Martha,' Grandpa said.

Elizabeth had left me. Just like Mam and Da. Like everyone did.

*

I opened my eyes. 'What time is it?'

'It's twenty-past-nine. And you might also like to know that it's Wednesday.'

Before I had a chance to answer, Elizabeth rushed into the room and said, 'Good, you're awake. You gave us all quite a fright.'

I turned my head towards the wall.

'Don't turn away, George. It's me, your Aunt Elizabeth.'

'I know who you are. You left me.'

'I didn't leave you. Look, I'm here.'

'You did. I woke up at night-time and you weren't here. And I heard Martha whispering that you'd gone. Go away.'

'I didn't leave you, George. I went down to see Victoria, and then came straight back.'

'Then why did you take a suitcase?'

She turned my head towards her and looked at my face. 'Look, George, I won't lie to you. Father upset me and for a moment I thought I wanted to leave but Victoria made me realise that you needed me.'

'So you did leave me. Go away. I hate you.'

143

'I think you should leave, Miss Elizabeth. He's getting far too upset and Lord Granville will be in here again to see what's going on.'

'What do you mean, again?'

'He came during the night. Now please, if you don't mind, my patient needs rest.' She slipped a thermometer under my tongue.

I thought Elizabeth loved me but she didn't care. She was just like Mam, and was going to leave me. At least I had Grandpa.

Nurse pulled the instrument out of my mouth.

Chapter 33

George

My legs were wobbly so I held on to the banister tightly as I treaded downstairs. The doctor warned me I might feel like this. In front of me, Annie stepped down backwards to make sure I didn't fall. By the time we reached the bottom my legs seemed stronger but still felt like jelly. The journey to the kitchen was like going on a hike, but Cook's smile made it worthwhile. She rushed over and smothered me under her big bosom.

'Thank the Lordie, Master George. We've been so worried. Come, sit down.' She shuffled me towards the wooden table. 'I'll get that breakfast.' She waddled over to the cooker and spooned a boiled egg into an egg cup and placed it in front of me along with a plate of toast cut into soldiers. 'Nurse said you have to eat lightly today otherwise your tummy will reject it after not eating for so long.'

'What, no butter?' I said.

'Just a scraping, Master George. We don't want you to be sick.'

Elizabeth walked in and sat on the chair next to me. I turned away.

'This is silly, George. You've been ignoring me for two days now. Don't you think that's long enough to punish me?' She grabbed my hand. 'I'm sorry I left but I did come back, that has to count for something.'

'You're just like Mam.'

'No, I'm not. I won't let you down again.'

145

It did seem a bit silly not speaking to her. I'd missed our chats. 'You promise?'

'I promise.' She poured orange juice into my glass. 'Here, drink this. We need to build up your vitamin C. You've had a nasty chest infection and you're not better yet.'

I sipped the juice.

'Isn't it a bit soon to be dressed?' Elizabeth pulled gently at my striped tank top.

I shrugged my shoulders. 'No one said I couldn't get dressed and I'm fed up wearing my pyjamas.'

'I understand but let's hope the doctor sees it the same way when he comes to check on you. Now, we need to talk about what happens next.' Elizabeth placed her hand over mine.

'Do you mean I can go back home?' I knew the answer before she answered by the look on her face.

'No, George. Father wants me to discuss future schooling with you. Whether you'd like to return to Oakleaf or prefer to go away to school?'

'I'm never going back to my old school, am I?'

'No. This is your home now.'

'Then I'll go back to Oakleaf.' At least I had one friend there. The silver car popped into my head and the driver in the balaclava chasing me. 'But suppose someone else kidnaps me?'

'We won't allow that to happen. In future the driver will wait for you inside the school gate.'

'But suppose he doesn't come? And why didn't the other driver come? He was supposed to be early. I heard Grandfather tell him so.'

'Unfortunately, the kidnappers coshed him on the head and he was given something to make him sleep.'

'They put something over my mouth to make me sleep too and when I woke up it was dark, cold and wet and I was really hungry. I thought I was going to die in that hole.'

"Poor little mite.' Cook rubbed my arm before picking up the dirty dishes from the table.

'It won't happen again,' Elizabeth said. 'Everyone will be looking out for you, especially the headmaster at school. He'll allocate someone to watch you until the chauffeur arrives to take you home. The important thing, George, Father insists that you mustn't ever speak to anyone about this episode. He said it will give people ideas and we don't want that. Understand?'

I nodded but I didn't really understand. It must have been in the newspapers that I was kidnapped. *Why hadn't Mam come back for me?* 'But hasn't it been in the newspapers?'

'No, Father took precautions to stop them identifying you. To protect you.'

'So Mam, didn't know?'

'Grace didn't know.'

'So she didn't come because she didn't know?'

'That's right. No one knew other than the police, the staff at Granville Hall, and your headmaster. Father made sure of that.' Elizabeth stared out of the window.

'Can I go outside and play footie?' I asked.

'Football isn't a good idea with wobbly legs. I also think it's a little too cold in the snow especially when you've been so poorly, but we can go and sit in the conservatory for a while, if you like?'

I nodded. 'Yes please.'

We went out into the summer room and sat in the bay window. I watched snowflakes fall to the ground turning the lawn white. It made me remember how I'd wished for a garden. Now I had a giant garden but no one here to play with.

'George.' Elizabeth waved her hand in front of my eyes. 'Father would like you to eat dinner in the dining room this evening if you're up to it.'

'In the dining room? Not the kitchen?'

'No, not in the kitchen. He said it's time you joined the family for meals, after all you have been living in Granville Hall for almost six months now. Things are going to get better for you.'

I suddenly became very tired.

'George, you've gone very pale. Are you feeling unwell?'

*

I don't know what happened, I must have blacked out because I found myself back in bed and the doctor was leaning over me.

'Trying to rush things, young man? I don't think you realise how poorly you've been. You need to rest.'

'Does that mean he can't come down for dinner, Doctor?' Elizabeth asked.

'Definitely not. Meals on a tray for the next couple of days. I don't expect to turn up tomorrow and find you out of bed, is that clear?'

'Yes,' I said. 'What am I supposed to do?'

'Rest,' the doctor replied.

Elizabeth waved the wad of comics over me. 'Don't forget you've got these. That will be all right, won't it Doctor?'

'Yes, but not now. He needs to rest. I suggest we all leave him alone and let him do that.' He gestured to Elizabeth, and to Martha and Annie who were hovering around. 'Someone draw the curtains.'

'I will.' Annie rushed over and pulled the drapes shut.

The room went dark. I closed my eyes and let myself drop off to sleep.

Chapter 34

Elizabeth

I met George in the hallway. Grey shorts showed off his spindle legs. Although fully recovered, he'd lost weight. His little frame shook. 'I'm scared.'

I wrapped my arms around him to calm the shakes. 'It will be fine, it's normal to be nervous but nothing's going to happen. I promise you. The driver's been told to drop you off outside the gates and a teacher will be waiting to take you in.'

'Will you come too? Please.'

'If you want me to, then yes of course, but won't that make you look soft?'

'I hadn't thought of that.'

'And don't you have that boy, what's his name, waiting for you?'

'Neil.' A half smile ran across his face.

'That's better. It will do you good to get back into the classroom and amongst some boys of your own age.' I held out a blue and white striped tie. 'Don't forget to put this on. And here's your satchel.' I passed him a bag identical to the one that got destroyed. 'The driver's waiting, you don't want to be late on your first day back.' I pecked a kiss on his cheek. 'Come on, I'll see you out.' I hooked my arm into his as we strolled towards the front door. He seemed to have forgiven me for abandoning him. 'Have a good day.'

My stomach skipped as I watched him slope down the steps, normally he'd be skipping. *How would I get through the day?* He had to go back sometime though and the first day was always going to be the worst. The culprits were behind bars so there was nothing to worry about but my legs still shook.

George climbed into the backseat of the black Rolls and gave a small wave. I waved back and watched the car drive away.

Charging back in, I ran upstairs to change, and picked up my wellingtons, before making my way around to the garage at the side of the house to seek out the head chauffeur.

'Good morning, Miss Elizabeth.' He unhooked his hat off the peg and brushed his ginger locks under the peak. 'How can I help you?'

'I was wondering if a driver was available to take me to Ashland's Farm. I'll be out for most of the day.'

'Yes, Miss. Harrison can take you. He's just popped out for a quick tea break but will be back in five minutes.'

'I'll wait.' I perched myself down onto a wooden seat. 'I don't think I caught your name.'

He scratched his head. 'James, Miss.'

'Pleased to meet you, James.' I shook his hand. I wondered if James was married. He'd been working for Father for at least twenty years. I imagined his wife, a round girthed woman, with grandchildren cramming around her feet.

'He's here now, Miss.'

Harrison walked towards me. A much younger man, probably around my age. He quickly removed the cheeky smile from his face when he noticed me. 'Good morning, Miss Elizabeth.'

'Good morning, Harrison. James tells me that you're available to drive me to Ashland's Farm today.'

'Yes certainly, Miss Elizabeth. When would you like to go? 'I'm ready now.'

*

150

The silver Rolls drove through the gates of Ashland's Farm and chugged up the muddy path.

'Pull up here,' I said to Harrison as we approached the stables.

He climbed out of the car and opened the back door. 'I'll get your boots, Miss.'

'Thank you.' I checked my watch. 'I'm going to be a couple of hours. Why not go for a stroll or drive? Be back by two o'clock.'

'Why, thank you.' A smile beamed across his face.

Simon plodded towards me. 'Elizabeth, good to see you again. Have you come to see that filly I mentioned on the telephone?'

'Yes, and I've come prepared this time.' I waved my wellington boots.

'Good girl, you're learning.' He winked.

I felt my cheeks blush so turned away to ensure Simon didn't see. Hooves trotted across the gravel. I turned to see Richard riding a tall chestnut brown horse. He yanked the reins to a stop and hopped off the horse. 'You, again. What is it this time?'

'If you must know she's here to see me,' Simon answered.

'Don't let her mess you about,' Richard said before wandering off guiding the chestnut beast.

'What's his problem?' I asked.

'Take no notice. Come on let's go and find that filly. Better put them on first though.' He pointed to my boots.

I sat down on an oak bench close by. I wasn't worried about my clothes as I'd come equipped in brown corduroy jodhpurs, and a khaki, tweed, hacking jacket.

'Let me help.' Simon eased off my flat shoes, gently handling my foot before pushing it into one of the Green Hunters.

Butterflies flapped inside me. Dear God, what was going on? *Why had I started having these feelings?* Feet sorted, I got up and looked around. 'Which way,' I asked, trying to compose myself. 'Did you manage to find Zena a new home? It was such a shame that we had to put back the purchase.'

'Yes, I did. She went to a ten-year-old girl. But don't worry, I think I've got just what you're looking for.'

Simon led me towards the stables. The wind blew my hair into my face as we trudged through crisp mud and iced puddles. I pulled my jacket closer. I wished I'd worn something warmer.

When we arrived, Simon opened the top half of the stable door for me to peep in.

'She's a beauty. Can I go in and see her properly?'

'Yes, of course.' He unbolted the bottom half and strode ahead towards a young jet-black horse and patted her back. 'It's all right, girl. I've brought Elizabeth to meet you.'

'She's gorgeous. George will love her. She's even nicer than Zena. What's her name?'

'Millie. I think it suits her. How's the lad doing now?'

'Well the doctor said he's fully recovered, but today was his first day back at school and he looked pale. I'm a nervous wreck wondering if he'll be all right which is the reason I decided to come here and do something constructive.'

Simon pressed my hand. 'I'm sure he'll be fine.'

Father had sworn everyone to secrecy about George's kidnap but I trusted Simon and confided in him when we'd last spoken on the telephone. He had that effect on me, making me want to tell him everything. I stroked the young horse's silky coat. 'May I give her some sugar?'

Simon passed me a couple of sugar cubes. Millie licked them from my palm. 'You're going to make one young boy very happy, lady.' I turned to Simon. 'What's your brother's problem with me? I don't understand why he's always so rude.'

152

'Take no notice.'

'I try but it hurts to be honest. I don't understand what I've done.'

'Look, there's a little cafe across the way. Why don't we chat over a pot of tea?'

The prospect of a hot drink was inviting. I followed Simon over a stile, across a field, and through a hedge bringing us out onto a country lane.

'It's just over there.' He pointed.

The teashop was free from customers so we chose a table by the window with a view of a duck pond. An old man, with thin grey hair and bald patches, approached us, clutching a small notepad and pen. 'What can I get you?'

'Elizabeth, how about a slice of cake to go with tea?' Simon signalled to the slab of Battenberg on the counter.

'That sounds lovely. And we'll have a pot of tea for two, please,' I said to the waiter.

'So tell me, what's Richard's problem?'

'He still carries a grudge because of Grace. I wasn't bothered to be honest. I was glad when it didn't happen because I'd rather choose my own wife but Rich, well he fancied himself being son-in-law of Lord Granville. Thought it would give him status. And he fancied your sister rotten.'

We stopped our conversation when the waiter returned and set a tray down on the table before shuffling off again. I poured the tea into the cups. 'And you didn't?'

'No, she wasn't really my type.'

'Didn't you think she was beautiful then? Everyone else did.'

'No doubt about it, but beauty isn't just on the outside, Elizabeth. What did happen to Grace?'

'She married a coal miner, unfortunately he was killed in a mining accident leaving her a widow.'

'None of us have had much luck in marriage, have we?'

'What do you mean?'

'Well you're a widow, Grace is a widow, and I'm a widower.'

'Except Richard. He's still married.'

'Yes, although to be honest I feel sorry for his wife. It's common knowledge that he's a bit of a philanderer.'

'I can't see what anyone would see in him.'

'Money, I suppose. Not everyone is as sweet as you.'

Again, I felt my face flush.

'You, and your husband, were you close?'

'Good God, no. I wasn't as lucky as Grace. My marriage was arranged. You must have known Sir Gregory Giles?'

'I knew of him, but to be honest, I moved away to Dorset when I married my wife ten years ago. A lovely little thing. Unfortunately she was knocked off her bicycle and killed outright.'

'Simon.' I squeezed his hand. 'I'm so sorry, that must have been awful for you.'

'It was at the time but it's been three years now so I'm trying to come to terms with it. Tell me about your marriage to Sir Gregory.'

'I was sixteen and he was in his fifties. That should tell you enough.' I felt anger rise up within me as I thought about Mother and Father allowing that match to happen.

'Did he treat you well?'

I shook my head. A tear fell down my face. 'I'm sorry.'

'No, don't be. There's no one else here besides you and me. Tell me about it.'

I shuddered and quickly changed the subject. This was too much too soon. 'When we spoke on the telephone, I mentioned the pony is a Christmas present for George.'

'Yes, you did. He's one lucky boy. Listen, Elizabeth.' He rested his fingers across the back of my hand. 'If you need to talk…'

'Thank you, I'll remember that. Are you able to keep Millie in your stables until then?'

'Of course. I can't believe it's only two weeks away. I'll tell you what, why don't I fetch her over myself on Christmas Day?'

'Is your brother going to have a problem with this?'

'My brother can go to hell. He's not my keeper. Anyway, it will give me a chance to see you again.'

I brought my cup up to my mouth and sipped the tea, partly to cover my face because I felt I was blushing again.

'How's the tea?' Simon smiled showing off straight white teeth.

I laughed. 'It's tea.' I looked at my watch. 'It's almost two o'clock, I should go. Do you mind?'

'Not at all.' Simon held up his hand to the waiter and mimed *the bill.*

Chapter 35

George

The car pulled up outside school. Groups of pupils crowded together in the playground made me feel dizzy. I spotted Neil waving to me at the gates so I took a deep breath and climbed out of the car. One of my teachers, his black robe floating behind him, came towards me. I dragged my footsteps and stumbled.

'Careful, Granville.' Mr Ellis helped me up and signalled to my driver who drove off. 'Your pal's over there waiting for you.' The teacher rested his hand on my shoulder for a second. 'Now stand up straight and I'll see you later in class.'

'Thank you, Sir.' I forced myself to straighten up.

Neil came up behind me and patted me on the back. 'Welcome back, chum. Are you all right? You look a little white.'

'Yes I think so. I'm just feeling a little tired.' I didn't tell him how sick I was feeling. A group of boys hovered around me pushing Neil out of the way. The lad that had instigated shoving me down the bog on the kidnapping day sloped over. I thought I was going to gag, I was too ill to cope with any bother, but he surprised me.

'George.' He shook my hand. 'Robert. We didn't get properly introduced last time. You've been through a tough time, pal, but don't worry, you're amongst friends now. Let's go into class.'

He must have been talking about my illness as Grandpa had specifically told me that I mustn't speak about the kidnap to anyone. The boys around me were all laughing and chatting but I couldn't take it all in. It was like walking through fog as I made my way inside school to the classroom.

'Here, George.' Robert tapped the desk next to him. 'Sit here.'

I turned to Neil. He mimed for me to go so I pulled out the chair to sit at the desk in the middle of the room next to Robert.

'Do you like football,' he asked.

'Yes, I love it.'

He rubbed his hands. 'Great stuff, you can be on my team.'

Why was he being so friendly, in fact why were they all being so nice?

Mr Ellis strode through the door. He thumped his desk. 'Quiet.'

There was instant silence. 'Now get out your exercise books. Granville, good to have you back, young man. We've heard how poorly you've been. Scarlet Fever wasn't it?'

I'd never heard of Scarlet Fever until Grandpa mentioned it and said that's what he'd told the Head Teacher to advise the staff at the school. I nodded. 'Yes Sir, but I'm better now, thank you.'

'Good, good. Come and make yourself useful, you too Sanders,' he said to Robert.

We walked up to the teacher's desk. He shoved a bundle of books at both of us. 'Give these out. One between two.'

We paced up the aisles placing books on the desks. Robert kept nudging me like we were best buddies. I became suspicious that Grandpa may have paid him to be nice to me. Our chairs scraped on the floor as we pulled them back. Robert nudged me again. Mr Ellis clapped his hands.

'Silence. Now we have a new book to study today. *Merchant of Venice*. Hands up those of you that have heard of it.'

Hands shot up, everyone's except mine, so I half-raised mine, and hoped Ellis wouldn't ask me anything about it.

The time went quickly and before I knew it the bell was ringing for morning playtime. After dinner break, we had PE with football. Robert picked me to be on his team. We'd only been playing for about ten minutes when I spotted him whispering to the two lads who'd tried to cause a fight at the end of my last day. As the ball came my way, I kicked it towards the goal. Suddenly, I went down like a brick. The lanky lad had deliberately tripped me up.

Robert sprinted over and shoved the streak of bacon out of the way. 'Did you do something to George?'

Mr Smith the sports teacher ran towards me. 'Are you all right, Granville? 'Did someone see what happened?'

The boys all looked away except Robert. 'I reckon Jarvis tripped him, Sir.'

'Is that right, Jarvis?'

'It was an accident, Sir. We were in a tackle.'

Mr Smith hoisted me off the ground and held me up while I hopped to the side of the court. 'Sit down on this bench and let's take a look at you.'

I pulled off my boot and sock. He took my foot in his hand and massaged it. 'Just a twist. It'll be fine in a while. Best sit out while we finish the game.' He blew his whistle and the rest of the boys carried on with the game. This was Robert Sanders's doing. I just knew it. Pretending to be nice while cooking up ideas to get at me.

By the end of the day my foot was fine but I was tired. I was also anxious about being picked up at the gate. However, unlike my last day at school, today was different, Robert was striding next to me and Neil hung back.

'You and I are going to be great pals,' Robert said.

I didn't want to be mates with him. 'What about Neil?'

'What about him?'

'Well he's my friend so if you want to be friends with me then he comes too.'

Robert turned up his nose. 'You've got to be kidding?'

I shook my head. 'No, I mean it.' Neil was there for me when the rest of them were being cruel. I wasn't going to abandon him and I didn't trust Sanders. 'So if you want to be my friend then you need to be his too.'

'All right, all right, maybe he's not such a wimp as he seems. Hey, Neil, you want to join us?'

Neil craned his neck looking around him.

'Neil,' I echoed, 'Come on.'

He ran and caught up with us and started chatting.

'We can get to know each other better while we wait for your ride.' Robert patted me on the back.

I looked towards the gate. 'That looks like him now.' I noticed someone get out of the back seat. *Elizabeth.* She must have known how nervous I'd be. 'That's my aunt. I'll see you both tomorrow.' I ran towards the car.

Chapter 36

George

Strangers were in the hall dragging a ten-foot Christmas tree through the back door. Two men stood it in a barrel while two more men slid another tree about the same size towards the ballroom.

'What's going on?' I asked Elizabeth.

'It's almost Christmas, George, so the trees and decorations are going up.'

'May I help to decorate?'

'Oh dear, I'm afraid not as Father hires people to do that. Why don't you go along to the kitchen and ask Cook for some hot chocolate?'

It wasn't fair, I didn't want hot chocolate, I wanted to help dress the tree but I wasn't allowed. Instead I sat on the stairs watching three young women dip into the boxes pulling out tinsel and coloured baubles while the men loaded more cardboard boxes on the floor. Other men carried more containers in the direction of the ballroom and women trailed behind them. I wished I was at home in Wintermore with our little artificial Christmas tree sitting on the sideboard. Da used to put me on his shoulders so I could reach to pop Tinkerbell, our fairy, on top of the tree. Then Da would switch on the coloured lights, and me, Alice and Mam would clap. This big tree was looking pretty but it wasn't special like ours. I ran upstairs to my room before anyone could see me crying.

*

It was Christmas Eve and the mansion was busy with maids running around with dusters. Extra staff had been called in ready for the big dinner and ball later this evening. I wished I didn't have to attend but Grandpa said he wanted me by his side. It was my chance to meet his acquaintances.

'Come along, Master George.' Martha appeared next to me from nowhere. 'Your bath's been run and a dinner suit is hanging up in your room.'

I went upstairs to the bathroom. I was now used to the luxurious gold taps and had almost forgotten about our old tinnie in the back yard. I closed the door, undressed and climbed into the huge shiny white tub. When I'd finished washing, I climbed out and dried myself with the fluffy towel just like I'd done every day since I'd been here except of course when I was kidnapped. Thankfully after my first day at Granville Hall, six months ago, Martha never came near the bathroom. I didn't need help getting bathed, I was nine-and-a-half after all.

Once back in my bedroom I spotted the black dinner suit hanging up with a white frilled shirt and a small black tie. This was no ordinary tie, it must be a bow tie like Grandpa wore most of the time but I didn't know how to tie it. I'd ask Elizabeth to help me. I stepped into the long black trousers and pulled the braces up over my shoulders across the white crisp shirt and slid into the matching suit jacket. I stared in the mirror and didn't recognise myself.

There was a tap on the door. 'Only me, are you decent?' Elizabeth asked.

'Yes, but I'm not quite ready.'

She pushed the door open and walked in.

'How do I do this thing?' I held up the bow tie.

'Don't worry, I'll do it for you. They can be tricky.'

She stood facing me, fastened the tie around my neck and tied the bow. 'Have a look.' She nudged me towards the mirror.

'It's perfect, how did you do that?'

'I'll teach you, as you'll be wearing them lots. This evening's event is the first of many. Are you excited?'

'Yes,' I lied. I couldn't think of anything worse. I wished I could go to my room instead of being shown off as Grandpa's prize.

'Where's your new shoes?'

'I don't know. I didn't know I had any.'

'Yes, I ordered them for you.' She looked all around the room. 'I'll be back in a moment.'

I sat on my bed just staring at the strange penguin boy in the mirror. My life had changed so much. I had changed so much. I didn't look like George Gilmore anymore, I was George Granville.

'Here we are.' Elizabeth marched back in with a box in her hand. She opened it and passed me a shiny pair of black shoes. 'These should fit.'

'What size are they?'

'Size 3 but we have other sizes for you to try if they don't suit.'

I slid my foot into the shoe. It pinched my toes. Elizabeth bent down and pressed on the toe area of the shoe. 'They fit perfectly and you have room for growth.'

The shoes squeaked and hurt as I walked across the floor area but I didn't say anything.

'Just walk up and down in them for a while to break them in. I must go and get ready so I'll meet you downstairs in an hour. Just remember to be polite and smile. This is your night to shine. Father wants to show off his grandson, the heir of Granville, to everyone.'

162

Chapter 37

George

I took a deep breath and walked down the stairs wishing the steps would never end. People paced into the ballroom chatting and laughing as they walked. My heart beat fast. This evening I was to sit at Grandpa's side and meet many of his acquaintances. I wished I could stay upstairs or eat in the kitchen with Cook. I was terrified. Elizabeth met me at the bottom of the stairs.

'George, you look delightful. So grown-up.'

I knew what she meant. I looked more like twelve or thirteen than nine. Elizabeth's dark brown hair was piled in soft rolls on her head and the rest of her hair flowed down to one shoulder in a curly ponytail. Her black silky dress had a long train, like Mam's wedding dress, and went all the way down to her shiny high heels. Was this really my Aunt Elizabeth? A string of white pearls hung around her neck. I couldn't take my eyes off her. If she wasn't my aunty, I'd marry her.

'Ready?' She held out her hand.

'Ready,' I said but felt anything but.

'You can walk me in, take my arm.'

I linked my arm into hers like the other couples in front and wandered into the ballroom. Grandfather had organised full length tables across both sides of the room and they were filling up fast. A huge Christmas tree stood in the corner with flashing lights, it was even bigger than the one in the hall. Instead of a fairy on the top it had a silver star. The tables were covered in red and white tablecloths, decorated with gold tinsel.

Grandfather was already seated in a throne-like chair at the top table on a platform facing the other tables where other people were sitting down and chatting. Grandpa raised his hand to signal me.

'George.' He pointed to the seat next to him.

Elizabeth glided up the two steps taking me with her. Grandpa patted the chair next to him. 'This one is reserved for you, and your aunt can sit the other side of you.' Grandmother was next to Grandpa. Her short dark hair must have had curlers in it because it was all wavy. She was wearing a red dress that was looser than Elizabeth's. Large diamond earrings hung from her ears and she wore a necklace and bracelet that matched. And Grandpa, well Grandpa looked like Grandpa but a bit grander than usual. His dinner suit was the same as mine with the wide satin belt that Elizabeth said was called a cummerbund. I sat down next to Grandpa, my legs still shaking. Elizabeth sat next to me and from under the table she clasped my hand. She must have known how scared I was.

A band played *God Rest you Merry Gentleman*. When all the chairs were filled up the music stopped and Grandpa stood up. Everyone started to clap.

Grandpa raised his hand. 'Thank you everyone for coming this evening. Tonight's a very special event as I would like to introduce you all to my grandson, George Charles Granville, the heir of Granville. I would like you all to stand and toast this young man. Please raise your glasses to George, the heir of Granville.'

'George, the heir of Granville,' everyone repeated and clinked glasses.

Grandpa signalled for me to stand up. *Please don't make me do a speech.* I stood up from my seat, my heart was banging and my hands shook.

'Just smile and nod,' whispered Grandpa.

I smiled and nodded and everyone clapped. Grandpa signalled me to sit down as the band started to play *Good King Wenceslas*. The waiters and waitresses rushed around the ballroom serving out food and pouring champagne, even in my glass.

Taking my small spoon and fork I ate the prawn cocktail and brown cut bread. I knew what to expect because Elizabeth had arranged for Cook to prepare the same meal for me to try beforehand.

'Are you enjoying yourself?' Grandpa asked me.

'Yes, thank you,' I lied.

Huge turkeys were placed at each end of the tables for men to carve and the waitresses passed it around on plates. I'd never seen so many waitresses in one room. They all looked the same with black dresses and white pinnies and little white hats. I spotted Annie. She was wearing one of the waitress uniforms too.

After dinner they brought out two types of gateaux. Black forest, and strawberry. Jellies and trifles were laid out too. I'd never seen so much food. And big baskets of fruit containing black and green grapes, oranges, bananas, apples and pears were spread across the tables. The room was so filled with noise from chatter, clinks of glasses and tinkling of cutlery, that I could barely hear the Christmas carols. Once everyone had finished eating, coffee was brought, and a lady with a harp appeared. She strummed the strings and started to sing *Silent Night* with a soft high voice. Everyone went quiet. She had pretty pink flowers in her hair. She looked about sixteen, and her white lace dress spread along the floor. Once she'd finished, everyone clapped. I clapped too because she was really good. I'd never heard a harpist play before.

The band started playing again. This time it was dance music rather than Christmas Carols. Grandpa took Grandma's hand

and led her to the dance floor and waltzed around the floor. Everyone clapped.

Elizabeth took my hand. 'It's our turn now. You remember the steps?'

I nodded. I did remember the steps but hoped my feet would. We joined Grandma and Grandpa and everyone clapped again. After we'd been around the floor once, everyone else started to join in. I stood on Elizabeth's feet twice. Soon the dance floor was full of couples waltzing and when couples got close to me, they'd whisper, 'Pleased to meet you, Master George.'

'Thank you.' I'd smile. My head felt a little light from the champagne but it helped me relax and my legs had stopped shaking.

We danced on and off until midnight. The band stopped playing and Grandpa stood up. 'Thank you, everyone for coming. Merry Christmas and Happy New Year to you all.'

Everyone raised their glasses. 'Merry Christmas and Happy New Year.' The people started to leave the room until there was only family left.

'You did very well this evening, young man,' Grandpa said, 'but now it's time for bed. Christmas tomorrow.'

'Thank you for a lovely evening,' I said, and meant it.

Elizabeth escorted me from the ballroom. 'Good night, George.' She pecked me on the cheek.

'Good night, Aunt Elizabeth.' I climbed the stairs. This was the first year I hadn't hung up a stocking and no one had mentioned me having one. I fell into bed and closed my eyes.

Chapter 38

Elizabeth

George did well last night at the Christmas Eve ball. I was proud of him and Mother and Father were too. He'd come a long way from the common lad that came to the Hall six months ago. I wondered what his reaction would be once he saw his main Christmas gift.

Simon trotted across the paddock as I reached the stables. I recognised him by the stunning steed he was riding, and the flick of blond hair hanging from his riding hat. He waved, dismantled Millie and reined her towards me. Father wanted to give her to George after lunch.

I held my hand out to shake Simon's but instead he kissed my cheek.

'Happy Christmas, Elizabeth.' He passed me a small package.

I sensed myself burning up. I hadn't thought of purchasing him a gift. 'You shouldn't have.'

'It's just a small token. Open it.'

I unwrapped the holly-design paper and revealed a bottle of *Floris*, Eau de Parfum. 'This is far too much, Simon.' I lifted the cap and sniffed. 'It's my favourite. How did you know?'

'I smelt it on you last time we met. Richard's wife wears the same fragrance.'

'Thank you. I'm sorry I haven't got anything for you.'

'See it as a client gift and a sort of a goodbye gift.'

'You're going away?'

'Yes, I'm going to Dorset for a while. My father-in-law is in bad health and I need to take care of the holding as there's no one else. It may only take a couple of months but on the other hand it could be a couple of years.'

'Sorry to hear about your father-in-law. I hope his health improves. Will you stay for lunch?'

'No, unfortunately I can't. Richard and his wife have invited me over and the children are looking forward to seeing their Uncle Simon.'

'Will I see you before you leave?'

'Unlikely, as I intend to leave directly after the holidays.'

'So this is goodbye then?'

'I'm afraid so dear lady. I do hope your young man loves his new friend.' He patted Millie on the back.

'Without a doubt I'm sure. He won't be able to ride her yet but he can take care of her. He's still got a lot to learn.'

Simon looked at his watch. 'I need to be off, Richard's waiting the other side of the paddock.' He kissed my cheek.

I watched him stomp across the grass until he was out of sight. A tear slipped. I wiped my eye. *Don't be stupid, Elizabeth. It's not like there was anything between you.* Maybe one day he'd come back and be over his wife.

Andy came up behind me. 'Morning, Miss Elizabeth. This must be Millie then?'

'Happy Christmas, Andy. Yes, isn't she a beauty?'

'I'll get her ready for Master George.'

'Don't make yourself late for the staff Christmas lunch though. You don't want to make Cook cross.'

'Don't worry, Miss, it won't take me long.'

'I'd best hurry. Master George will be wondering where I am. Good day to you, Andy.'

*

As I headed into the house laughter was coming from the kitchen. The staff were getting excited about their Christmas lunch and Father's gift to each of them in the form of a brown envelope containing cash. He could be generous at times and always made sure the staff were treated well at Christmas, and that included a nice little bonus in their pay packets.

I paced upstairs to quickly freshen up and change before making my way down to the dining room. George was just ahead of me about to go downstairs.

'Happy Christmas, George.' I kissed his cheek.

'Happy Christmas, Aunt Elizabeth.' He didn't look very happy. The white of his eyes looked pink like he'd been crying. I suppose he was missing his old family. Millie would cheer him up.

'What's wrong?' I asked.

'Nothing.' He turned his face away from me.

'Aren't you excited about Christmas?'

'What's there to be excited about?'

'Presents of course.' I stroked his arm.

He shrugged his shoulders.

'I imagine it's hard for you. Missing your mother, father and sisters.'

He nodded his head, opened his mouth to say something and then changed his mind. 'Go on, say,' I said.

'It doesn't matter.'

'Yes, it does. Say.'

'Well I never got to hang a stocking. We have huge Christmas trees here but no presents.'

'I'm sorry, I didn't think. But don't worry, there will be gifts. It's just that we do things a little different at Granville Hall. You'll see. Come along, I can smell lunch.' The aroma of roast beef tickled my nose.

Chapter 39

George

When I walked into the dining room with Elizabeth, I was surprised to see a round table in place of the regular rectangular one that seated lots of people. The decorated candles in the middle made it look pretty and it was set for four people.

It was certainly different to what it would've been like at home with Mam and Da. For starters we called it dinner not lunch. I squeezed my eyes to stop getting weepy. I missed my family so much. I loved Elizabeth, Grandpa and Grandma, as they were nice to me now, but still hoped to live with Mam and my sisters again one day.

Grandpa sliced the beef and passed the plates to Martha to fill with roast potatoes, cabbage and carrots. Annie left a big tray of Yorkshire puddings in the centre and a jug of gravy to help ourselves. The beef was delicious, it wasn't new to me as we had it at Granville Hall quite regularly.

For afters we had Christmas pudding. Grandpa struck a match to it and sent it up in flames. Da used to do that too but that was the only thing the same. I missed not having a stocking. I didn't even get the tangerine that was always stuck in the bottom of the sock. That was probably because I could have one any time but I missed the fun, and I got no new cars or tractors. Da always managed to get me the latest ones. Alice and I would dig into our stockings and then grab our pillowslips packed with presents and drag them into Mam and Da's bedroom and climb on the bottom of their bed taking turns to open the presents one by one. I had nothing like that today.

Not even one present and it was now three o'clock in the afternoon.

After dinner we sat in the drawing room by the fire and played cards. Grandfather was teaching me to play Gin Rummy and said I was a quick learner. I'd just laid down a run of hearts and a set of queens when I heard jingling. I looked up from the game to see Father Christmas waddling through the door. 'Ho Ho Ho,' he said, and placed a present in front of each of us.

'Open yours first,' Grandpa said to me.

I unwrapped the patterned reindeer paper to find a small gold box.

'Open it,' Grandpa said impatiently.

I lifted the lid and glared at a Timex watch. Not wanting to look ungrateful, I smiled, but thought it was a boring present, not the sort of present that Mam and Da always gave me. They always surprised me with what they bought even though we didn't have much money. I already had a watch which Elizabeth had given me when I first arrived at Granville Hall, so I didn't see why I needed another one.

'It's the latest one out,' Grandpa said. 'I hope you like it.'

'Yes, thank you.'

'Open yours, Elizabeth,' said Grandma.

Elizabeth unwrapped her package. It was perfume and handkerchiefs. Grandma's looked the same and Grandpa had Old Spice aftershave. I suppose they had so much money that they didn't really need presents.

Grandpa stood up. 'We need to go for a little walk to give you your main present,' he said to me.

I gave a big grin and hoped I wasn't going to be disappointed. Maybe we were going on a mystery trail.

'Come along young man.' Grandpa gripped my hand. I'd never seen him so excited and Grandma and Elizabeth were smiling too.

'It's snowing outside so we'd better put on boots,' Grandpa said.

After we popped on our coats and wellies, we plodded outside the back door and crunched on the snow towards the stables.

'Are we going to make a snowman?' I asked.

'Definitely not,' Grandpa said. 'You're still convalescing. We can't risk you getting ill again.'

Grandpa stopped at the stables. The groom came out but there was no sign of Andy. I expect he was having his dinner. 'Close your eyes,' Grandpa said, 'I'll guide you.' He led me into the stables. I wasn't sure what to expect. He let go of my arm. 'You can open them now.'

In front of me stood a beautiful black pony with a plaited mane and tail and a big red ribbon around its neck.

'She's yours,' Elizabeth said. 'Her name's Millie.'

'For me?'

'Yes,' Grandpa said. 'Do you like her?'

'I love her.' I hugged the horse. 'May I ride her?'

'Not yet because you still have lots to learn.' Grandpa said. 'Once the weather is warmer you'll be ready and in the meantime you can take care of her.'

It was a lovely present and I did love her but felt sad too. It was Alice who'd always wanted a horse. I'd never thought about having one. Maybe in time Grandpa would allow Mam and my sisters to come and stay.

'Right, let's get you back inside, young man. We don't want a relapse.'

The snow splattered my face and hid my tears as we trudged back to the house.

Chapter 40

Elizabeth

I was late downstairs for breakfast which meant George had already left for school. Apart from the recurring nightmares, he seemed to have put the last few months behind him. Breakfast was still laid out on the side. I buttered a couple of slices of cold toast from the rack and poured out a small glass of fresh orange juice. I'd just sat down and taken a sip of the drink when Father marched in.

'Elizabeth, I thought I might find you in here. Late start?'

'Sorry, Father, I didn't sleep well last night.'

'Never mind that now. Finish up here and come and find me in the library. There's something I'd like to discuss with you.' He hurried out as quickly as he'd entered. I wondered what he wanted to discuss. It might've been to do with sending George away. I'd got so attached to him that I didn't want him to go anywhere. He was happy and becoming quite an expert rider. Such a quick learner. Only last week we rode across the estate together and he managed to keep up with me.

I chewed a mouthful of toast before deciding I didn't want it anymore. My stomach turned. What was Father going to say?

I went upstairs to the bathroom to clean my teeth and pull a comb through my hair before piling it into a bun then dabbed a couple of drops of Chanel No. 5 onto my wrists. I made my way downstairs to the library.

The door was open so I gave it a tap and walked in. Father was sitting behind his desk.

'Do sit down.' He signalled to the empty chair opposite him.

'What can I help you with, Father?'

'I've been making enquiries about George going off to school this September and managed to reserve him a place at Sandalwood.'

'But so soon?'

'Elizabeth, the boy's ten now.'

'But what about his bad dreams?'

'The problem is sorted.'

'How?'

'Robert Sanders is due to start this year too. I've arranged that George will share a room with him. That way if he has a nightmare the whole dormitory isn't going to know. I shall brief the Sanders boy. Oh and that little wimp, Neil Pendlebury, has a place too. You know the one that George seems to have befriended?'

I hadn't realised that Father had taken so much interest in George's friends. I certainly hadn't appreciated that he knew about Neil, although he had been up to the mansion a couple of times to play with George.

'Elizabeth, did you hear what I said?'

'Sorry, yes Father. You're right. It makes sense for George to go the same time as Neil and Robert. But wouldn't it be better for George to share a room with Neil? Neil's far more sensitive. I'm concerned Robert may make difficulties for George. And he's still vulnerable.'

'The last thing I want is for George to share a room with that namby-pamby. He needs to be around tough lads. So we're in agreement?'

'Yes Father.'

*

174

Dinner was being served at 8pm. Father had requested we dress formally as he'd invited guests but wouldn't declare who.

I stepped into a black silk dress. The gown brushed against my stilettos as I moved. A single string of white pearls lay in front of the mirror on my dressing table. I fastened them around my neck and glared at my reflection. My dark brown hair fell in waves and my blue eyes stared back at me.

As I walked towards the staircase I was met by George looking dashing in his black dinner suit and bow tie. His blond curls hung slightly across his forehead. When he first arrived, he had a mop of curls but Father ordered them to be chopped. I was glad his curls had grown back.

'Good evening, young man,' I said. 'You're going to be a real lady killer.'

'Don't,' he said bashfully. 'Do you know what's going on?'

I sensed George was nervous from his slow words and breaths. He worried about strangers coming to the house after the kidnap saga.

'You're as wise as me. I've got no idea but let's go and find out.'

We entered the dining room arm in arm. Mother was standing near the fireplace talking to a man I didn't recognise. She looked lovely this evening. Her emerald dress accentuated her dark hair and she too was wearing pearls but a triple layer. She stroked the beads around her neck while chatting. I wondered who she was talking to, and what was being said.

'Why's he here?' George asked.

I stared across to the other side of the room and noticed Robert Sanders so realised that must be his father speaking to Mother. So that's what this was all about.

'We'll have to wait and see.' I felt like I was betraying George because I had an idea this evening was to discuss schooling, but surely shouldn't Father have spoken to George in private first?

Father entered the room and everyone turned to face him. 'Thank you everyone for coming. We still have one more guest to come, so do have a drink while you're waiting. The waitress is serving drinks.'

Martha walked in carrying a tray of champagne filled goblets. A woman with a tiny frame, dressed in a bright green evening gown, glided in behind. Her face was more youthful than Mother's. Mother wasn't going to be happy as the colour of the woman's gown almost matched hers. The woman strode next to Robert and placed her hand over his. So this was Lady Sanders. Therefore, who was the extra guest? The table was set for eight. Mother, Father, The Sanders, George and me, that was seven. My stomach bubbled inside. Please let it be Simon. But I wasn't even sure if he was back, and surely Father wouldn't invite one brother without the other?

'Ah, here's our late guest now. Sir William and Lady Sanders, let me introduce you to Simon Anson. He owns the best equestrian centre, Ashland's Farm, for miles. He's your man if you need a new horse. We bought one for George at Christmas and we've not been disappointed.'

Father took my arm and led me away from the group. 'I've invited Simon to make up the numbers. I trust that's not going to be a problem for you?'

'No, not at all, Father,' I said, trying to get my words out as I was shaking.

'You seem nervous?'

'I think I'm just a little chilly. I hope I'm not coming down with something.'

'I hope not too.' He turned away and moved towards the dinner guests. 'Friends, shall we dine?'

Father sat at the head, with Mother at the other end, Sir Henry on her left side and Simon on the other. George sat next to me, and on my other side, Simon. Lady Sanders sat next to

176

Father on his right, and the boys sat opposite each other with George next to Father. Annie served vegetable soup while Martha poured white wine into the glasses.

Simon kissed my hand. 'It's very nice to see you, again, Elizabeth.'

'You too, Mr Anson. Have you completed your business in Dorset?'

'Simon, please. I thought we were on first-name terms. For now. My father-in-law made an unexpected recovery but I'm not sure for how long.'

'I hope he continues in good health.'

'I don't suppose you'd consider coming on a picnic with me tomorrow, would you?'

'I might.' I smiled.

Father made small talk with Lady Sanders while she kept her voice low and fidgeted with her wedding ring. Mother seemed engrossed in Sir William. The boys stared at each other across the table.

'Do you know what this is about?' Robert asked.

George shrugged. 'No idea.'

I could see Father's point. A friendship with Robert would be more value at Sandalwood than Neil, and they appeared to be getting on well this evening.

Father patted Lady Sanders' hand. 'Excuse me. I see the boys are getting impatient to find out what this is all about.'

Robert and George nodded.

'Robert, your father and I have been chatting. And this concerns you too, George. We've managed to reserve places for you both at Sandalwood from this September. Isn't that good news?'

'That's excellent news.' Robert rubbed his hands.

'Sandalwood? Isn't that the public school in Westbridge?' George asked.

'That's right. It's the best educational establishment around,' Father said.

'But I thought you said I didn't have to go away?'

'What's the matter, lad?' Sir William interrupted. 'This is a big chance for you. Look how excited Robert is.'

'But…'

Father interrupted George. 'You're ten now, George. Time to learn to stand on your own two feet. Your friend Neil Pendlebury has a place too.'

'Oh? Why isn't he here this evening too?'

'Oh God, not that little weakling that hangs around you all the time.' Robert picked up his glass and took a swig of wine.

'Don't be so offensive. Neil's all right,' George said, 'and he was my first friend at Oakleaf when no one else wanted to know.'

'Does that mean you're happy to give it a go?' Father asked.

'It doesn't look like I have a lot of choice.'

'Good. I've arranged for a visit next week.'

'It will be fine, George,' I said. 'I'll be along for the visit too.'

'There appears to be a misunderstanding, Elizabeth,' Father said, 'Sir William will go with the boys. George doesn't need an old aunt holding his hand. Do you, George?'

'No Grandfather.'

Chapter 41

George

Everywhere was silent except for the odd rustle of a tree and my footsteps as I padded towards the stables. It was too early for the stable hands to be around. I saddled Millie and led her out. 'How are you girl? I'm going to miss you. Let's have one last ride.' I climbed on her back and trotted across the meadow moving to a canter as the sun started to rise with a burning yellow. It was going to be a nice day. The ride was just starting to settle my nervous shakes when galloping hooves came up from behind me. My chest hurt. I shook the reins to let Millie know to go faster. Who was after me? Was it happening again? How could I have been so stupid to have come out when no one else was around? I thought I was safe on Grandfather's estate.

'George,' Elizabeth called, 'it's only me.'

I tightened my knees against the saddle and gripped the reins. Millie started to slow down to stop. 'Aunt Elizabeth,' I panted, 'what are you doing here?'

'I couldn't sleep either. I was looking out of my bedroom window when I saw you creep out. You know you shouldn't be out at this early hour on your own, don't you?'

'Sorry, I didn't think.'

'Well we need to get you back.'

'I'd like to watch the sun finish coming up first if I may? It's so spectacular.'

'It is, isn't it? We'll watch it together and then get back before someone notices.' She dismounted her horse and I did the same. The sky got lighter. Orange and yellow shone with hints of blue. Da always told me this was the best time of the day and he was right.

'Time to go.' Elizabeth climbed back on to her horse.

I wanted to stay longer but knew I had to go. I mounted Millie. By the time Elizabeth and I trotted back to the stables it was daylight.

'Good morning, Miss Elizabeth, Master George. Shall I take your horses?'

'Thank you, Andy.' Elizabeth passed him the reins from her chestnut brown pony.

'Please can I stay to brush Millie down?' I asked.

'No, George, you need time to bathe before breakfast. Father will be cross if you arrive late.'

I sank my head into Millie's coat. 'Bye girl. See you soon.'

*

A silver limousine pulled up outside Granville Hall, just like Grandfather's. A chauffeur stepped out of the car.

'Master George.' He tipped his hat.

Elizabeth, Cook, Martha and Annie all stood on the steps watching me.

Elizabeth moved closer to hug me as Grandpa came out of the house. 'Elizabeth, what are you doing?'

'Just saying goodbye to George, Father.'

'Well I hope you don't intend hugging him in front of his peers.'

Elizabeth stuttered. 'No of course not.'

'Good.' Grandpa strode towards me. 'Now young man, Sandalwood will be the making of you. It will teach you to become independent and confident. And you'll be back home in time for Christmas. Don't let anyone push you around. Do you understand?'

'Yes, Grandfather.' I stretched out my hand to shake his before moving towards Elizabeth. 'Don't worry, Aunt Elizabeth, I'll be fine and I'll write to you.' I kissed her cheek. 'Where's Grandmother?'

'She's here,' Grandpa said as Grandma came out of the front door and stood by his side.

'Goodbye, Grandmother.' I kissed her on the cheek like I'd done with Elizabeth having been told that was acceptable.

I sloped down the steps and when I reached the bottom, I turned back to waving hands and smiling faces. I waved back before climbing into the back of the car next to Neil. Robert sat by the other window.

'Isn't this fun?' Robert said.

I shrugged. I wasn't sure it was going to be fun. How did I know I wouldn't get kidnapped again? Neil didn't seem that impressed either. In fact I spotted a tear on his face, even if he did try to hide it. Thankfully Robert missed that, otherwise he'd have given Neil a really hard time.

The driver started up the engine. Robert started jabbering. 'Isn't this fab?'

Shut up, Robert. I peered out of the side window. Elizabeth and the others continued to wave and eventually faded to black specks. It was just like the day I was forced to leave Wintermore. Once again, I was being snatched from a home where I was happy.

Part II

Chapter 1

George

Friday 9th August 1968

Just before I turned out of the Strand, I took one last look back and watched Elizabeth go through The Savoy's entrance. I was sure I might throw up. Mam was here. After all these years she was finally here. But even now she hadn't come for me. She'd only come because Grandfather had asked her to. He'd persuaded me to help convince her to come. 'I'm on borrowed time,' he'd said as I sat by his bedside in the dark room, listening closely as, under his rasping breath, he tried to get his words out. Why hadn't anyone warned me that he was dying? And now this. He wanted to make peace with Mam. I'd tried to argue but he started spluttering. The nurse rushed over to his bedside and held a bowl under his chin as he spat out blood. Feeling sick and faint, I staggered over to the window, drawing the curtains a fraction to pull up the window for some air, staying away from his bed while the nurse took care of him. How could I deny a dying man his last wish? I wondered how long he had left to live, and what Mam had done that was so awful she was never allowed back to Granville Hall.

I pushed the glass door and walked into the pokey café. I laughed under my breath at the comparison with The Savoy. The place was empty so I took a seat by the window.

'Hello dearie,' the middle-aged woman in a white tunic and mob cap, said. 'What can I get you?'

'Just a cup of tea, please.' I turned to the window.

'Want it in a mug?'

'That would be nice, thank you.' I hadn't drunk from a mug since I was a kid in Wintermore.

The woman waddled off behind the counter and started clanking china. 'Want an iced bun or scone with that?' she shouted.

'No thanks.'

She paced her way back with a tray containing a jug of milk, sugar cubes, and a mug almost as big as Da's old one. 'What's the matter, Pet? You look like you've lost a pound and found a penny.'

'Nothing, I'm fine thanks.'

'Well you don't look fine. Where's your mam, is she meeting you here?'

I was wishing I hadn't come in. Nosey old bat. Why couldn't she just leave me alone? She stared right at me. It was obvious she wasn't going to go away without an answer. I longed for someone else to come into the café to keep her busy. 'My aunt's meeting me shortly.'

'Oh aye, where's she then? Shoppin?'

She was persistent, I'd give her that. 'She's meeting a client over at The Savoy.'

'The Savoy, eh? Bit different than ere, aye?'

I nodded and turned to the window hoping she'd take the hint to leave me alone. I wished Patsy were here. Patsy had been my girlfriend for a year now. I couldn't believe my luck when she chose me rather than Robert.

Using my handkerchief, I wiped away the beads of sweat from my forehead. It was too hot. I shouldn't have arranged to meet Elizabeth here. I picked up the mug and sipped the tea. Good God, it was like dishwater. I placed the mug back down on the table and decided to go for a wander. I'd be back on the Strand by the time Elizabeth came looking for me.

I stood up away from the table and headed towards the door. 'Bye.'

'What you going already? But you aven't finished your tea.'

I didn't hang around. Poor old woman, she must be lonely but I wasn't in the mood for chit-chat. Not today. Not when my stomach was churning. I wasn't sure whether it was from excitement about the prospect of seeing Mam again or because I didn't want to see her. I wondered what Alice and Beth were like. Beth would be six. Did she look like me? Did she even know about me? Alice would be twelve. I wondered if she still had her curls and what Mam was like. She'd done well for herself so she hadn't come for money this time. Only yesterday I'd picked up a newspaper with her and her new boyfriend all over it. *I'm going to throw-up.* I put my hand over my mouth and gagged. I checked my watch. I'd been thirty minutes, Elizabeth would be worried. I picked up my pace and strode back towards The Strand.

I reached The Savoy just as Elizabeth was coming out of the door.

'George, what are you doing wandering around in this heat? You'll get heatstroke?'

No wonder I felt sick. I hadn't thought about that. 'The woman in the café was asking too many questions. Is Grace in there?'

'Yes, and she's eager to meet you. Give her a chance, George.'

'What's she like?'

'She's beautiful, and she's missed you so much.'

'Don't give me that. If she'd missed me so much she'd have come and found me. Not even a phone call in six years. Does that sound like someone that cares?'

Elizabeth placed her hand on my shoulder. 'She does, George. Give her a chance.'

'You shouldn't have made me come.'

'If you don't come in, you'll never know the answers to your questions. And you promised Father, remember? I'm pleased I've found my sister again.'

'I'm going to be sick.' I rushed to the Gents and just managed to get over the bowl in time to heave. I pulled the chain, washed my hands and swilled warm water around my face, staring into the mirror. I wondered what she'd make of me. Perhaps she wouldn't recognise me.

Elizabeth was standing outside the Gents waiting when I came out. I took a deep breath and wiped my hand across my mouth, licking my lips. I needed a drink of water.

'Are you ready?' She touched my hand.

'Give me a couple of minutes. You go on in. I promise I'll come through.'

'All right, but don't be long.' Elizabeth walked back inside the restaurant.

I paced up and down for a while. My legs felt like jelly. *Was that nerves or from throwing up?* I'd better go and face it. I took a deep breath and walked inside where the Maître d' greeted me.

'Good afternoon, Master Granville. Your aunt is this way.' He walked on in front.

I could see Mam a mile off. She was wearing expensive clothes and her hair was meticulous but I could see it was her, she had that same smile. For a moment my resistance slackened and I quickened my steps but then the thought of what she did hit me again so I slowed down but still reached the table too fast.

She stood up, leaning on the table and greeted me. 'George, darling, it's so good to see you.' She went to hug me but I backed away. 'You're the image of your father.'

I shrugged my shoulders.

'Come and sit down, George?' Elizabeth said.

I eased the chair from under the table watching Grace watching me.

'I've waited so long for this day,' she said sitting down.

'Really? I can't think why,' I said quietly, wanting to scream. 'What do you mean?'

'You sold me. You're a Judas, only you got a bit more than thirty pieces of silver for me, didn't you?'

Just at that moment the waiter appeared at the table. There was silence as he arranged finger sandwiches, scones with jam and cream, and small delicate cakes. I focused on her face the whole time, waiting for her answer.

Shaking her head, she said, 'I didn't sell you. I was put in a predicament where I had no choice but to let you go with Mother.'

Elizabeth tried to defuse the situation. 'George, look at all these lovely cakes.'

I ignored her and focused on Mam. 'Have you any idea what it was like to be ripped away from your family, straight after your father's died?'

'I can imagine.'

'No, I don't think you can. Stolen away. Stolen away not just from my mother, but my sisters. Where are they anyway? Or did you sell them too?'

'Alice is at home, eager to meet you.'

'And Beth? Not that you gave me the chance to know her. She must be six?'

Mam wiped her eyes. 'I'm sorry, darling, but I'm afraid Beth died.'

'What? When?' So she'd stolen the chance of me getting to know my baby sister. I thought about how I used to feed and change her. And now I'd never get to know her.

'It was Scarlet Fever when she was nearly two.'

'Oh my God, it gets better. It didn't occur to you to let me know? I should've at least been allowed to attend the funeral.'

'I tried, George, really, I did. I haven't stopped trying. Not just to tell you about your sister but to get you back home. I've been trying since the day Mother took you, six years ago. I've been to *Granville Hall*, I've written to you, Mother, and Elizabeth.'

I looked at Elizabeth. She nodded back in acknowledgement.

'Then how come I never got a letter?' I sat back in my chair. 'I saw you come to the Hall, once. I tried to wave to you but the maid pulled me away from the window. I thought you'd come to get me but you hadn't. You left me there. Abandoned me. You deserted me yet again. Elizabeth said you'd come for more money.' I remembered that dreadful day when Martha had snatched me away from the window and rapped my legs with the ruler.

'I did come to get you. But Mother wouldn't let me in.'

'I phoned you once.' I leant forwards in the chair. 'But you were too busy. When I found out where you were living it took me ages to pluck up the courage to phone you and then you didn't want to know.'

'I don't understand. No one told me.'

'I didn't say who I was because I could hear you shouting in the background that you didn't want to speak to anyone. Too busy for me. After all I was only your son. Why would I count?'

'You've always counted. If only I'd known... The last few years have been dominated by trying to get you home.'

'I'm sure. Don't make me laugh.' I picked up the newspaper and waved it in front of her. 'You've been far too busy with your fancy man.' I flung the paper at her face.

'He's my business partner.'

'It didn't take you long to replace my da, did it?'

189

'George, don't be too harsh on your mother. There are things you don't know. Not just about the letters, but other things that I didn't know about before today. You need to give her a chance.'

I sat still for a moment before dragging my chair back. 'I don' wanna know. I've 'ad enough of this. I wanna go 'ome. I told you I didn' wanna cum.'

Grace rummaged into her bag and pulled out a large wad of envelopes. 'George, before you go, take these. Read them and then hopefully you'll understand.'

I snatched the batch from her hands, stood up and stormed out of the restaurant without looking back.

*

Elizabeth found me leaning on a wall. She put her hand on my arm. 'Are you all right? You look very pale. It must have been a shock.'

'No, I'm not.' I pushed her away. 'But what do you care? You forced me to go when I said I didn't want to.'

'I do care, and so does your mother. Read those letters and you'll see. Mother and Father gave her no choice but to hand you over. They threatened to notify the authorities that she was neglecting you all and to be honest George, she wouldn't have stood a chance. Father would have made sure of that. At least this way you had a good home and so did your sisters.'

'And now one of my sisters is dead and I didn't even know.' I wiped my sleeve across my eyes.

'I know. Look the car's here. Get in.'

I climbed into the back seat and Elizabeth followed. The driver did a three-point turn and we were on our way back to Granville Hall. I wanted to run away.

'Read those letters when you get in,' Elizabeth said again. 'Look, she's given me a bundle too. I thought she'd forgotten all about me too but it looks like she tried. See, they say *Return to Sender*, that means they must have come to Granville Hall first and Father sent them back.'

'But why would he do that?'

'He wanted you, George. He was obviously so desperate for an heir that he went to those lengths and I presume that's what he wants to make right with Grace.'

'Even so, she should have found a way. I'll read the letters but I'm not going to forgive her. I can't.'

Once the car stopped at Granville Hall, I climbed out and ran up the steps clutching the bundle of envelopes. Grandmother stopped me. 'Did she say she'll come?'

'I don't know. You'll have to ask her.' I pointed to Elizabeth behind me.

'No good can come from this.' Grandmother moved towards Elizabeth.

*

I threw the bundle of letters onto the bed. I wanted to scream. I was about to rip them up but thought better of it. I flipped through the different sized envelopes, some greeting card-sized whilst others larger, and opened one of the big ones marked *Return to Sender*. It was a birthday card with the number ten on it.

> *Happy tenth Birthday, my darling George. I hope you're happy. Mother tells me you are. If ever you want to leave Granville Hall and come home, just call or write. Our new address is above.*
> *I miss you so much and so does Alice. We love you.*
> *Mam*
> *xxx*

191

I opened the first small letter in the bundle.

Dear George,

I visited Granville Hall today to see if you were ready to come home. Mother told me that you're happy. If this isn't the case please contact me at this address…

It certainly sounded like she'd been telling the truth but even so, she was my mam, she should've found a way. And this was Grandmother's doing, I don't suppose Grandfather knew anything about it.

If Patsy were here she'd help me decide what to do. I missed the way her long blonde hair tickled my face when we kissed, and how it smelled like the apple trees in Grandfather's orchard. It was hard being away from her but necessary so I could visit Grandfather. I packed up the letters and put them in the top drawer of the chest. I'd think about this later after seeing Grandfather. It seemed that every time I got close to someone they left me.

After a short sleep I was heading downstairs when Elizabeth appeared. 'George, are you all right?'

I shrugged my shoulders. 'You shouldn't have made me go?' Memories of my first day at Granville Hall came flooding back. Martha and her aggressive behaviour, Grandmother not letting me speak, and Grandfather making me call him *Sir*. Who'd have thought I'd have grown to love him, all of them, and this place too. 'How is he?'

'Father? He's got a nasty chest infection. The antibiotics will help. We're not going to lose him yet.'

'Thank goodness. Is he awake?'

'He was sleeping when I left him but that was a while ago. Why not pop in and see him before dinner?'

I took the remaining stairs down while Elizabeth carried on up. When I reached Grandfather's room, I found the door open. It was dark and Grandmother sat by his bed holding his hand.

'How is he?' I asked.

'Not good, but at least his temperature's gone down. Nurse reckons he should be up and about again in a couple of days.' She started to sob. 'I can't lose him.'

I'd never seen her like this. She'd always been so strong. I wanted answers but now wasn't the time.

'George.' Grandfather beckoned me.

'Hello, Grandfather. How are you doing?'

'I'm fine, lad. You know me, I'll be up and about again in no time. There's lots of work to be done. You need to learn more about the business.'

I didn't want to go into the business, I wanted to be an architect but every time I mentioned this it caused a row so instead, I smiled. 'You get yourself better then. Rest now. Grandmother, dinner will be served in a few minutes. I think you should come and eat.'

'I'll have mine in here with your grandfather.'

*

After dinner I headed out to the stables to find Millie. 'Hello girl.' I saddled her up, and led her out before mounting her and trotting across the estate, stroking her mane before moving into a gallop. It was thanks to grandfather that I'd learnt to ride and had this beautiful horse. I didn't think of Mam much at all these days, she'd left me here, and when I'd been kidnapped Grandfather did everything he could to rescue me. And then that Christmas he'd given me Millie.

The sound of hooves came from behind. I slowed to a trot. Elizabeth was at my side.

'Why didn't you tell me he was so poorly?' I asked.

'I didn't want to worry you. The doctor said he'd got six months and I knew you'd be home from school in the holidays.'

'But I could have come home sooner.'

'He looked much better last week. Now let's not waste time arguing. I'll race you to Bluebell Meadow.'

'You're on.' We cantered off.

Chapter 2

Elizabeth

I waited outside the door until it opened and the doctor walked out.

'Your father hasn't long, Elizabeth. He needs to tie up loose ends. He's asking for Grace.'

Grace again. I was here but he wanted her. Why? 'She upset him last time.'

'Nonetheless, he's asking for her. And Elizabeth, utter urgency is required.'

'I'll see what I can do.'

'Well you need to hurry because he hasn't got long.'

'What, weeks?'

'No, hours. It's imminent.'

'But he was doing so well.'

The doctor shrugged his shoulders. 'I'm sorry but sometimes it can go like this. Where's Lady Granville, I need to check on her?'

'She's in the sitting room. We practically had to drag her away from Father for a while.'

'That's what I'm worried about. She's going to take this badly. You'll need to look after her and perhaps Grace can help.'

He disappeared along the hallway and I strode into Father's room. He looked like he was sleeping. His breathing was shallow.

'Grace,' he whispered.

'No, Father, it's Elizabeth.' I tucked his arms into the sheet. 'I'll ring Grace now.' I kissed his cheek and left the room as the nurse went in.

Grace's last visit hadn't exactly been a success, in fact she'd caused Father to have a bad turn but he was still asking to see her. I telephoned Grace's number, a woman answered and said she'd pass the message on. I tried to emphasise the urgency but whether Grace would come or not, I had no idea.

*

'Grace you're here. Thank goodness you've come.' I hugged my sister.

'You said it was urgent.'

'Grace, this is his last wish. Please don't upset him again.'

Grace shrugged. 'I'll try not to. It wasn't my fault last time.' She walked down the hallway, and through Father's bedroom door. I followed her in.

'It's a bit dark in here isn't it?' Grace put her hand over her mouth.

'Be prepared. He's gone downhill since your last visit.'

Mother sat by the bed clenching Father's hand. She turned around. 'What are you doing here? Haven't you done enough?'

'It's what Father wants,' I said.

Father whispered something. I couldn't make out what he was saying as I was too far away but I did catch 'Grace.'

'Go to him, Grace. Mother, give her a few minutes.'

Mother kissed Father's hand before resting it on the bedcovers, and stood back from the bed next to George. I followed Grace and held her hand, staying with her once she reached Father's side.

'Grace,' he managed to whisper.

'Yes Father, it's me. I'm here.' She took his hand.

'I'm sorry,' he whispered.

'Sorry?'

'Sorry, Grace.' He touched her hand and closed his eyes. The machine bleeped. Mother gasped. The doctor hurried over. We backed out of the way to let him through. He lifted Father's eyelids and shone his torch. The bleeps stopped, leaving a straight line.

Mother rammed past me and shoved Grace out of the way before falling on Father, wrapping her arms around him, and screaming, 'No, Charles. No. You can't leave me.' She became hysterical so I lifted her away.

'Come along Mother.' Rain pounded on the window and a roar of thunder sounded like it was hitting the house. I steered Mother out of the room and George followed.

'Take her upstairs,' I told him, 'and I'll get the doctor to come to her room with a sedative.' Mother was muttering incoherently. 'George,' I asked, 'are you going to be able to cope on your own?'

'Yes, I'll be fine.' He held Mother in his arms and she sobbed on his shoulder. 'It's all right, Grandmother.' With his arm around her waist, he led her to the stairway.

Grace stood outside the drawing room. I hugged her. She showed no emotion. 'Don't you feel anything?' I asked.

She shrugged. 'I don't know.'

I pushed past her into the drawing room to find the doctor. 'I think Mother needs a sedative. Are you able to sort her out?'

'Yes of course, Elizabeth. I'll just finish off the paperwork here. 'I'm sorry for your loss. Do you need anything?'

'No, I can cope. Just take care of Mother.' I moved over to the bed for one last goodbye to Father. I held his hand and kissed his cheek. He wasn't the best father to me but I loved and respected him even if I'd never lived up to Grace. 'Goodnight, Father. Sleep in Peace.'

Chapter 3

George

After hearing the news that Grandmother and Grandfather had betrayed me and fed me lies these past six years, I wanted to hate them but I didn't. The truth is I'd miss the old man, he'd been kind and always looked out for me. The last funeral I'd attended had been my own father's and I wasn't allowed to grieve with my family but ripped away to Granville Hall.

Elizabeth sat the other side of Grandmother as we travelled in the back seat of the black limousine following the hearse. I gripped Grandmother's hand as the hearse slowed and the funeral director stepped out. He walked ahead as the car snail-paced into the churchyard. Our vehicle crept behind. The lettered wreaths, *Husband* and *Father*, piled onto the coffin, showed through the window. Crowds of people stood either side of the road. Our car stopped when we reached the entrance of St James' Church.

We climbed out of the car and waited by the door with the Minister. Grandmother's black suit accentuated her weight loss. Elizabeth's face was concealed by her netted hat. Not unlike the one Mam had worn at Da's funeral except more expensive. I spotted Mam. Elizabeth did too. She made her way towards her.

The pallbearers began their journey down the aisle, Grandmother and I followed behind. I linked my arm into hers. I was back in 1962 at the church in Wintermore when Mam was clutching my hand so badly that her wedding ring stuck into me. I shed silent tears.

Grandfather's casket was set down and we were directed to the front. Elizabeth ushered Mam to the other side. I was glad. She didn't deserve to sit here as family. I waited for Elizabeth to join us but she sat with Grace.

The church filled up so much that they left the door open for the overflow to continue outside. Choir boys, in red and white, led the congregation in song. It was so different to Da's funeral. A friend of Grandfather's stood up to read a eulogy. I wondered if he really knew him or whether he was just a casual acquaintance.

The pallbearers picked up Grandfather's coffin and began the procession towards the graveyard. I remembered one of the pallbearers sneezed when lifting Da and I thought they were going to drop him. Nancy had squeezed my hand. This brought more tears to my eyes. Tears for Da, tears for Grandfather, and even tears for Mam. All those special years we'd missed. Even if my grandparents had tricked her then she should've fought more. I would never give up my child. I'd missed out on so much with my baby sister.

It was time to throw in the rose. I stepped forward with Grandmother. Elizabeth and Mam went next. Mam threw a white rose onto the coffin and stepped away. Not like when Da was buried and she almost fell in the ground with him. She was devastated when he died but I don't think that was any excuse to hand me over. Even if it wasn't for money. She let me go.

The Minister opened his prayer book. 'We commend to the Almighty God, our brother, Charles Andrew George Granville, and we commit his body to the ground, earth to earth, ashes to ashes, dust to dust. The Lord bless him…'

Elizabeth led Mam away from the grave. I hoped Mam wasn't going to come back to Granville Hall as I didn't think that Grandmother would cope. Grandmother was motionless.

She'd stopped crying but hadn't said anything. She just stood there. I led her away from the graveside towards the limousine.

Chapter 4

Elizabeth

After saying goodbye to Grace, I joined George and Mother in the car. Mother just stared into space. I patted her upper arm. 'We're going back home now, Mother.' She continued to stare at nothing like I wasn't there. 'Has she spoken at all?' I asked George.

'Not a thing. We should call the doctor when we get back.'

'Yes, I think we should.'

'I'll call him if you like?'

'That would be helpful.'

The driver pulled into the drive. Lots of mourners had already arrived and Martha was standing at the door showing them in.

The chauffeur opened the passenger doors to the car. His eyes focused on Mother. 'Do you need some help, Miss? Maybe I can get someone from the Hall?'

'I think we can manage, thank you, but perhaps you could try and clear these crowds?' I signalled to the guests on the steps. 'Before I take Mother in.'

'Certainly, Miss. I'm so sorry about Lord Granville. He was a good employer.'

'Thank you, that's very kind.'

The chauffeur moved towards the steps, chatting to people on his way. The crowds started to disperse. Some went into the house and others stepped down and moved to the side.

I took Mother's arm and led her to the front door with George shielding her as we climbed the steps. I sensed numerous pairs of eyes behind us, watching.

As we strode into the entrance, I said to George, 'Take her straight upstairs and I'll see to the guests but come back down as soon as you can because I could do with you by my side.'

George guided Mother to the staircase and she managed to put one step in front of the other as they climbed the stairs. I took a deep breath and made my way down the hallway and into the reception room. It was crowded. I peered around to find a familiar face, so many of these people were colleagues or clients of Father's. I had hoped Victoria would come but she said she wasn't a hypocrite, that she couldn't stand the man in life so she certainly wasn't coming to send him off. I could have done with her support.

Suddenly I saw a friendly face. Simon walked over to me.

'Elizabeth.' He took my hand and kissed it. 'I'm so sorry about your Father.'

'Thank you.'

'How are you coping?'

'To be honest, I'm more concerned about Mother at the moment.'

'Of course. I imagine she's taken it badly. I know it's not the right time, but I'd like to see a lot more of you if you'll let me?'

'I'd like that but you're right, now isn't the time. Excuse me as I should mingle. Ah, there's George. It will be easier if he's by my side.' I moved towards George but not without turning my head back towards Simon and smiling. At least something nice had happened today.

'George.' I took hold of his arm. 'Mingle with me. We need to shake hands with everyone and thank them for coming.'

He was a natural. Martha and Annie were laden with trays holding glasses of sherry and orange juice. The caterers had set out a buffet on long tables covered in white cloth. There was a ham, smoked salmon, and turkey, along with salad including potato and coleslaw.

Colleagues of Father's stood up and made a speech. They asked if I would like to say something but I declined. George took the floor for a while.

'Thank you everyone for coming and honouring my grandfather today. My grandmother sends her apologies but understandably, she's indisposed. Please join me in a toast to my grandfather. To Lord Granville.' George raised his glass of sherry.

'To Lord Granville,' the guests said simultaneously raising their glasses.

The room was filled with chatter and people loaded their plates with food. An orchestra played background music. I decided it was a suitable time to make our escape. 'Let's get out of here,' I said to George. As we were making our getaway, a voice came from behind.

'Elizabeth, is now a good time?'

I turned around. 'You go on up, George. Hello again,' I said to Simon.

'Fancy getting out of here for a while. Perhaps we could stroll the grounds?'

I was exhausted. The day had been draining both physically and emotionally but maybe a walk was just what I needed. 'Yes, thank you. That would be nice.'

Simon led me outside. The evening was warm with a sky full of stars.

'I've missed you,' he said.

'I've missed you too.'

We'd moved far away from the mansion when Simon took my hand. 'I've really missed you.'

'What are you saying, Simon?' I didn't want to get this wrong again.

'The time away from you has shown me just how much I've missed you. Elizabeth, I think I'm falling in love with you.' He moved closer to me.

'And your late wife?'

'It's time to move forward and I'd like to move forward with you. Do you feel the same way about me?'

My heart raced. I sensed the smile on my face but this wasn't right. I'd only just buried Father. This was disrespectful. 'I do, Simon, but now is not the right time. We can meet up in a few days but right now I need to be back to George and check on Mother. You do understand?'

'Yes, of course. I'll ring you in a few days but know this, I'm here to stay. I'll walk you back.'

We walked back in silence. How I wanted to kiss him but that would happen soon.

Chapter 5

George

Eager to get back to Patsy, I returned to school before the summer break had finished. She hadn't written to me while I was away but then she never was very good at conversing by letter. The limousine pulled into the school gates and dropped me off at the top of the drive. I jumped out of the car and went straight around to Patsy's quarters. Her mother would be working so there'd be no danger of her catching me. I tapped on the door but got no answer.

It was a scorcher of a day so I decided to go to my room, get changed and then make my way down to our oak tree. Robert wasn't in our room so I presumed he hadn't returned from vacation yet, although I thought he'd planned not to go home this summer because his parents had gone to America, but I must have got that wrong. It didn't surprise me as my head was all over the place. The revelation that Grandfather had stopped Mam seeing me kept going around and around in my head. I hated him, yet grieved for him at the same time. And as for Grandmother, on the day of the funeral I wanted to hate her too, but she looked so fragile I couldn't abandon her. Maybe Karma had caught up with them both but that didn't excuse why Mam hadn't fought for me more. I felt betrayed by everyone. I needed Patsy. She would understand.

I slipped into a pair of shorts and a plain red t-shirt and made my way over the meadow towards the oak tree, our favourite place, hoping Patsy would be there. In the distance I could see what looked like a couple, only as I got closer I noticed the girl's blonde hair was just like Patsy's but it couldn't be her. I stopped, uncertain. The couple were embracing… they parted. She turned towards me. It was Patsy. My Patsy with another bloke? He saw me and rose. Robert. The double-crossing bastard. I marched up to them and, without a word, hauled Robert away. Catching him by surprise, I threw my fist in his face.

'What was that?' Robert soothed his cheek, glared at me, then pounced.

Patsy was shouting, 'Stop it. Stop it, please.'

Robert and I rolled over and over on the grass, each trying to get the better of the other. I held him down but he pushed me and we bowled again, this time leaving me underneath. Patsy was running around us, still shouting, 'Stop it. Please.'

I was just in the process of getting back on top when strong hands dragged us apart.

'What's going on?' I looked up through a haze of sweat to see Mr Basson, the Dean's assistant.

Mr Basson held us both at arm's length. Robert's mouth was wide open, but neither of us spoke.

Patsy stammered, 'They're fighting over me but I didn't ask them to, I was telling them to stop.'

'I'm not sure what's been going on here but, you lassie, get yourself home now.' He sighed. 'And don't think I won't be speaking to your mother.' He sighed again, shaking his head. 'Leading these lads astray.'

Patsy picked up her sandals from the ground and ran off without looking back at Robert or me. I shook with anger. How could they have done this? At the same time tears welled up in my eyes as I watched her run away. I'd trusted her and now she was gone.

Heads down, we followed the teacher back to the school building. My stomach churned. I wanted to lash out at Robert, but stayed silent in front of the teacher, so not to shame the Granville name. Mr Basson tapped on the Dean's door, opened it and pushed us in.

'Sir, I caught these lads brawling and they've been messing around with Mrs Cable's lass.'

The Dean stood up shaking his balding head, tutting. He reached into his top drawer, removed a packet of Players, and extracted a cigarette. His silver lighter burst into flame after he flicked it. He still said nothing. Finally, he sighed and took a deep breath. 'You boys do realise that you could be expelled for this?' He puffed on the cigarette. His grey moustache twitched, round metal framed spectacles bounced on his nose. I bit my lip to stop myself laughing.

'This isn't a joke, Granville.'

'No, Sir. Sorry, Sir.'

'And Sanders, you can wipe that smile off your face too.'

'Sorry, Sir,' Robert said.

'Do you want to be expelled?'

I just shrugged my shoulders. I didn't care.

'Granville, you perhaps have an excuse for this aggressive behaviour. I'm sure you weren't thinking properly what with the death of your grandfather but you Sanders…' He let out another big sigh.

'Sorry, Sir,' Robert said with his face down.

'Stand up straight, Sanders. You're both on a warning and very lucky that I'm not using this on you.' He lashed the cane in the air after pulling it out from under his desk. 'This is what you should be getting, and would be too, if you hadn't just lost your grandfather, Granville… I can't let you off without being lenient on Sanders too, therefore your punishment is to work together. You can clean the dormitory toilets for one week. Do you understand?'

We nodded simultaneously.

'And I don't want to see either of you with that girl again or any other girl for that matter. The next time I won't be so lenient. I shall use this. Is that clear?' He swiped the rod across the desk.

'Yes, Sir,' we both said together.

'Right, off to your room and try not to kill each other.'

'Thank you, Sir,' I said.

'Thank you, Sir,' Robert said after me.

Mr Basson opened the door. 'Just be thankful the Dean was soft with you. Off you go.' I rushed through the exit and Robert followed. I marched on in front because I knew if I looked at his face, I'd want to thump it again. The cheating bastard.

'Look, wait, George. I'm sorry.'

Ignoring him I headed on back upstairs towards our room. He was close on my heels. I unlocked our door and strode in. Robert followed closing the door behind him. 'I've said I'm sorry, what more do you want? It wasn't my fault and it was only a kiss. What's the big deal?'

I turned around and held my fists up, took a deep breath and dropped them. 'The big deal is, she was my girl. So why would you hit on her?'

'It wasn't me. It was her. She came on to me.'

'That's right, blame Patsy when she's not around to defend herself.'

'Look pal, it's true. Honestly, she kissed me first. You caught us at the wrong time, that's all.'

'Sure, it looked that way too. That's why she was fastening the buttons on her blouse. Have a good fumble, did you?'

'What can I say? I'm sorry. She's not even my type.'

'You bloody liar. You've always been after her, but she chose me.'

'Well it isn't my fault if you're not man enough for her.'

That was it. I couldn't stand to hear anymore. I raised my fist. One thump, he fell into the wardrobe door and ended up with a bloodied nose.

'Now look what you've done.' Robert got up, leant heavily on the bed, sat down and pulled a hankie out of the drawer. 'That must make us even now.'

'How could it make us even? I never want to speak to you again. Furthermore I'm going back to the Dean now to see if I can share with Neil instead of you. You can join the others in the dormitory.'

Robert laughed. 'Don't be so stupid. It doesn't work like that. My father paid for this room, just like your grandfather.'

'We'll see about that.' I charged out of the room and left him with his head tilted back trying to stop the bleed.

As I was hiking along the path a voice called out.

'George wait.'

I turned around and spotted Patsy. She was running towards me. I didn't know what to do. My insides felt like they'd been torn out. I longed to hold her but she'd cheated on me.

'Please, George. Meet me in half an hour by our tree and let's talk. I'll wait for you.' She disappeared from sight.

I continued to the Dean's office and knocked on his door.

'Come in.'

'Sir, may I have a word, please?'

'Certainly, Granville. Sit down. I'm always here to listen. You've been through a tough time. I trust you've got over your squabbles with Sanders?'

'Well no, Sir. I was wondering if it would be possible for me to share the room with Neil Pendlebury instead.'

'And how do you think that would work?'

'He could swap with Sanders.'

'Pendlebury's father pays for a dormitory room while Sander's father pays for a twin. You think Sander's father is

209

going to continue to pay higher fees for the dormitory when Pendlebury's parents can't afford the shared room? As it is he's here on a scholarship.'

'Then can I have a room on my own? I'm due to inherit Granville Hall now my Grandfather has died. I can pay.'

'I'm pleased to hear that you've inherited, but it won't make any difference. We don't have an empty room. Just pull yourself together and go and make it up with Sanders. You need friends around while you're grieving. Now was there anything else?'

'No, Sir. Thank you for seeing me.'

I checked the time and decided that I would go and hear what Patsy had to say. I didn't want to go back to my room yet so I ran down to the oak tree. She was already there, lying under the shade. My heartbeat quickened. I loved her so much but I hated her for doing this to me.

She caught sight of me and waved. I waved back and ran towards her. I flopped down onto the grass and sat beside her but I didn't kiss or touch her.

'So?' I asked.

'I'm really sorry. I just got lonely and he was there.'

'So every time I'm not around you're going to get off with some other chap then? Because you're lonely?'

'No, I was stupid.'

'Yeah you bloody were. I trusted you.'

'I know, I'm sorry. Please give me another chance. It never meant anything and we only kissed.'

'How come your blouse was undone then? You think I didn't notice?'

'But we didn't really do anything.'

'And how do I know you haven't been doing all sorts, things that you and I haven't even done, while I've been away. You do know my grandfather died, don't you? I wrote to you and thought you might answer but you were too busy with bloody Sanders.'

Patsy leant over me. 'I'm sorry. What can I say?' She brushed her lips against mine. Her blonde hair tickled my face. I needed to be strong but she was so gorgeous with that sweet smile, long slim legs and tiny waist. Her smell was inviting, earthy and warm. I turned towards her and kissed her back, slowly at first but then hard. I unbuttoned her blouse and inserted my hand to stroke her soft breasts then imagined Robert's filthy paws all over her. I pulled away. 'It's not going to work.'

'I've said I'm sorry.' She tried to kiss me again but I pushed her away.

'No. I can't trust you. We're over.'

I got up, stumbled away, wiping away my tears, and didn't look back.

Chapter 6

Elizabeth

It was quieter than normal in the house with Father gone and Mother not leaving her room. She'd just sit or lie on her bed in the dark and barely touched anything to eat or drink. I wasn't sure what to do. I entered her room and drew back the drapes. 'Mother, you can't go on like this.' She didn't answer but continued to lie staring at the ceiling. It was unusual for the day nurse I'd employed to be so late. I rang the bell. Martha arrived within a few minutes. 'Has the nurse arrived yet?' I asked.

'A taxi's just dropped her outside.'

'Thank you.'

The nurse entered the bedroom as Martha left. 'Sorry I'm late Miss Elizabeth. Something unavoidable came up. I'll get your mother freshened up a little and then perhaps you can help me get her into the chair before the doctor arrives?'

The nurse disappeared into Mother's bathroom and came out armed with a bowl of hot water and a towel. Using a flannel she wiped Mother's face and under her arms to lightly freshen. Afterwards we guided Mother to sit down on the royal blue Queen Anne armchair by the window. The nurse picked up the bowl to empty in the bathroom while I helped Mother into her cream, satin-quilted, bed jacket. She pushed her arms into the sleeves voluntarily.

Martha returned to the room with Mother's breakfast. 'I'll put this down here.' She placed the tray on the side. Is it convenient for me to strip the bed now?'

The nurse answered, 'If you could leave it until after the doctor's been?' She turned to me. 'Are you able to feed your mother while I grab a cuppa and a piece of toast as I haven't eaten yet and I'm feeling a little faint?'

'Yes, go. I don't want you passing out. Oh and by the way, Martha, I'm expecting Mr Anson shortly would you mind letting Cook know that I won't be around for lunch?'

'Yes, Miss Elizabeth.' Martha left the room and the nurse followed.

I dabbed Tweed on Mother's wrists. 'There, isn't that better? How about a bit of breakfast?' I took the dish of stewed apple from the dressing table and teased open her lips with the spoon. She accepted the fruit instinctively but after a few mouthfuls shoved my hand away. 'You don't eat enough to keep a bird alive.' I tutted and put the bowl down. 'How about something to drink then?' I picked up a glass with a straw and held it to her mouth. She sucked the fresh orange juice, continuing to stare vacantly, not saying a word. Once it was clear she wasn't going to drink anymore I placed the beaker down, and moved back to the window to open it. 'Shall we listen to the birds?' Mother stared through me. 'Look at the flowers. The roses are especially beautiful.' September and the weather was still warm.

There was a tap on the door. 'Doctor's here, Miss Elizabeth,' Annie said.

The doctor came in. How's our patient doing today?'

'Take a look for yourself. She's not said a word since Father's funeral. All she does is sit like that. She barely touches her food.'

'Is she eating anything?'

'A few spoons of stewed apple or mashed banana.'

'How about fluids?'

'Water and orange juice, but even that's drunk in this trance-like state. She just refuses to speak. I know she's in there somewhere because she pushes the spoon away when she's had enough to eat and helps to get herself dressed.'

'Concentrate on the fluids. Just keep getting a few sips down her at regular intervals to prevent her getting dehydrated.'

'I'm trying, doctor.' I could feel my eyes filling up.

'I know, Elizabeth, and you're doing everything right. I see that you're making sure she sits up to prevent a pneumonia.'

'The day nurse I've employed insists on it. I keep hoping by sitting Mother at the window it will spring some life back into her. She used to love the garden.'

'It's grief, Elizabeth. I think we should try her on a course of Valium to see if that helps. Is there somewhere to wash my hands?'

'Mother's bathroom is through there.' I pointed

The doctor stepped into the en-suite and returned a few moments later, opened his black bag and took out a syringe and phial. He filled the barrel. 'You may want to hold your Mother's hand to reassure her.' As I took hold of Mother, he patted her inner elbow and injected the drug into a vein. 'You say you've got a nurse in?'

'Yes. I was hoping with plenty of professional care that she'd come out of this.'

'Let's hope so but if there's still no response after a few weeks then I fear we may need to look at residential psychiatric care. She can continue taking the medication in tablet form. I'll prescribe Minadex to help build her up while she's not eating.' He wrote out a prescription and handed me the slip before packing up his bag. 'I'll call again next week.'

*

It was two o'clock when a car pulled up outside. My hair was wrapped into a bun but I decided to unwind it and let it fall below my shoulders. The bun had given it a slight wave. Simon liked it loose. I took one last glance in the mirror, pleased at the fit of the light-blue dress I'd chosen. I particularly liked that it brushed across my knees when I moved. I came downstairs as Simon walked through the front door.

'Good afternoon,' I said.

He wolf whistled. 'It certainly is. You look gorgeous, darling.' He leant towards me and kissed my cheek.

'Don't, the staff will see.' I felt myself blushing.

'Does it matter?'

'We said we'd wait out of respect for Father. Remember?'

'Have you got a wrap in case it turns colder later?'

I unhooked a navy shawl from the peg in the cloakroom. 'I have now.' We wandered outside and Simon strode around to the passenger side of his jaguar with a wide grin on his face. He opened the door for me to climb in. Such a gentleman, so different to Gregory.

'An E Type, isn't it?' I said, sinking into the leather seat.

'Yes. I only picked it up a couple of weeks ago. What do you think of the colour?'

'It's my favourite shade of blue.'

'Azure, apparently. Are you going to be warm enough if I leave the hood off?'

'Yes I'll be fine. I love the wind picking up my hair and don't worry, I've brought a comb. Aren't we lucky to have such fine weather at the end of September?'

'They say it's going to suddenly turn so let's make the most of today. How's your Mother?'

'No change unfortunately. I don't know what to do. The doctor's talking about getting her into psychiatric care. I thought maybe she could stay with my cousin, Victoria. What do you think?'

'I don't know. What's Victoria like? Will she take her?'

'I think so.'

'The first thing to do is check with your cousin that she's prepared to have her there. Don't you think it would be a good idea to ask Grace to help?'

'Mother won't like that.'

'No, but maybe Grace can take a look at your mother, and see what she thinks about the Victoria plan?'

'You're probably right. I'll give Grace a ring later.'

'What's happening with her and George? Has he come around at all?'

'I don't think so but he's been writing to his sister, Alice.'

'I'm sure things will right themselves.' Simon drove into the car park of The Black Horse, a country pub. 'This is it.'

We climbed out of the car. 'You may need this inside.' Simon wrapped my shawl around my shoulders before locking up. As we headed into the dark pub, a strong smell of hops hit me. The counter area was smoky from a young couple sitting on bar stools smoking cigarettes. An older couple sat by the window.

'Good afternoon,' the barmaid said, 'you're not from these parts are you?'

'No,' Simon answered. 'We're out for a drive. Your pub was recommended by a friend so I thought we'd drop by and see for ourselves.'

'That's nice to hear. We try our best.'

The sound of laughing and shouting came from the Public Bar. I turned to look but turned away again.

'I'm sorry about that,' the barmaid said. 'There's a darts match next door, so a little busier and noisier than usual. If you sit over there in the corner it may be quieter for you.' She darted

216

to the other side of the bar to serve a young man waving a pound note in the air.

'What would you like to drink?' Simon asked.

'Babycham please.' I moved towards the small table in the corner leaving Simon to order our drinks. He joined me carrying a tray, and placed the saucer-shaped glass, a small bottle of sparkling liquid, and a pint of beer, onto the table.

'I took the liberty of getting us some nuts.' He playfully threw a packet of peanuts to me which I managed to catch.

'Thanks.'

Simon raised his pint glass. 'Cheers. To us.'

'To us.' I clinked my glass against his.

A group of noisy men and women stomped in. 'My round. I'll get the drinks,' one of the men said. 'What would you like?'

A young woman asked for a pint of shandy. It was frowned on for ladies to drink from a pint glass but she obviously didn't care. She picked it up and sipped it while the man next to her gulped his back in one go.

'Did you see that?' I asked Simon.

'Yes.' He laughed. 'And the woman's got a pint. What's the world coming to? Anyway, never mind them. Let's talk about us.' He took my hand. 'I meant it the other day that I want more. Do you feel the same?'

'You know I do. But are you sure that you're over your wife?'

'Yes, for the first time in a long while I feel free, able to look forward, see a future. A future with you.' He placed his hand on top of mine.

My stomach fluttered. I smiled.

We nibbled our peanuts, sipped our drinks and chatted. A young lad wearing a white apron approached our table carrying two plates of food.

'Two cheese ploughman's?'

'Yes, that's us.' Simon took the plates off the boy. 'Thank you.'

The bread was home baked just like Cook made it. I hadn't realised how hungry I was until I started eating.

'Can I see you tomorrow?' he asked.

I nodded, finished eating what was in my mouth. 'Yes, I'd like that.'

'How about the Pictures? We could go down to Kensington. I'm not sure what's on but I can check the newspaper when we get back.'

I hadn't been to the Pictures since I was at Greenmere. 'I'd love to.'

The barmaid rang the bell. 'Last orders.'

'Would you like another drink?' Simon asked. He still had half a pint.

'No thank you. I'm fine.' I bit into the last bite of bread. 'That was very tasty. Maybe we should come here again?'

Before long the barmaid rang the bell again. 'Time please.'

'We should make a move.' Simon swigged back the rest of his beer.

Chapter 7

Elizabeth

The mansion felt strange with only me and the servants. Mother was in Victoria's care. If anyone could bring Mother out of her darkness, Victoria could. Grace and Alice were coming for lunch. Alice was a dear little girl, well not so little really as she was approaching thirteen. It was good to finally get to know her. George was excited about meeting up with her in the holidays but he still hadn't warmed to Grace.

The November wind was bitter so I'd dressed in a tartan skirt and dusky-pink mohair jumper to keep warm but my neck itched from the knitted fabric. Looking for company, I walked down to see Cook. As I opened the kitchen door the sun blasted my eyes. Such a lovely lit room. The stainless-steel kettle whistled on the stove. Cook always had boiling water on the go to make a pot of tea. Melted cheese, ginger, and baked sponge aromas filled the air. I loved this time of day when Cook's kitchen was quiet before the staff crowded it at mealtimes. It was a time I could find solace now that there was no one here to tell me not to be too familiar with the servants.

'Morning, Cook. How are you today?'

'I'm well, Miss Elizabeth. Just preparing luncheon for you and your guests.'

'I can smell the baking. What's in the oven?'

'Quiche Lorraine and potatoes in jackets, along with muffins and cookies.' She offered a huge smile.

'Smells divine. I'm sure Grace and Alice will love whatever you serve.'

'How is Miss Grace?'

'She's fine. I'm sure you've seen from the newspapers that she has a series of shops.'

'That young lady always knew what she wanted. Do you remember that day Lord Granville was so angry about her needlework that he confiscated all the sewing machines in the house, including ours down here? She's done well though. A good head on those shoulders.'

'Yes, I remember that day too. I still have the pair of trews she made for me. I wonder if she still has hers.'

We both laughed.

Cook stirred the tea in the pot before pouring me out a cup. 'There you are, Miss Elizabeth. Just the way you like it. You must be swimming around upstairs with just you.'

'It's quite lonely to be honest.'

'I can imagine, but you're always welcome in my kitchen for a natter. How about one of my chocolate muffins to go with that cuppa?' Cook opened the oven door to the freshly baked smell.

I touched my stomach. 'I shouldn't really but go on, why not? Will there still be plenty left for our guests? I'm sure Alice will love these, especially if she has an appetite like her brother's.'

Cook passed me a chocolate muffin from an earlier batch cooling on the counter. I sipped the tea and took a bite into the soft sponge. 'You're such a good cook. Granville Hall is very lucky.'

Cook beamed a big smile. 'There's ample for your guests. I made them especially. And thank you. I've been cooking for a long time.'

'How's your Jimmy doing?'

'Very well, thank you. He leaves school in the summer. Got himself an apprenticeship lined up as a motor mechanic with the local British Leyland garage.'

It was a shame that George and Jimmy never got the chance to become friends. Jimmy was more interested in cars than horses and he certainly didn't have any interest in drawing.

Footsteps thumped along the hallway. 'Is the kettle on?' Andy asked. He'd been promoted from stable boy to groom last year when his predecessor died quite suddenly. Heart gave out it seemed. No one had known he was ill.

I looked up at the clock. 'Early today, Andy?'

'Yes, Miss Elizabeth. I've got a carpenter coming in half an hour to give me a quote.'

'I see. Nothing serious I hope.'

'Not at all. Just a few joists in the stables starting to rot. Want to sort it now before they worsen.'

'Yes of course. Well I'll bid you both good morning.' I stood up from the table. 'Thank you for the tea and muffin, Cook. I'm off for a stroll now before my guests arrive.' I left the kitchen, went upstairs to the cloakroom and snatched my navy coat off the hanger along with a woolly hat and scarf.

*

Annie was sweeping the grate as I headed into the dining room. She'd lit a fire and the flame was just starting to catch. It wouldn't take long for the room to warm up. I looked up at the clock. One o'clock. They'd be here in a minute. On that cue the doorbell clanged. In a loud voice Martha said, 'Good afternoon, Miss Grace.'

Grace didn't have any time for Martha, and the way she'd treated Grace in the past, I didn't blame her. I walked into the hallway to greet my guests.

221

'It's all right, Martha, I'll take it from here.' I turned to my sister. 'Grace.' I kissed her on the cheek. 'Alice. How about a hug for your aunt?'

Alice put her arms around me. 'I'm famished. What are we having for lunch?'

'Alice,' Grace chastised.

'You'll have to see what Cook's rustled up.'

'Can we play Monopoly?' Alice asked.

'I don't see why not. Grace?'

'Yes, if you like, but after we've eaten. I must admit I'm quite hungry too.'

Sometimes Grace just dropped Alice off and she'd spend her time asking question after question about George but when Grace was around she asked to play board games. I didn't mind as I liked playing them too.

'How's Mother doing?' Grace asked.

'No change I'm afraid. Victoria is so patient with her. The doctor wants her to go into a psychiatric unit but Victoria won't allow it. Not sure how long she'll be able to keep it up though.'

'Karma, that's what it is,' Grace said under her breath.

'Don't start, Grace.'

'You're not going to start fighting again, are you?' Alice said.

'No, dear. We're not. Come and sit down at the table. Annie's lit the fire so it should be nice and warm in there by now.' My guests followed me into the dining room. We sat at the long table with me on the end and Alice and Grace either side.

'So how are things going with you and Simon?' Grace asked, rubbing her hands to get warm.

'Very well thank you, but we're still keeping things quiet.'

'Let me make your wedding dress.'

'I think that's a little premature, Grace, but if we get that far then I'd like that.' It would certainly be different to my last wedding. 'He may not even be interested in me that way.'

'Then he's a fool.' Grace laughed.

'Aunt Elizabeth, did you hear me? I said, please can I be your bridesmaid?'

'Of course, Alice, if I get married then I wouldn't have it any other way, and your brother will give me away. I understand you've been writing to each other a fair bit?'

'Yes, every day.'

Grace turned her head away. I placed my hand on hers. 'He'll come around. You'll see. Just be patient.'

Annie pushed in the hostess trolley. She placed a bowl of piping hot soup in front of each of us and a basket of sliced white bloomer in the centre.

'This is lovely.' Alice sipped another spoonful. 'Your cook is smashing. Tomato's my favourite. We have Joan, she's a great cook too. Isn't she Mum?'

'She certainly is. She's an absolute gem. I couldn't do without her or her husband, Ted. They've been with me from the start.'

Annie came back in to clear our plates and replace them with a cheese and bacon quiche complimented by a green salad and tomato.

Alice chewed a forkful. 'Yum. I love quiche. We never had this when I was small. Does George like it, Aunt Elizabeth?'

'He does.' Once again, I noticed Grace fiddling with her hands. 'If it's all right with your mum I could send a car to collect you once George is home. I'm expecting him next week and I know he's really looking forward to meeting you.'

'Mum?'

'Yes of course, although I could always get Ted to drop her off. Or I could drop her off myself and maybe come in for a few minutes?'

'I think it's best if I send a car, Grace. Remember, you have to be patient.'

We finished the meal with chocolate muffins and fresh whipped cream.

'Time's getting on,' Grace said. 'I've a meeting at four o'clock.'

'Can I stay?' Alice asked. 'Please.'

'It's all right with me,' I answered. 'It's up to your mum.'

'Yes but I'm not sure what time Ted will be free.'

'She could always stay the night. There's plenty of room with only me here and she can borrow a nightdress of mine or wear one of George's shirts.'

'Please, Mum. Please.'

'Very well. In that case I'll leave you and Elizabeth to play games as I must do some preparation before my meeting. Thank you for the lunch.' Graced kissed me on the cheek and then moved over to Alice and hugged her. 'You be a good girl. I'll send Ted to collect you at midday tomorrow.'

'Thanks, Mum. See you tomorrow.'

I walked outside to the hall with Grace. 'George will come around. Just give him time.'

Chapter 8

George

I folded the last shirt into my suitcase.

'How long are you going to keep this up?' Robert closed his case and placed it by the door. 'I think you've sent me to Coventry for long enough. Don't you?'

It did seem a little petty to have gone on this long without speaking, especially when we had to share a room. And it was Christmas, after all, as they say, *Goodwill* and all that.

'You're right.' I held out my hand to shake his. 'But if you ever double-cross me like that again, there won't be any more second chances.' It wasn't like he was ever a best friend. More of an acquaintance, really. Neil was more of a friend. I wondered if one day I'd ever see Ben again. Possibly not if he'd gone to America to his aunt's like he always said. I'd never find him. Strange how even years later I still missed the old mucker.

'Thanks. You're a real pal, George. I know I buggered things up but let's make a pact not to let a girl come between us again.'

'Sure.' I didn't want to think about how he'd split me and Patsy up. She wanted us to try again but it just didn't work. I couldn't trust her and I didn't feel the same about her after I knew she'd been playing around with Robert. Even if she did say they'd only kissed, I didn't believe a word of it.

'I'm meeting my sister, Alice, when I get back. It will be the first time we've seen each other in over six years,' I said. 'And I need to get her a Christmas present but no idea what to buy a twelve-year-old.'

'I can get some ideas from my sister if you like? She's thirteen. Do you know what Alice's interests are?'

'No idea. The last time I saw her she was only six and an annoying little brat to be honest. She used to like singing but that may have changed.'

A toot came from outside. Robert peered out of the window. 'That's our ride. We'd best make our way down.' By the time we reached the ground floor, and walked out of the front door, numerous cars, taxis and limousines were lined up with boys piling into them. We headed towards Robert's father's silver Daimler. The chauffeur greeted us and loaded up our bags while we climbed onto the back seat.

'Wait a minute,' I said, as the driver started the car up. 'Neil's not here yet.' I spotted Neil struggling with his luggage, trying to get it down the steps. 'Here he comes but he keeps on stopping and starting.'

'What the hell's he got in there, bricks?' Robert said.

I got out to help him. 'Come on, mate. What you got in there?'

'Books to study over the holidays.'

The driver came to our assistance. 'I'll sort this. You boys get yourselves into the car.'

'Thank you,' Neil said.

I let Neil slide into the middle as he was the smallest, and we were on our way. Granville Hall was the first drop off. I punched Robert and Neil in fun before climbing out of the car. The chauffeur took my small suitcase from the boot. Martha was standing at the front door ready. 'Master George. Welcome home. Should I arrange someone to bring your luggage?'

'No, thank you, Martha. It's very light. I can manage. Is Miss Elizabeth in?'

'Yes, she's in the drawing room.'

'I hope the fire's roaring because it's freezing out there.'

226

'They're predicting snow tonight.'

I left Martha to close the door, popped my bag on the floor in the hall and made my way down to the drawing room to surprise Elizabeth.

The door was closed but voices came from behind it. She must have a guest. I didn't think Simon was coming until this evening. I tapped on the door before opening.

'Come in,' called Elizabeth.

I entered the room slowly, unsure who was on the other side. A young girl with long blonde hair was sitting next to Elizabeth. The young girl stood up when she saw me.

'George, this is Alice,' Elizabeth said.

She didn't look like my Alice. Where had her Shirley Temple curls gone? Maybe it was another Alice. 'Alice?' I said.

'Yes.' She rushed over to me and took my hand. 'I'm Alice. Your sister.'

I stood there with my mouth open. 'But…' I eventually managed to get my words out. 'You look so different.'

'So do you, but it's been a long time and I was only six, remember?' She hugged me. I put my arms around her too. 'We've got so much to catch up on,' she said. 'I know we've been writing letters but there's loads more for us to share.'

'Why don't you young ones sit down by the fire and I'll organise hot chocolate.' Elizabeth left the room. She'd used that as an excuse to leave us alone because normally she'd ring the bell.

Alice eased back down on the chaise longue and I sat down next to her. I picked up a few strands of her hair. 'What happened to your curls?'

'They grew out. Well except my fringe. I have to put Sellotape on it overnight after washing it.' She giggled. 'And your curls have gone too. Well except your fringe.' She giggled again.

'They cut my curls off when I first arrived here. I remember crying because I didn't look like me. But unlike your curls, mine always grow back when my hair gets longer. Now that Grandfather's dead and Grandmother's indisposed, I may well grow it.'

'Cool. Like a hippy?'

'Yep.'

'But what about your school? Will they allow that?'

'Probably not.' We both laughed.

'George, do you think you might come to my house over Christmas and meet Mum? Just for a while? It would make her so happy.'

'How come she's Mum and not Mam?'

'When we first moved to London, Mum thought it better if I called her Mum or Mummy. So will you?'

'Will I what?'

'Come and meet her?'

'I don't know. We'll see. I'm not sure whether I'm ready. She left me here for all those years without contacting me.'

'But the letters…'

'Yes she gave me a load of letters before Grandfather died. I have read them but even so…'

Alice took my hand. 'She hasn't had it easy. Give her a break.'

'And you think I have?' I pushed her away, got up, marched over and stood in front of the fire. 'It's all right for you. You're not the one who was torn away from his mother and sisters straight after Da died. And then after trusting my grandparents, I discover they've been lying to me all these years. Have you any idea how it feels to be so betrayed?'

'I'm sure it's not been easy, but it hasn't been easy for me either.'

228

'I can't do this now.' I stormed out of the room leaving Alice alone, grabbed my coat off the hat stand, went downstairs, and out of the backdoor into the garden.

'George…' Cook called after me but I didn't want to speak to anyone.

It started snowing. Snowflakes landed on my nose. It was far too cold to stay outside so I rushed back into the house and found Cook looking out of the window watching the snow. She turned around when I walked in.

'How about a cup of my hot chocolate, young man? The kettle's on ready.'

'Thanks but I'd better not as my sister's upstairs.'

'Yes, I know. Your aunt asked me to make refreshments for you both. But what I don't understand is if your sister's upstairs then what are you doing down here?'

'She annoyed me but I suppose I should go back up.'

'I should say so. Off you go young man and I'll organise those hot chocolates with my special ginger cookies.'

'Thanks, Cook.' I skulked back upstairs to the drawing room, part opened the door and peeped in. Alice was sitting on the chaise longue. Was she crying?

'I'm sorry,' I said, on entering the room. I sat down next to her and put my arms around her. 'Everything still hurts. My whole world fell apart in the summer when I found that I'd been living a lie for all these years. It was like being abandoned all over again. Also…' I wasn't sure whether to mention Patsy or not but decided against it.

The door opened and Annie wandered in holding a tray.

'Look what Cook's sent up,' I said. 'Do you still like hot chocolate?'

'Yes.' Alice dried her eyes. 'I just wanted you to see Mum. It would be the best Christmas present she could have.'

'I'll think about it.' I suppose I hadn't really given Grace a chance to explain. I'd ignored her when she came to see Grandfather, but then, I didn't know he'd lied to me. I hated her for shouting at him but just before he died he told her he was sorry. I didn't want to believe it but Elizabeth said it was true. They'd treated Grace badly too. 'All right, Alice, I'll come.'

'When?'

'Christmas Eve. You come over here at lunchtime and we'll go back to your house early evening. I'm not going to stay long though.'

Alice flung her arms around me. 'Thank you, George. It will be the best present ever.'

The rest of the afternoon we played snakes and ladders, and Ludo. Maybe I'd speak to Grace about my drawings.

Chapter 9

Elizabeth

George was up and about early this morning. I wondered if he'd decided to drive down to Dorset with me to visit Mother. Last night he was adamant he wasn't going to come. I eventually found him sitting in the kitchen eating cornflakes.

'There you are. I've been hunting all around for you. What are you doing in here?'

'Chatting to Cook. I like being in here.'

'Sorry Miss Elizabeth if I've encouraged him. The kettle's on if you fancy a cuppa?' Cook lifted a cup and saucer down from the shelf.

'No, I'm fine, thank you. I don't blame you, George. I like being in here too but we can't do it once Mother's back.' I sat down next to him. 'Are you coming with me to see her?'

'No, I don't like seeing her like that.'

'But George.' I took his hand. 'I'm sure she'll be pleased to see you.'

'She won't know whether I'm there or not. And anyway, I've already arranged to meet Alice. We're going Christmas shopping. You go. I'll be fine.'

'Fair enough but I'll get Simon to pop around this evening to keep you company as it'll be late by the time I get back. I'm hoping to miss the snow. I'll see you in the morning.'

As I left, George didn't even lift his head away from his cereal. I made my way down the steps to the car where the chauffeur stood waiting. He opened the door and tipped his hat. 'Miss.'

231

I passed him two large bags containing Christmas presents for Victoria and Mother. Although I hoped to persuade them both to come back to Granville Hall for the festivities.

'Do you think we'll make it down there before the snow?'

'I hope so Miss. It's predicted to arrive early hours in the morning.'

*

We pulled up outside Victoria's cottage. The garden looked bare except for the holly swaying under the window. I tipped the flowerpot and picked up the key to unlock the front door.

'If you go around the back, I'll open up, and organise refreshment.' I wasn't sure whether Victoria would be busy with Mother. I missed the fun chats that Victoria and I used to have before Mother moved in with her. Now it was always all about Mother.

'Thank you, Miss.' He plodded down the side path.

'Victoria, it's only me.' The sitting room was empty. She must've been upstairs with Mother as I'd thought. I entered the kitchen and unlocked the door for the driver. The aroma of a stew on the stove reminded me I was hungry.

Light footsteps came down the stairs. I met Victoria at the bottom. 'How are you coping?' I hugged my cousin. She looked tired. Maybe looking after Mother wasn't good for her.

'You know.'

'How's Mother doing?'

'No change. I've just been sitting on her bed talking to try and get a response but as usual she just stares into space.'

'I've brought Christmas presents. I see you've put the tree up.' Victoria's tree was nothing like the trees at Granville Hall but more like the tree George spoke about having when he lived in Wigan. It was around three foot and sat on the sideboard. Gold, pink and purple baubles of different shapes hung from the pine branches and cotton wool was spread like snow. A few presents of different sizes sat under it.

'I'll get some tea and sort your driver out. I know you want to get back sharpish but you need to eat so I've made a stew and it'll be ready in about half-an-hour.' Victoria padded into the kitchen. I stood by the fire warming my hands.

'Here we go.' She sloped back in with tea on a tray. 'Would you like to be Mum?'

'Of course.' I poured milk into the mugs followed by tea and sat down on the couch. Victoria sat in her usual highbacked armchair. 'I'll have this and then pop upstairs to see Mother. Listen, Victoria, I was thinking. Why don't you and Mother come back to Granville Hall for Christmas?'

'I don't think she's up to it.'

'But maybe being back in her own home will help jog her out of this, whatever this is.'

'Or make her worse.'

'I worry about you being here on your own. You need a break.'

'I'm all right, pet.' She patted my hand. 'No need for you to worry. It will only spoil everyone's Christmas if she's there. You know it will.'

I knew she was right but I felt so guilty leaving my cousin to look after Mother when it should be my responsibility. Victoria wouldn't even agree to a nurse coming in. I really didn't know how she coped. I drank my tea and placed the cup down on the coffee table before going upstairs to find Mother.

As I reached the landing I thought I heard her moving around. That had to be a good sign but when I entered the room she was sitting in a chair staring into space. Just the same as every other time I'd visited over the past months. 'Mother.'

I touched her arm. She turned and stared. 'It's Elizabeth. How are you?'

She turned away, stood up and gazed out of the window.

'I've brought gifts. Would you like to come down and open yours?'

She didn't answer but stood playing with her hands. I took the brush off her dressing table. 'Sit down and I'll brush your hair.' I led her to the seat by the mirror. She stared into the glass, her face blank. I brushed her hair, teasing it behind her ears. 'Shall I put some make-up on you?' Mother always wore cosmetics. I picked up a red lipstick and traced it around her lips. 'There, now you look more like Lady Granville.'

She didn't answer, but wiped her mouth before shuffling over to the bed, lying down and closing her eyes. It was no use trying any further so I went back down to Victoria. The table was set with two plates of steaming stew.

'Come and eat. Your driver has his and I'll take Margaret's up later. Not that she eats much.'

'She's so thin.' Tears streamed down my face. 'Do you think she's going to die?'

'Now, now, girlie. The doctors don't think she's in danger of dying. In fact they've said she could go on like this for years, just eating and drinking enough to keep her alive.'

The stew was warming but I felt dreadful, I was so wrapped up with guilt. I couldn't stop crying. It was wrong that I let Victoria do everything while I got on with my own life. What about her life? I tried to pull myself together. 'Would you like to open your presents while I'm with you? I brought some for Mother too but I don't suppose she'll open hers.'

'Let's see how much time we have left. I have gifts for you to take back too.' She pointed to the parcels under the tree. 'For George, of course, but also one for Grace, and one for Alice.

Maybe you can bring them with you next time. I'm surprised George isn't with you today.'

'He refused to come. He says he can't face seeing her like that and in his mind she won't know he's there anyway. And maybe he's right?'

'Probably, but who knows, seeing him could prompt a change in her.' We finished eating dinner and Victoria stacked our plates. 'Would you like some dessert?'

'No thank you.'

'How about a coffee or a sherry?'

'No I'm fine. Open your present.' I passed her a large package in cream glossy paper covered in a snowman design.

She squashed and turned it.

'Just open it.'

Eventually she pulled off the ribbon and paper and lifted out a pink cashmere robe. 'This is a bit extravagant.' She tried it on. It was a perfect fit. 'I love it though. Not that anyone will get to see it.'

'Only the best for my favourite cousin. Victoria, don't you get lonely? Now that Mother is here it must make it difficult for you to get out.'

'I'm fine. I can leave her alone for short periods and if I need to be longer then the woman down the road pops in. She used to be a nurse.'

'Well if there's anything you need. For instance, I know you've refused before, but I could employ a nurse, full or part-time.'

'And like I've said before, I don't want strangers in my house. If it comes to a point where I can't manage anymore, I'll let you know. Now, look at the time, five o'clock, you need to be making your way back to Gerrard's Cross.'

Chapter 10

George

Ted dropped Alice off at the mansion.

'Shall we go Christmas shopping?' I asked.

'Ooh yes. I'd like that. Are there many shops around here?'

'I was thinking we could go into London on the train.'

'I don't think Mum would be happy for me to use public transport without her. She keeps reminding me that I'm only twelve. If I'd known you wanted to go into London I could've asked Ted to drive us in.'

'No worries, I'll arrange one of the Granville drivers to take us. Shopping in town is fun this time of the year. All those crowds, music and lights.' I was excited because I hadn't been shopping with Alice since we were children when we shopped in our little village of Wintermore. Our last Christmas together we'd had half-a-crown each. We bought Da a wallet, not leather, because we couldn't afford that, but it didn't look cheap and for Mam, lavender soap. They loved their gifts. I bought Alice a colouring book and wax crayons and she bought me little green soldiers. It always made me sad when I thought back to those times.

We rushed outside to the garage to find a driver.

'Please can someone drop us in London?' I asked the Head Chauffeur.

'Certainly, Master George. Smith, are you free?'

'Yes, Sir.'

'Can you drive this young man and lady into town?'

'Yes, Sir. I'll just finish checking the Rolls.'

'If you go back to the Hall, he'll be with you in ten minutes. Too cold to hang around here.'

*

Men, women and children crowded the pavements, rushing and milling in and out of shops.

'Let's go into Selfridges,' I said. 'It'll be warm in there, we can do a bit of shopping, and then go to the restaurant for hot chocolate.'

A long queue had formed outside the Grotto to see Father Christmas. Young children huddled against mums and dads. 'Shall we get in the queue?' I teased Alice.

'I'm not six anymore you know.'

We both laughed but I felt sad for the years we'd missed. We wandered around the store looking at pullovers, dresses and skirts. Alice picked up a bright red cardigan. 'If you're thinking of buying something for Mum, I think this will suit her.'

I hadn't planned to purchase a gift for Grace. It was too soon for that. 'No, I wasn't. I just want to buy a present for you.'

'Oh. All right. What would you like?'

'Hmm. I know. There's a new Batmobile and batman out. You can buy me the Batmobile if you like. Let's go down to the toy department and see if they've got it.'

'Aren't you a bit old to play with Batman?'

'Well I don't see the Batmobile as a toy because I'm a collector and one day my collection may be worth something. I'll leave it to you in my will.' I laughed. 'How about you? What would you like?'

'I'll think about it. I may see something once we're down with the toys. I'm almost grown-up so don't want anything babyish. I'm thirteen next year, remember.'

On our way down to the toy department we passed Electricals.

'Stop.' Alice picked up a little black transistor radio off the shelf. 'I'd love one of these.'

I took the radio from her to study. It was set inside a black leather cover with lots of holes. 'Panasonic,' I said. 'That's a good make. I'll buy this for you but I'll get a surprise gift too.' I handed it over to the assistant. 'Please can you wrap this and charge it to George Granville.' Aunt Elizabeth had set me up an account with twenty pounds.

The assistant stared at me. 'Do you have any form of identification?'

'Well no, but I'm George Granville.'

'George Granville?'

'My grandfather was Lord Granville. Look, I don't have any form of identification but I have this.' I pulled out a newspaper cutting with a write-up and photograph of me and Grandfather. 'Will this do?'

'I'll check with my manager.' The assistant rang a bell next to her till. An elderly lanky man came over. 'What seems to be the problem?' He rubbed his nose.

'This young man's aunt has set up an account for him but he has no identification. He does however have this. Can we accept it?'

The manager looked backwards and forwards from the photograph to me. 'I don't think there's any doubt. I'd say he's definitely the boy in the photograph.' He handed the cutting back to the assistant.

'So is it all right to process the transaction?'

'Yes. I'll sign it off for you.' He turned to me. 'Your grandfather was a good man. My brother worked for him for over thirty years. Never had a bad word to say about him. I'm sure he'll be sorely missed.'

The assistant wrapped the radio up in snowmen Christmas paper, and wrote the transaction down in a ledger which the manager signed. She handed me the package. 'Merry Christmas, Sir.'

As we walked away from the counter Alice said, 'You get an allowance?' She slipped off her shoe and rubbed her foot. 'My feet are killing me.'

'Only just. Elizabeth set it up yesterday because she didn't want me carrying lots of cash. Let's go and get that hot chocolate and something to eat so you can sit down for a while. Don't worry, I've got money.' I pulled out a note and loose change from my pocket. 'See. The restaurant's up there.' I sloped towards the stairs.

Alice hobbled behind me.

'Only a girl could come out shopping with new shoes on,' I teased.

'Shut-up, you.' Alice nudged me playfully. I'd missed that.

A waitress smiled when she came to our table. 'What can I get you young people?'

'Two hot chocolates, please, and can you recommend something light, but warm, to eat?' I asked.

'That's got to be our soup of the day.'

'Which is?' I asked.

'Potato and leek. Would you like your drinks before or after?'

'Alice?'

'After I think. So long as the soup isn't going to be long.'

The waitress scribbled on her little pad. 'It shouldn't take long.' She headed towards the kitchen.

'Well, are you going to keep your promise?' Alice twiddled the front strands of her long hair.

'Promise, what promise?'

'About coming back with me today to see Mum.'

239

'Oh. I don't know. I'd forgotten all about it.'

'It's Christmas Eve, George. It would make such a special present for her. Do it for me?'

'Let's eat and then I'll give you my answer.'

'When we first moved to London, it was to a flat over a shop. Did you know that?'

'I think you mentioned it. Elizabeth only said that you'd moved to London.'

'Well I don't know whether you know or not but Mum spent almost every day going backwards and forwards to Granville Hall, each time hoping to bring you home.'

'I saw her once. I thought she'd come to get me but she went away again. Elizabeth said she'd come for more money.'

Alice shook her head. 'No, she never asked for money, she came for you. She had your bedroom ready for you. I chose the wallpaper.'

'She had a bedroom for me? Really?'

'Yes. I chose The Beatles paper. You know why?'

'No.' I didn't really like The Beatles. I preferred The Rolling Stones.

'I chose it because the pattern was a picture of the group with their names. So it meant George was written on it. That's why. Mum made your room so lovely. It had Matchbox and Corgi cars on the chest of drawers. And those little green soldiers you liked. And some cowboys and Indians.'

I'd no idea that she'd done any of that for me. Alice was right, I should make the effort and see her. After all it was Christmas Eve. I'd talk to her but that's all. I still wasn't going to buy her a present.

'Did you hear what I said, George?'

'I did. I had no idea. All right, Alice, you win. We'll get the driver to take us back to Cheam but I can't stay long as

Elizabeth's arranged for Simon to keep me company this evening until she gets back home.'

She swung her arms around my neck. 'I love you George Gilmore.' And smacked a big kiss on my cheek.

I hadn't been called that for a while. So much so that I was used to being Granville now. It had a nice ring to it though. Maybe now Grandfather was dead I could go back to my old name. I'd speak to Elizabeth. 'I love you too, little sister. I've missed you so much.'

*

Alice unlocked her front door and we stepped into the hall.

'Shh.' Alice placed her finger on her lips and tried not to giggle. 'I'll go in first and then come back to get you. Don't make a sound,' Alice whispered.

I glanced around the hallway. This was a big house. The staircase was wide and spiral the same as at Granville Hall. It had pictures on the wall of Grace's designs, at least I thought that's what they were.

'Come on.' Alice took my hand and led me into a large drawing room. The whole of downstairs in our house in Wintermore could be fitted into this one room. I took it all in. A huge Christmas tree in the corner. Expensive furniture. Photographs on the sideboard. A chaise longue just like the one at Granville Hall. Had she tried to replicate it all?

Alice nudged me. Grace was blindfolded. Alice gently twisted her around in circles.

'I'm getting dizzy, Alice. Aren't you a bit too old for blindman's buff?'

'Shh, Mum. I have a surprise for you.'

'Well you'd better wrap it up and put it under the tree and take this blindfold off me. I'm in the middle of sewing.'

'This present can't be wrapped and I want you to have it now.' Alice pulled me so I was standing in front of Grace and mimed me to speak.

'Hello, Grace,' I said.

Grace's mouth twitched. 'It can't be.' She removed the blindfold. 'George.'

'Happy Christmas.' I kissed her on the cheek.

She went to hug me but I stepped back. I still didn't trust her. I didn't trust anyone except Elizabeth and now of course Alice. She was my little sister after all.

'This is the best present I could ever wish for. Sit down and I'll get some tea or would you prefer coffee?'

'Isn't Joan here to do that?' Alice said.

'No, I gave her and Ted the night off as Nancy and Charlotte are out and you weren't about. I thought I'd enjoy some quiet time by the fire sewing. I haven't had a chance to sit and sew for pleasure for a long time. Always so busy. But having George here is much better than sitting and sewing on my own. What a wonderful gift. Thank you. I'll get that tea.' She was all fingers and thumbs. She kept talking but I didn't really hear her, I was thinking about how it was before Da died.

'I'll do the tea, Mum. You spend some time with George, he's not here for long,' Alice said.

'Thank you, Darling. George, come and sit next to me.'

I sat down on the chaise longue but I was too fidgety. I stood up and sloped towards the tree. 'This is huge.' I guessed she employed decorators to dress it. 'Do you remember our little tree in Bamber Street?'

'Yes I do. If I'd known you were going to be here you could have helped me decorate this one.'

'You did it yourself?'

'Yes, I always do. Alice helps sometimes, but she's never been that interested in doing it, unlike you used to be.'

242

'Is that our…'

'Tinkerbell? Yes. It is.'

I glared at the top and thought of Da lifting me on his shoulders to pop her up there. My jaw tightened. 'I need to go in a few minutes.'

'But you've only just got here.' She strode over to me and stroked my face. 'You're so like your father. He'd have been proud of you.'

Alice charged back in. 'Look who I found on the doorstep. And it's snowing out there now.'

'Hello, Grace.' An older man walked in laden with Christmas gifts. 'Pop these under the tree, sweetheart,' he said to Alice. He slipped off his grey wool overcoat which was covered in melting snowflakes and Alice rushed back over to relieve him of it. 'It will need hanging up to dry,' he said. He was obviously a regular visitor as he hadn't dressed up for the visit looking very casual in a royal-blue V-neck cardigan and no tie. 'I told Alice this was a bad idea. Sorry to interrupt your cosy arrangement.' I glared at the man.

'George, this is…'

I didn't let Grace get any further. 'He's old enough to be my grandad. I'm out of here.'

'Stop it, George, and listen to Mum,' Alice pleaded.

'Well?' I stared at Grace.

'This is your Uncle Max, but he's also been like a father to me.' She smiled affectionately at him.

'Oh.' I sensed my face turning pink. 'Sorry.'

Max gripped my hand to shake. 'Your father's Pa was my brother which I believe makes you my great nephew. Has anybody ever told you, that you're the spitting image of your pa?'

'Yes, Grace did. So you knew my da?'

'Oh yes, he spent most of his childhood around my house in Bolton. I could tell you lots of stories about him but let's make that another time, eh? But for now, perhaps you should get reacquainted with your mother. I'll go and help Alice make tea.'

'Sorry,' I said again once I was alone with Grace. 'I thought he was your boyfriend. I shouldn't have judged you so quickly.'

'No, you shouldn't have, but understandable.' She smiled at me.

'Nevertheless, I'm sorry.'

'No apologies necessary.' She took my hand and then dropped it when I inched away. I moved over to the chaise longue to sit down and she sat down next to me.

'When did you know that you wanted to be a designer?' I asked.

'From very young. I think I was about ten or eleven. My father thought it was a load of nonsense.'

'I like designing too. Not clothes but buildings. I want to be an architect.'

'You should follow your dream. Has anyone seen your drawings?'

'One teacher at school. He says I have talent. But Grandfather didn't like me doing them, wanted me to take over the estate instead.'

'Well he's gone now. You must do what you want to do. Follow your heart.'

'Do you really think I could? What about Granville Hall though?'

'Elizabeth's got Simon working on the estate, hasn't she? I understand he's taken over your grandfather's duties until you're old enough, so I'm sure that could become a permanent arrangement. This is your life, darling.'

'I'll bring some of my drawings next time if you like?'

'I'd love that.'

Alice came back in the room with refreshments. 'Tea up.' She set the tray down on the coffee table.

'And some of Joan's sponge cake.' Max sunk into an armchair.

I took a bite of the cake. 'Wow, almost as good as Cook's.'

It was like being a family again except we were six years older.

Chapter 11

Elizabeth

Straight after New Year, George went on a ski-trip with his school and then directly on to Sandalwood. It had therefore been a long twelve weeks since he was last home and I was excited about him returning today. I glanced out of the window into the garden. The pink and salmon-coloured peonies had started to open reminding me that it was the first day of Spring. I was pleased that George had made the initial steps of reconciliation with Grace last time he was at Granville Hall. It was a new beginning for us all.

Butterflies fluttered in my tummy as I remembered last night when Simon had gone down on one knee. His hand stretched out towards me as he held an open ring-box containing a glistening white precious stone.

'Elizabeth, would you do me the honour of becoming my wife?'

I was overwhelmed and speechless. Simon's face paled. His smile disappeared. 'Elizabeth?'

I took a deep breath. 'Yes, yes darling. Yes, I will.'

He held his hand to his heart. 'Thank goodness. I thought you were going to say no. You almost gave me a heart attack.'

I laughed. 'Sorry, I was taken aback, but I'd love to marry you.'

He eased himself upright, took my left hand and slid the diamond ring on my third finger. 'You won't regret it, I promise.'

I believed it was the happiest day of my life but knew there'd be lots more to come. Half past two. George should be here shortly. I walked down the hallway to find Martha.

'Make sure you call me as soon as Master George arrives.'

'Yes Miss.'

I took the stairs down to the kitchen to find Cook and tell her my news.

'Good afternoon, Miss Elizabeth, you look nice and bright. What a beautiful smile. Has something or should I perhaps say, someone, made you happy?'

I lifted my hand.

'Congratulations. It's beautiful, when's the big day?'

'We haven't set a date yet but it will most likely be August when Master George is home from school.'

'I shall look forward to making a huge wedding cake. And there's the catering to organise.' She rubbed her hands. 'About time we had something nice to celebrate at Granville Hall.'

Martha appeared at the doorway. 'Master George's car is on its way up the drive now, Miss.'

'Thank you, Martha. Cook, I hope you've got George's favourite cookies.'

'Freshly baked this morning.' She chuckled.

I rushed upstairs, opened the front door as the Sander's limousine drove off and George came up the steps.

'Aunt Elizabeth. What are you doing out here?'

'Enjoying the sunshine and waiting for you. It's been a while. Come in. Come in.' I practically dragged him through the door and into the drawing room, only allowing him time to drop his suitcase on the floor in the hallway. 'Martha can see to that. I want to speak to you.'

We sat down next to each other on the chaise longue in the drawing room. Annie entered with a tray and placed it on the coffee table.

'Thank you, Annie, I can take it from here.' She left the room and I poured tea into the Royal Albert china and passed George a cup. 'And look what Cook's made for you.'

'Ginger cookies. My favourite.' He bit into one with a loud crunch. We both laughed. 'Cook's cookies win top prize as the crunchiest.'

'George, you like Simon, don't you?'

'You know I do. Why?'

'How would you feel if I married him?'

George's smile broadened. 'Has he asked you?'

'Last night.' I lifted my hand to show off the ring.

He whistled. 'Wow that's one mighty stone. So you must have said yes?'

'I did. Is that all right with you?'

George hugged me. 'Of course it is, Aunt Elizabeth. You deserve to be happy.'

'There's one more thing. Will you give me away?'

'I'd be proud to. When's the wedding?'

'We haven't set a date yet, but it's likely to be August this year when you're on vacation from school.'

'Cool.'

Chapter 12

George

Elizabeth and I had been charging around all over the place since I came home which meant I still hadn't visited Grace. However, I decided to take the opportunity today. I tucked my A3 portfolio under my arm and went to find my aunt.

'Good morning, Aunt Elizabeth. Oh, no. What's happened to your hair?'

She touched her head. 'What's wrong with it?'

'You have a white streak across your right brow.'

She rushed out to the hallway to check in the mirror.

'April Fool. Got you.' I laughed.

'George Granville. You…'

'You have to admit it was funny. Now this is a serious question, and not an April Fool, I promise, but I want to go over and visit Grace, and I understand you'd planned to see her today.'

'Yes that's right. She's got some samples of fabric for my wedding dress.'

'Are you having a fitting?'

'No, nothing like that. I don't have time as I've arranged to meet Simon for a business lunch. Why?'

'I thought I'd tag along. You can leave me at Grace's and pick me up after lunch or send a car.'

'Sounds like you have it all worked out. I shall be leaving in a minute.'

'I'm ready.'

'What's that tucked under your arm?'

'Nothing. Just something I want to show Grace.'

'Very secretive.'

I laughed and sauntered out ahead of her towards the car. She didn't drive very often which was a shame as she had a lovely red MG sports car and I loved riding in it. Next year I'd be old enough to learn to drive and once I passed my test, I planned to buy an MG just like this one. Elizabeth said she'd arrange for money to be released from the trust fund.

My aunt walked down the steps and unlocked her car. I climbed in the passenger side. She drove out of the drive, turned right on to Princes Avenue, left at Kings Road, and headed South on the dual carriageway towards where Grace lived. We chatted but mostly it was Elizabeth quizzing me about what was going on at Sandalwood. I hadn't mentioned Patsy. Finally after an hour, we pulled into Grace's drive.

'What made Grace choose to live in Cheam?' I asked.

'I don't know, George. You'll have to ask her.'

We climbed out of the car and made our way up to the front path when I realised I'd forgotten my portfolio. 'Oh no, can I borrow the keys please? I've left something in the boot.'

Elizabeth threw the keys at me. 'Don't forget to lock up.'

'I won't.' I ran back towards the car as she carried on up to the front door where a plump woman who reminded me of Cook invited Elizabeth in. I quickly grabbed my A3 portfolio out of the boot, locked the car, and sprinted back up to the entrance to the house. The woman who let Elizabeth in was standing on the step holding the door open. 'Come on in, young man. You must be George.'

I followed her down the hallway and into the drawing room. It looked much bigger without the huge Christmas tree taking up loads of space.

Grace rushed over. 'George, it's so good to see you again. You didn't tell me he was with you, Elizabeth.'

'My fault.' I pecked her on the cheek. 'I wanted it to be a surprise.'

'Well it's certainly that. A wonderful one.'

'I'll just take those samples and be on my way,' Elizabeth said to Grace. 'I've promised to meet Simon for lunch.'

'Of course. I'll get them.' Grace disappeared out of the room and Alice bolted in.

'I thought that was your voice, George. Why didn't you tell me you were coming?'

'It was a last-minute thing. I wanted to talk something over with Grace. And I've brought these.' I held up the portfolio.

'What's in there?'

'Sketches. Remember I told you about my building designs?' Alice looked vacant.

Grace returned. She handed a small package to Elizabeth. 'Telephone me once you've decided so I can order the fabric. Have you got someone to help you choose?'

'No, I don't think I have.'

'Well, take a look, and we'll meet for lunch one day next week and talk it through together.'

'Thank you, that sounds like a good plan. I'll check my diary later and let you know when.' Elizabeth turned to me. 'We'll pick you up at three. Be ready though as we can't stop because dinner guests are due this evening.'

'Yes, Aunt Elizabeth.'

She kissed Grace and walked out of the room. I moved over towards the window and peered out. Grace followed me.

'I'm getting a car like that once I pass my test,' I said.

'You have good taste,' Grace said.

'Can you drive?'

'Yes. I've been driving for a few years now. I drive a black Mercedes sports. You'll have to come for a ride in it one day. Sit down and we'll have tea.'

The fire was lit. I sat down on the chaise longue next to Grace. 'I've brought some of my drawings.' I lifted the portfolio in the air.

'Can I see?'

'Yes, that's why I've brought them.'

'Can I see too.' Alice hovered.

'Of course, but you might not find them very interesting.' I pulled out the A3 drawings and placed them on Grace's lap. She perused them one by one but didn't say anything. I hoped she liked them. Eventually she put the papers down. 'George, these are exceptionally good. You obviously have a lot of talent.'

I smiled. 'Thank you. What do you think, Alice?'

She shrugged.

'Why not go and see about that tea, Alice?' Grace asked.

'Sure.' Alice left the room.

'While Alice is out of the room,' I said, 'there's something I wanted to ask you.'

'Of course, anything.'

I took a deep breath.

'You can ask me anything.'

I took another deep breath. 'Do you think you could take me to Da's grave?' I asked hurriedly. 'Grandfather said he didn't know where Da was buried, and I only remember it was near where we used to live.'

'I can take you but it's a long way from here which will mean an overnight trip.'

'That's all right. I'll clear it with Elizabeth.'

'When would you like to go?'

'Soon. I go back to school on the twenty-first of April so it'll have to be before then. But please don't tell Alice, I'd rather it just be me and you, the first time.'

'I'll make the arrangements.' She patted my hand and I didn't pull it away. She turned her head but before she did I noticed tears welling up in her eyes. Maybe she really did care.

*

One of the Granville drivers dropped me at Euston where I met Grace. We made our way to the station platform and our train was ready. We climbed into the first-class carriage and had the space to ourselves.

I picked up my book, *Brighton Rock,* and Grace was reading *One Flew Over the Cuckoo's Nest.* In-between I napped so I didn't have to converse too much. I opened my eyes when the train stopped. 'Crewe. Do we have much further to go?'

'No, about another half hour and we should be there.'

I placed a piece of paper to keep my place in the book before putting it away in my duffle bag. 'Alice mentioned Nancy lives with you?'

'That's right. Do you remember her?'

'Yes of course.'

'Would you like to meet her? She'd love to meet you.'

'I'd like that very much. Maybe when I come home in the summer holidays. Nancy was always very good to me.'

'Yes, she was. She loved all of you like her own. She's been a great support to me over the years. I have a business partner that lives with us too. Charlotte. Perhaps you'd like to meet her sometime. I think you'll like her.'

'Possibly. We'll see.'

The train pulled to a halt. 'Wigan, this is it,' Grace said. 'Let's get a cab from the rank outside.'

The taxis were lined up outside Wigan station. We hopped into the one in front. 'The Bellingham at Wintermore, please,' Grace said.

It only took a few minutes to reach the hotel. Grace paid the cab and we headed to the foyer and reception desk. I stayed back while she sorted things out. As she beckoned me a porter came along and took our small overnight bags. I wondered if she recognised my duffle bag.

'The porter will drop our bags in the rooms so we can go straight to the cemetery. It's within walking distance.' She gave the porter a tip.

My stomach rolled. I wanted to do this, yet at the same time I was nervous. This would be the first time I'd seen Da's grave since they lowered him into the ground. 'I'd like to buy some flowers first?' I said.

'Yes of course you would. There's a florist outside the cemetery. Look.' She pointed. 'There it is.'

A bell chimed when Grace pushed open the door. An assistant rushed into the shop.

'Good afternoon, what can I get you?'

'What was his favourite flower?' I asked Grace.

'Roses but they're not out yet. He loved daffodils too.'

'A bunch of these please.' I took the daffodils from a bucket. 'What are you getting, Grace?'

'I shall get daffodils too.'

We paid for the flowers, walked out across the road to the cemetery gates and strolled along a gravel path.

'Is Beth in the same place?'

'No, she's in London. I'll take you there another day if you like?'

'I'd like that.'

We turned left at a yew tree and Grace said, 'Here we are, just up this path.'

The gravestones stood in line. Some low, some high and upright, and others looked bent. Da's was tall and straight.

Grace placed her daffodils on the ground. 'I'll leave you to it for a few minutes.' She hurried off towards a bench.

'Hello Da.' I felt silly talking to a gravestone but suppose he could hear me and I didn't say anything. 'I couldn't come before because I lived with Mam's Mam and Da and they wouldn't let me. Now Grandpa's dead and Grandma is sick. I miss you so much.' I started to cry and couldn't stop. Grace came up behind and put her arms about me. She was crying too.

Chapter 13

Elizabeth

The months flew by. It was almost my wedding day. I carefully took the wedding dress off the hanger, held it up against me, swaying, and watching my reflection in the mirror. Grace had done a wonderful job. She was so gifted. What was I gifted in? No wonder Father had always preferred her to me. Well that didn't matter now as I had Simon and George. Although I wondered how long I'd have George. How long before he'd leave me to go to her? She didn't deserve him. No matter what the circumstances she'd still deserted him. I was the one who held his hand at night when he had nightmares following the kidnap.

There was a tap on my bedroom door. 'Miss Elizabeth, Mr Anson is downstairs.'

'Thank you, Martha.' I hung the gown back up and spent a moment staring at it. In a week's time I'd be in the limelight, all eyes focused on me and not Grace.

I made my way downstairs. Simon was standing in the hallway talking to George. I wondered what they were plotting.

'Hello, my favourite men.' I kissed them in turn on the cheek. 'What are you two up to?'

'Nothing,' George said, 'I was just making sure Simon's written his speech and checking that he's supervised the best man's. We don't want his brother spoiling things for you.'

'Will he?' I asked Simon.

He took hold of my hands and lifted them to his lips. 'Nothing is going to spoil our special day, not even my brother.

So relax, darling. Are you ready? We have an appointment with the vicar, remember?'

'As if I could forget.' I laughed.

'Are Alice and Grace meeting us at church?' Simon asked.

'Yes, Grace said it would be better if they met us there.'

The Rolls and driver were outside.

*

It was a gorgeous August day. Granville Hall bloomed with summer flowers. Cactus dahlias, sunflowers, lilies and marigolds filled the Hall's borders in orange, red and yellow as we drove out of Granville's gates. Simon and George sat either side of me, both holding a hand. We reached the church and stepped out of the Rolls as Grace's driver pulled up behind. Alice and Grace got out and came towards us.

'Are you excited, Aunt Elizabeth? I am. I've never been a bridesmaid. What will I have to do? Will I have to say anything?'

'You won't have to say anything, Alice,' Simon said, 'but you will need to know what to do, where to stand etc and that's why we're having this rehearsal.'

'I hope I don't get anything wrong. Are you nervous, Mum?'

'No, dear, and you don't need to be either.'

'Alice, don't worry.' I squeezed her hand. 'They'll walk us through everything today. You have a very important job because you head the bridal trail.'

'Thank you, Aunt Elizabeth. I hope I don't let you down.'

'You won't.' I turned to my sister and smiled. She looked stunning in her midnight-blue georgette outfit that fell just below her knees and was set off perfectly with a wide brim hat. 'New suit?'

'Yes. It's one of my latest designs. Do you like it? What do you think of the slit?' She turned sideways and showed off a bit of leg. 'It should hit the shops in a couple of months. I thought I'd try it out today.'

'It's wonderful.' I looked down at my lime-green, A-line, crimplene dress. Would Simon have misgivings about marrying me when at one time he thought he'd marry her?

'Come on, let's get inside.' Grace hooked her arm in mine and we wandered on in front. 'Are you feeling nervous?'

'Yes and no. I don't feel nervous like the last time.'

'Was that very awful for you? I'm sorry I wasn't there.'

'It was more than awful, Grace. One day I will tell you but not today.'

'Are you sure about this marriage? Simon's a nice man but he is rather old for you.'

I unhooked my arm from hers. 'Stop it. Stop trying to spoil things. He's not too old at all. We love each other.'

She moved closer to me and took hold of my hand. 'That's good. I was just checking that you weren't making a mistake.'

'Well I'm not.' I slowed my pace until Simon caught up with me.

This wedding would be so different. A man I'd chosen myself, Alice as my bridesmaid, and George to give me away. This time, my sister close. Although if she kept asking silly questions like that then she needn't bother to come.

Chapter 14

Elizabeth

I stood at the mirror. My dark brown hair was piled high, not abrupt into a bun, but loosely, and my spiral curls caressed my white diamond earrings. The hairdresser had done wonders. Was this really me? And Grace had not only designed my wedding dress, but made it, sewing everything by hand. She hadn't let anyone else near it and spent numerous hours embroidering the pearl bodice. The gown hugged my waist and flowed to the ground.

I strode down the staircase carefully in my satin stilettos to where Grace, Alice and George stood waiting. Alice chanted, 'Here comes the Bride.'

Grace kissed my cheek. 'You look stunning. Doesn't she George, Alice?'

'Yes, she does,' Alice and George said in chorus.

Grace lowered my netted veil across my face. 'Are you ready?' She lifted the huge bouquet of white roses adorned with green foliage from the sideboard and passed them to me.

'Thank you. I'm ready as I'll ever be.' The bouquet trembled in my hands.

Max walked in the front door. 'Let's go. Your chariot awaits.'

Outside stood the black open-topped Rolls. The bonnet was dressed in a garland of pink roses with ivory silk ribbon. A pattern of matching rosebuds trailed around the sides.

'I'm so happy,' I said, gripping George's hand.

*

'Are you ready?' George asked.

'Yes,' I said, willing my body to stop shaking.

Alice went first, carrying a basket of flower petals against her rose silk gown that stopped just below her knees. When she reached the aisle the organ played the wedding march. It was our turn. George took my arm and led me down to Simon who was standing next to his brother, Richard. Simon turned around as we reached him and mouthed, 'You look wonderful.' Grace followed behind in a matching dress to Alice's. Grace moved towards me and lifted my veil. She looked beautiful. We smiled and hugged.

The vicar welcomed the congregation with prayers, beginning with 'The Grace of our Lord Jesus Christ…' Then the preface, how everyone had come to witness our marriage, followed by the declaration.

'First I am required to ask anyone present if they know a reason why these persons may not lawfully marry to declare it now.'

The church was silent. Simon smiled at me and I smiled back. The vicar advised us both of the importance of the vows we were about to make in the presence of God. 'Simon Archibald Anson, will you take Elizabeth Anne Granville to be your wife? Will you love her, comfort her, honour and protect her, and, forsaking all others, be faithful to her as long as you both shall live?'

'I will.' Simon gripped my hand.

'Elizabeth Anne Granville, will you take Simon Archibald Anson to be your husband? Will you love him, comfort him, honour and obey him, and, forsaking all others, be faithful to him as long as you both shall live?'

'I will.' Tears dampened my cheeks.

Simon would take care of me. I could see the love in his eyes. I deserved this. He held my hand as he placed the ring on my finger.

'I now pronounce you husband and wife,' the vicar said. 'You may kiss the bride.'

Simon tilted my chin and brushed my lips with his. Everyone clapped. 'All Things Bright and Beautiful' played as we, the wedding couple, followed by Grace and Richard our witnesses, were paraded into the vestry.

Chapter 15

Elizabeth

It had been a magical few months, living together as man and wife, and although I'd been looking forward to spending Christmas day at our home, I'd been persuaded by Simon to accept George's request to spend Christmas day at Grace's.

As we headed into Grace's dining room, I was drawn to the pine Christmas tree almost reaching the ceiling decorated with coloured baubles and flashing lights. Christmas crackers lay on the table at each place setting. Grace's surrogate father, Max, sat at the head.

'George, you're next to me.' Grace led him to his seat. 'And you and Simon sit opposite.' She sat down and took George's hand. 'This day will stay with me forever.'

George kissed Grace's cheek. I smiled. Of course George should sit with his mother, but I'd expected he'd sit next to me too.

Max carved the turkey while waitresses weaved in and out serving roast potatoes with vegetables. The waiters served red and white wine. I couldn't believe I was sitting comfortably at the same table as Grace's housekeeper and driver. I'd never have imagined doing this while Father was alive but I supposed it was nineteen sixty-nine. The whole table was full of Grace's close friends. Nancy, a coal miner's widow and old neighbour of Grace's, Charlotte, Grace's well-connected business partner, and Adriénne, whom Grace insisted was merely a business partner, but I wasn't convinced. I don't think anyone was. I was pleased she'd had their support while estranged all those years.

The more recent additions were a father and daughter. The daughter, Rebecca, shared a room with Alice at Greenemere. To Grace, these people were family. Laughter and chatter filled the room punctuated by the sound of pulled Christmas crackers.

After dinner Grace, Adriénne, Max and Charlotte went off for a stroll while the rest of us played Monopoly. After they returned, Grace switched on the television set ready for the Queen's Speech. Her housekeeper, Joan, and driver, Ted, sat by the roaring fire snoring. Grace whispered to George and he followed her out of the room.

*

When George and Grace re-entered the room, Alice was in the middle of the floor taking her turn at Charades. George interrupted. 'We have an announcement.' Alice sat down leaving George the floor.

'Well,' said Charlotte. 'Get on with it.'

Grace took a deep breath. Her eyes were moist. 'My son has come home.' George and Grace faced each other holding eye contact.

Everyone started clapping. I managed to clap along. Simon mouthed, 'Are you all right?'

I nodded but I was anything but all right. I was losing George to Grace.

She raised a glass. 'Please everyone join me in a toast. Not only to my son, George, but to the New Year. A few days premature but to nineteen-seventy.'

I secretly held my stomach. My announcement could wait. 'To George. To nineteen seventy.' I joined in with the others clinking glasses.

Chapter 16

George

14th August 1970

'I told you, I'm not going back.' I slammed my fist down on the Chesterfield chair.

'Calm down, George.' Simon held my shoulders at arm's length. 'You're upsetting your Aunt.'

Elizabeth held her swollen stomach. She was just over eight months pregnant and glowing.

'I'm sorry Aunt Elizabeth. I don't want to upset you but I'm not happy. And Neil's allowed to leave. He's got himself an apprenticeship at Furman's, the garage down the road. I could get an apprenticeship too.'

'Doing what?' Simon asked.

I shrugged my shoulders. 'I don't know. Something.'

'I thought you wanted to be an architect,' Elizabeth said. 'How are you getting on with the new tutor? Mr Bennett, isn't it?'

'I do want to be…but…'

I'm back in Bennett's office. I unroll my latest sketches onto his desk. He flips through them one by one. 'These just won't do, Granville.' He glares at me.

'What's wrong with them?'

'Slapdash.' He screws up my drawings and throws them into the waste-paper bin. 'Do them again. And I want them by four o'clock, tomorrow.'

'I can't do it by tomorrow. I spent days on them and I'm supposed to be going out this evening.'

'Then cancel your plans, boy. And pull your socks up. You're wasting my time and yours.' He stood up away from his chair.

'Mr Higgins thought my work was exemplary.'

'Mr Higgins isn't here anymore and all I can conclude is that you performed better than this.' He kicked the waste-paper bin over. 'Off you go now. Remember on my desk by four, tomorrow.'

'George, I'm speaking to you.' Elizabeth broke my thoughts. 'What is it exactly that you want?'

'Maybe I could get an apprenticeship as a draughtsman?'

Elizabeth moved over towards me and took my hand. 'You'd be much better off staying on at school.'

'What's it got to do with you anyway?' I pulled my hand away. 'You're not my mam. I'll speak to Grace.'

'George, don't be like that.' Elizabeth looked like she might cry. She held her stomach and sat down. Simon rushed over towards her.

'Are you all right? It's not the baby is it?'

'No, I think he or she is just having a good kick.'

They forgot all about me, lost in baby talk. I would speak to Grace about moving in with her. I knew she'd jump at the chance.

*

'You want to do what? Adriénne have you heard this?' Grace called out.

'What's that, darling?'

'George wants to quit school.'

265

'But you're doing so well. What's brought this on?' Adriénne said.

'What's it got to do with you?' I stormed over to the window. 'I'm sick of everyone telling me what to do. She did what she wanted.' I pointed to Grace. 'She went off and married my da. So why can't I do what I want?'

'Don't be rude, George,' Grace said, 'I'll support you in whatever way I can but I'm asking you not to be rash. You don't have a plan of what you want to do. There's no reason for this.'

'There is. I hate it there.'

'But why?' Her voice softened.

'I just do.'

'But your drawings have so much promise and even the school think that, otherwise they wouldn't be offering one-to-one tuition.'

'I don't want that anymore.'

'But why? Is it the teacher? I'm sure Elizabeth can speak to the Dean. I'd happily speak to him, but Elizabeth is down as your guardian.'

I'm back at school. Bennett's behind his desk puffing on a fat cigar. 'Sit,' he says to me.

I pull up the chair next to him.

'Have you done your homework?'

'Yes, Sir.' I pull out the A3 drawing from my portfolio. 'It's a departmental store.' I smile.

'Good God, boy.' He leans over me to pick up a piece of charcoal from the desk. The stench of his body odour makes me want to gag. He scrawls across my sketch. 'No. No. No. It's no use. It can't be improved. You'll have to start again.' He rips it up.

'But, Sir.' I stare down at the shredded template I was so proud of.

'My predecessor may have been happy with sub-standard work, but I'm not. And if you want to go to that conference next term then you'd better buck up your ideas. Make sure that assignment is back on my desk before you leave for the Easter break.' He breathes out smoke rings in my face.

I hold my hand over my mouth to stop being sick. 'Can I go now, Sir? I don't feel very well?'

'Off you go then, boy.' He ushers me away with his hands. 'Namby-pamby,' he mutters under his breath.

Grace shook my arm. 'George, answer me. Is it the teacher? We can sort that out if it is.'

'No, it's just that …'

'It will be worth it when you're a successful architect. Trust me,' she said.

I could see I wasn't going to get anywhere so I charged out.

*

The telephone rang.

Martha strode into the drawing room. 'It's Miss Alice for Master George.'

I jumped up to go into the hallway.

'Maybe that will put you in a good mood,' Elizabeth called after me.

'Hello Alice…'

After putting the handset down I swaggered back into the room. 'Alice is going to the funfair at Mitcham Common. Ted's going to pick me up on the way. I've to be ready for two o'clock. That's all right, isn't it?'

Elizabeth set her embroidery down on her lap and Simon peeped his head over the newspaper. 'Are you packed to go back to school?' he asked.

'Yes.'

'Good lad. We're proud of you making the right decision to return. You'd have regretted it otherwise.' His face was back in the newspaper.

'You might think so,' I muttered under my breath.

'What was that?' He put the newspaper down.

'I said you might think so.'

Elizabeth sighed. 'I thought this was sorted.'

'It is. But it doesn't mean to say I have to like it. And after a year, I'll be eighteen so then it's up to me what I do after that.'

'Yes, that's what we agreed.' She came over to me, and took my hand. 'You're doing the right thing.'

Simon sat upright. 'I heard you're joining the cricket team.'

'Yes, they've been after me for years. I'd always refused before because I didn't have time.'

'So what's changed?' he asked.

'I'm giving up the one-to-ones. I decided to have a bit of fun for a change.'

'That seems fair enough, although I'm sure the Dean may have something to say about that.' He sat back into his chair.

'I don't give a damn what he says. You asked me to stay another year and I agreed but I need to make new friends and how am I going to make new friends if I'm in stupid one-to-ones all the time?'

'That's true, lad. I'm sure you'll enjoy the cricket.'

'Hold on. What do you mean, giving up the one-to-ones? I thought you wanted to be an architect?' Elizabeth asked.

'Maybe, maybe not. I don't see why I can't do it without the extra tuition. Anyway, if you've both quite finished with the interrogation, I need to get ready.'

'Leave the lad alone, Elizabeth. Architecture isn't going to help him once he's on board with the estate. Let him have some fun.' Simon wandered over and patted me on the shoulder. 'We just worry, lad. Go and get yourself sorted. It'll do you good to let your hair down for a while.'

I reckoned he was just pleased that I'd be out of the way for a while and not upsetting Elizabeth.

*

As we headed down the road, Derek, Alice's boyfriend, slipped his arm around her. She'd met him last Christmas at a dance and they'd been corresponding while she was away at school. He was sixteen so I was surprised that Grace let her see him. I'd even mentioned this to Grace but she said she trusted Alice. I trusted Alice but I didn't trust him hanging around with a fourteen-year-old. We'd nothing to worry about, Grace assured me. His mother was a friend of hers. 'If I start objecting, I know Alice, she'll dig her heels in, but if I go along with it, the friendship will sizzle out before we know it.' I hoped she was right because I didn't like him and if I'd known he was coming today then I wouldn't have bothered.

'Let's go in the ghost train,' Alice said.

'Nah. You two go,' I insisted. I didn't want to sit squashed in a car playing gooseberry with those two. 'I'll have a meander and meet you at the hot dog stand around half-past-three.'

'Okay.' They paid the man and jumped into one of the cars.

I wandered around the fair and bought five tickets for a tombola from a woman standing inside a circular stall.

'Hey, it's a WIN.' I handed over the ticket.

'Here you go, darlin.' The woman passed me a floppy toy dog. I clutched it under my arm. I'd give it to Alice.

'Hey, what do you plan to do with that?' A female voice called after me. 'You're a bit old to play with cuddly toys, aren't you?'

I turned around and was mesmerised by the vision. 'Maybe it's for you if you tell me your name.'

'Juliette. Does that mean the dog's mine? I just love his green suit.' When she smiled her blue eyes sparkled. Her blonde wavy hair reached her shoulders and she wore a rosebud band across her forehead.

'Yes. Here you are.' I passed her the toy. 'What are you going to call him?'

'Err. I know. How about Floppy Dog? Are you here on your own?'

'I am at the moment but meeting my sister and her boyfriend around half-past-three. Are you with someone?'

'I am now.' She hooked her arm into mine. 'What shall we do next?'

'How about the big wheel?' I steered her to the large ride not believing my luck. We stood in line until it was our turn and then climbed into a swing. The guy made sure that we were locked in with a bar, our legs dangling out.

The music played Edison Lighthouse's, 'Love Grows, where my Rosemary Goes.' 'I love this one,' I said.

'Yes, so do I.' She swung the seat as the wheel turned.

'When it was number one, I annoyed my roommate by playing it continuously. Brilliant record. Stayed at number one for five weeks.' The wheel stopped to let more people get on. We sat on the top.

She kissed me on the lips. 'I like you.'

'I like you too.' I kissed her back. I hadn't kissed a girl since Patsy.

She lifted the curls around my forehead. 'I love these. Why don't you grow your hair?'

'I have to keep it short for school.'

'But they are so you. All my boy pals have long hair. You must come and meet them.'

270

I really wanted Juliette all to myself but I smiled and said, 'That'll be nice. I only have a week before I return to school.'

'Where's that?'

'Sandalwood.'

'Never heard of it.'

'It's in Westbridge not far from Cambridge.'

'Then we'd best make the most of our time.'

The big wheel turned and came to a halt when we reached the ground. The attendant unhooked our bar and as we climbed out he helped Juliette down. I wasn't sure why but it irritated me. After all he was only doing his job. I checked my watch. Quarter-past-three. 'I've only got fifteen minutes before I meet Alice.'

'That's a pretty name,' Juliette said. 'How about a ride on the ghost train?'

'Okay.' I quite liked the idea of being in the dark with her for a few minutes. As we approached the ride I noticed Alice heading my way.

'George, hi.' She ran towards me and Derek tailed her. 'Are you having a good time? And who's this?'

'I'm Juliette. You must be George's kid sister. There's been a change of plan, he's hanging around with me for a while instead so won't be going back home with you.' She really hadn't given me the chance to say that's what I wanted to do.

I just smiled. 'Will you let Elizabeth know I'll be a bit late. Juliette lives just up the road.'

'But how will you get home?'

'He can arrange a lift later,' Juliette said clutching my hand.

I wasn't sure about this. I'd no idea what her friends were like but I went along with it. What was the worst that could happen?

'Neither Mum nor Elizabeth are going to like it.' Alice stood with her hands on her hips.

271

'Then that's tough. I'm going back to school, aren't I? The least they can do is let me have some fun in my last week before doom.'

Alice shrugged her shoulders. 'Fair enough but your funeral. I'd have thought you wouldn't have wanted to upset Elizabeth though in her condition.'

'Condition?' Juliette asked.

'She's eight months pregnant,' I answered.

'So what? Women have babies all the time. I wouldn't worry about that.'

Alice glared at me. 'George.'

'She won't even notice I'm not there. I'll see you later.' I pecked Alice on her cheek. 'Bye Derek.' At least I didn't have to spend another minute with that plonker. I was nervous about meeting these new friends though. As Alice and Derek walked away, I felt guilty, this wasn't right. Elizabeth would be worried and I couldn't have her losing the baby on my conscience. I called after Alice. 'Get Ted to come back at six o'clock for me?'

'This way.' Juliette took my hand and we headed for the ghost train.

*

Juliette stopped at the side of the road. Her tiered, flowery-patterned skirt brushed the ground. A huge dilapidated house with windows boarded up stood in front of us.

'This is it,' she said.

'But…'

'It's a squat. You've heard of squats, haven't you?'

So was she saying that they lived in this old place and it didn't belong to them? She pushed the run-down door open. I followed her across broken floorboards. Was this place even safe? She must have sensed my concern.

'It's fine so long as we don't go upstairs. The stairs are really ropey.'

The inside was dark and musty but there was another smell that I didn't recognise. We walked along the corridor and stopped at the doorway of a large room. Sleeping bags were strewn around the floor. A group of youths sat on huge cushions in a makeshift ring and I could smell incense burning. I recognised the fragrance as jasmine because it smelt just like the white bush in bloom at Granville Hall. Harry, the gardener, said the scent put a person in a good mood.

'What's he doing here?' said a lad with straggly hair.

'This is George. Look, he won me this.' She placed Floppy Dog down in the corner. 'You can trust him. George meet Alex.' She took my hand as we went into the room and pointed to the group in turn. 'Donna, Kev and Tristan.' The blokes had long, straggly, unwashed hair. Donna's blonde hair also hadn't seen a shampoo for a month by the look of it, yet Juliette's shone. The blokes and girls took turns to blow into some kind of pipe. I stared.

'It's a hubble bubble,' Juliette said, 'sit down and try it.'

'Nah, you're okay. I don't smoke.'

'This is no ordinary smoke, man.' Alex handed the pipe to me as I crouched down onto the cold floor easing a rank cushion under my backside.

'I'm not sure.' I pushed it away.

'It'll make you feel good. Just give it a try.' Juliette put the pipe in my hands. I blew into it. I felt dizzy. 'Not for me thanks.'

'Try this then.' Alex passed me what looked like a homemade cigarette.

'No thanks.'

'What are you doing here then?' Alex stood up behind me.

'Let him be,' Juliette said. She cuddled up and started to kiss me.

273

'Ah, I see,' Alex said. I wasn't sure what he meant by that.

Donna laid down by my side too and started stroking my hair. 'You've got lovely curls, Georgie boy.'

I pushed her off. I didn't like being called Georgie boy for a start and I wasn't sure about having two girls all over me.

'Relax,' she said. 'Try the pipe again.' She passed it to Juliette and gave her some kind of signal.

'I think I should be getting back.' I stood up.

'But I thought you liked me.' Juliette pulled herself up beside me and stroked my neck and put her hand down into my shirt.

'I do. But what about them? Can't we go into another room?'

'There isn't another room that's safe. But how about we go over in that corner where no one will see us, and if they can, well, they're too spaced out to care.' Juliette picked up a blanket and guided us across the room. She threw the blanket on to the ground and moved me down, lay on top of me, and kissed me while holding my hands on the floor so I was trapped and couldn't move. She was really turning me on. My brain told me I should leave but lust insisted I stay. Heavy metal music was playing on a cassette player.

Common sense told me she was after me for money, but what was the harm in a bit of fun? It was just what I needed. I was dizzy from necking. I put my hand inside her blouse and stroked her small breasts and she didn't stop me. There was no need to worry about unhooking a bra because she wasn't wearing one. We snogged and petted and she slipped her hand down my trousers and rubbed me. Boy, I thought I'd died and gone to heaven. Patsy had never done that. When we came up for air, I checked my watch. Half past five. I ought to make my way back to the funfair if I didn't want to miss my ride.

'I have to go,' I said. I got up and moved towards the doorway.

'Where do you think you're goin in such a hurry?' Alex stood up and headed towards the doorway blocking the exit.

'I'll miss my lift if I don't go now.'

'Not before you pay up twenty quid.'

'What are you on about?'

'You don't think you got her for nothing, do you?'

I turned to Juliette. She shrugged her shoulders. 'What did you expect, a freebie?'

'But I thought…'

Two more blokes gathered around me. 'Let's see your money,' one said.

'I don't have that sort of cash.'

'Now that's not true, Georgie boy, is it?' Donna said, 'we saw you get out that posh car.'

So they'd been watching me. I needed to think quickly. At this rate I'd be held for ransom again. How could I have been so stupid? 'I hitched a lift, that's all.'

'And what about your kid sister, and the Ted guy that's picking you up?' Juliette put her face up to mine. How could I have thought she was pretty?

I shoved her ugly face out of my way. 'She hitched a lift too, and Ted's our next-door neighbour. I don't know what I saw in you. You're nothing but a cheap whore.'

'Don't speak about my Missus like that. Hold him,' Alex said to the two blokes. They grabbed an arm each.

Out of nowhere Alex punched me in the nose making me choke and cough. I spat blood. 'Bloody hell, mate.'

Alex ignored me and rummaged through my pockets. 'Seven and six. Where's the rest?' He turned to Juliette. 'I thought you said he was loaded.'

'He is. I know he is.' She stared at me.

'I told you I don't have any money,' I stammered. 'That's all I have you dirty pimp.'

Alex's fist was ready for another punch when the front door banged open. I struggled to wriggle myself free. A man's voice called, 'What the hell's going on in here?' Max stormed in with Alice and Derek in tow. Max grabbed Alex by the collar jerking him away from me. I took the opportunity to kick one of the others, who squealed and let me go.

Max held Alex in his grip. 'The police are on their way and you lot are trespassing. I'd run if I were you.'

'You're bluffing.' Alex tried to free himself from Max's hold.

'Try me,' Max said.

Alex signalled to the others who scarpered in seconds. Max released Alex and he darted out of the door.

'You're all right now, lad.' Max passed me a handkerchief. 'To wipe the blood. And boy, you're going to have a couple of shiners by tomorrow.' He led me out of the house to his car at the bottom of the footpath.

I managed to stutter, 'Thank God, Max. I'm sorry for being so stupid.'

'Just get in. It's your Alice and Derek you have to thank. If they hadn't called me when they did…'

I climbed in the back seat with Alice. Derek sat in the front with Max. I held my head back to stop the bleeding.

'But how did you know where I was?' I asked through the handkerchief.

'I didn't trust her, so we followed you,' Alice said. 'It looked suspicious so we went back to the phone box down the road to call Max. How's your nose?'

'Sore. Thank goodness you and Derek had the foresight to get help.'

'I suggest you stay at Grace's tonight as she's away on business for a couple of days with Adriénnee and Charlotte. You don't want Elizabeth seeing you in that state.' Max drove the car away.

'I'm not going to have to make a Police statement, am I? I'd rather just forget about it all.'

Alice laughed. 'We didn't call the police. Uncle Max was very convincing though, wasn't he?'

'Yes, he was.' I moved the handkerchief away from my nose. The bleeding had stopped.

We drove up to Grace's house and left Alice on the doorstep saying goodnight to Derek. Maybe he wasn't such a bad lad after all. Max and I went through to the drawing room.

'Thanks Uncle Max. I should have known it was too good to be true. Every girl I meet is a liar or cheat. I'm done with them.'

'You can't generalise girls because of a couple of incidents.'

'But it's all of them. First, Grace, then Grandmother, Patsy, Juliette, and even Elizabeth's let me down at times. The only girl I trust is Alice.'

'Sit down, lad.' He moved to the chaise longue and patted the space next to him. 'You can't generalise. Men can be liars and cheats too. Charlotte's not had it easy, I can't say why because it's her story to tell, but she learned to trust me, and then there's Elizabeth. From what I can gather her first husband was a bit of a fiend, but she's found Simon. And as for your Mother lying and cheating, one day you'll see that all she ever did was put you first. Now I suggest we get Joan to clean up that nose and that will be the end of it.'

'You won't tell Grace or Elizabeth?'

'No one will. But we'll have to make up some excuse for the black eyes.'

Chapter 17

Elizabeth

I put Vikki to my breast to silence her hungry cries. Since she arrived two weeks ago, I'd been stuck almost constantly on the chaise longue. The photographer had been around this morning to perform a photo shoot. I planned to send some pictures in the post to introduce George to his new cousin as he'd returned to school before she arrived.

'Ouch.' My toes curled up. 'I'm not sure how much longer I can do this.'

'Persevere for a while longer, darling. It's only been a couple of weeks and the midwife did say it would get easier. Much better for our little girl if she has Mummy's milk.'

It was all right for him to say that, he wasn't the one with sore nipples and desperate for sleep. Grace and Adriénne were due any minute, I'd talk to Grace about it.

'They've just pulled up outside,' Simon said. 'Perhaps your sister can give you some guidance on feeding.'

'I hope so.' As soon as I lifted Vikki off my breast she started crying. I tried winding her but she still screamed.

The drawing room door opened. 'Miss Grace and Mr Adriénne, Miss.' Martha showed them in.

'Grace, how wonderful to see you. Did you have a nice break? I said, unable to move from the couch.

'Lovely. But never mind that, let me see my gorgeous little niece. Look at that head of dark hair. May I hold her?'

'Of course. Come and sit next to me.'

Grace lifted Vikki against her shoulder. 'There, there, now.' Vikki instantly stopped crying. 'That's better. What was all that noise about?'

'How come she stopped crying for you? She never stops for me unless I feed her. I'm such a useless mother.'

'No you're not.' Grace put her hand on my arm to reassure me. 'It's all perfectly normal. It's because she can smell your milk. It will get easier. I found the first six weeks the hardest.'

Six weeks like this. There was no way I could do it. Simon and Adriénne were chatting in the corner of the room. 'Sherry, Grace?' Simon asked.

'Just a small one.' She rocked Vikki.

I noticed the gold band on her finger. I picked up her hand. 'What's this?'

'We decided to get married.'

'What? When?'

'Last Saturday at Redmont Registry Office. Complete surprise to me too but Adriénne had it all sorted. Witnesses off the street can you believe?'

'I'm not sure I know Redmont?'

'It's just north of Hastings. Lovely little village. Anyway, he'd arranged it all and I thought, why not? It was different for you when you married Simon as you hadn't had a happy first wedding but I had so I didn't need a big event. I wanted to do it quietly and Adriénne had realised that. So I'm now officially Mrs Ardant but I shall stay Grace Gilmore for the business.'

'I'm really happy for you.' Vikki was fast asleep on her lap. 'Why doesn't she do that for me?' I burst out crying.

'Come on now.' Grace put her arm around me. 'Like I said, she can smell your milk. All new mums feel like you're feeling now.'

'Really?' Elizabeth dried her eyes.

'Really. Now don't you think we should make a toast to the new arrival? Grace picked up her glass of sherry.

'We should,' Simon said. 'Elizabeth, are you able to have a small one?'

'I'd better not.' Another thing I was being deprived of. I didn't think I was cut out for this motherhood lark. My baby didn't even seem to like me. 'Pour me some juice instead,' I said.

'What day was she born?' Adriénne asked.

'September fourth, making her a Virgo and strong willed.' Simon passed me a small juice.

'Well she's certainly strong willed. She must get that from you, or maybe…' I faced Grace. '… from her aunt.' I turned to my husband. 'Simon, has Adriénne mentioned we have more to celebrate?'

'No, what?' Simon turned to Adriénne and Adriénne looked at Grace.

'We got married while we were away.' She showed off her ring.

'Do George and Alice know?' Simon topped up his glass.

'Not yet. But hopefully they'll both be happy for me. It's not like they didn't know it was coming. To baby Victoria.' Grace raised her glass.

'To Vikki,' I said, 'and to Grace and Adriénne. I was thinking about getting a nanny. What do you think?' I was praying she'd agree with me and wouldn't think bad of me for suggesting it.

'It's up to you. How do you feel about that, Simon?' Grace asked.

Why was she asking him?

'Well we both grew up with a nanny and it didn't do us any harm, and Elizabeth needs to resume estate business as it's too much for me on my own and what with all the business dinners etc.'

'Sounds like you have your answer then, Elizabeth,' Grace said.

I breathed a silent sound of relief and wondered how soon this new arrangement could be put into place?

Martha wandered into the room. 'Dinner is served. Would you like me to get Annie to put baby Vikki to bed?'

Before I got a chance to answer, Simon said, 'No, we'll take her in with us. She can go in the carrycot.'

'Very well, Sir.'

Grace carried Vikki into the dining room and Simon picked up the green carrycot, sat it in a stand by the table and Grace laid Vikki down, still sleeping. At least I might get to eat a meal without interruptions. 'There was something else I needed to discuss with you.' I pulled out a letter from my pocket. 'I received this yesterday.'

Grace took the letter. 'Mother's worse and Victoria's doubting whether she can continue to look after her. What are we going to do?'

'Well she can't come back here, so I suppose she'll have to go into some sort of institution. Victoria said there's one about five miles away from her house. Simon and I are taking Vikki down there tomorrow so I thought we could check out the hospital at the same time. Will you come too?'

She pressed my hand. 'Of course.'

*

We drove down to Devon in two cars as Vikki's carrycot took most of the backseat of Simon's boring banana yellow Ford Cortina. We could have had one of the chauffeurs take us down in a Rolls but Simon insisted he'd rather drive. Grace and

Adriénne pulled up behind us when we arrived at Victoria's, in their new scarlet, Porsche 911. I suppose our sports car days were over.

Simon carried the carrycot up the path while I lifted the plant pot to get the key from underneath. Pink climbing roses brightened up the cottage along with blue hydrangeas either side of the path.

'Only us.' I unlocked the door and then returned the key to its hiding place.

'Come in.' Victoria went straight to the carrycot, looking dishevelled as if she hadn't had time to comb her hair properly. 'Oh she's such a bonny thing, and sleeping too. Isn't she good?'

'Well she is today. I think she likes travelling in the car. Now we know what to do, Simon, when she won't stop screaming.'

'I told you, it will get easier,' Grace said to me before turning to our cousin and kissing her on the cheek. 'You're looking tired. Why did you leave it this long to let us know you're struggling?'

Victoria moved towards the kitchen. 'Sit down and I'll put the kettle on.'

'I'll do that.' Adriénne took hold of her. 'You sit down and talk to the girls.'

I'd never seen so many of us in Victoria's little sitting room before. I was pleased to find the fire lit as it was pretty nippy outside with the cold winds. The orange and yellow flames were very welcome.

'I suppose you're not getting any younger, Victoria,' Grace said.

'It isn't that so much, Grace, but your mother appears to have given up. At least before she'd let me feed her and she'd drink through a straw but now I can barely get her to touch anything. She's withering away.' Victoria sobbed. 'I'm sorry girls, I've let you down, but I couldn't be the one to make the decision to send her away.'

'It's not your fault, Victoria. You've done so much for us.' I stroked her arm. 'Don't worry, I'll go up and see her.' I crept upstairs and knocked on Mother's door before tiptoeing in. I gasped. She was lying on the bed staring at the ceiling. Her face was ghostly white and more drawn than when I'd last visited. She looked so thin. Thinner than Father on his death bed. I went to the door and called downstairs, 'Grace, can you come up please?'

Grace rushed up and hovered at the door. 'What's going on?'

'I think we need to do something. Come in and see.'

Grace entered the room and moved to the side of Mother's bed. 'We must phone the doctor straight away and get an emergency placement. She needs expert care.'

*

I followed the doctor upstairs. He rested his hand on Mother's forehead. 'Well she hasn't got a temperature so that's a good sign. What's going on Lady Granville,' he asked. 'Why've you stopped eating?'

Mother lay there motionless.

'I'm sending you to hospital to get better. There's an ambulance outside and the men will be here in a minute.' He tutted. 'She should never have been allowed to get to this stage. I told Victoria to let me know immediately if she couldn't cope.'

I wiped my eyes with a handkerchief. 'It's me you should blame, not Victoria.'

'No one's blaming anyone,' the doctor said.

Heavy footsteps traipsed upstairs. Two uniformed men carrying a stretcher trudged in. 'Hello, darling,' the taller one said to Mother, but she lay unresponsive. She'd have hated being called darling. 'Don't worry, we're just going to slide you on here,' he continued. They slid her on to the stretcher and picked it up to take her down. I followed them.

'Mother's going now,' I called into the sitting room where Grace was consoling a sobbing Victoria. I trailed Mother out to the yellow vehicle. The men slid the stretcher inside.

'Is it all right if I say goodbye,' I asked.

'Of course,' the taller one said. 'Let's just get her settled first.'

Once they'd backed out of the vehicle, I climbed the steps and approached Mother. Her eyes were closed. 'I kissed her cheek. Get well soon, Mother. I love you.' I stepped out on to the pavement where Victoria and Grace were now standing. Victoria mounted the small steps and leant over the stretcher towards Mother. 'I'm sorry, Margaret.'

Grace clasped my hand. 'Simon and Adriénne took Vikki for a spin in the car to stop her crying. I think they felt in the way, but they'll be back shortly.'

One of the ambulance men entered the vehicle and touched Victoria's shoulder. 'All right my love,' he said, 'we'll take good care of her for you.'

Victoria trod down from the vehicle, sobbing.

The ambulance driver closed the back doors on Mother and his colleague. 'Don't worry, dear,' he said to Victoria, 'she'll be well looked after.' He made his way to the front of the vehicle and ascended the cab.

We all stood back, watching, as the yellow ambulance drove off and disappeared from view.

Chapter 18

George

21ˢᵗ May 1971

I knocked on the Dean's door.

He coughed. 'Come in.'

I strode in and stood in front of his desk.

'Sit down Granville.'

I eased myself down into the seat opposite him, slouched down and twiddled my thumbs gazing at the portraits on the wall of former Deans. They all looked as pompous as this one.

'Sit up, lad.'

I arched my back and shoulders to sit up and faced him. 'Sorry, Sir.'

'Do you know why I sent for you?'

'No, Sir. Is it something to do with my aunt?'

'Nothing like that. It's come to my attention that you've been refusing to get your hair cut.'

'Yes, Sir. I don't want it cut.'

'Well, Granville, as a student in this school you don't have a choice. We have our reputation to protect. And looking at the length of your hair, no wonder the tutors are concerned.'

'I'm leaving after the exams so I don't see why it matters.'

'It matters. You know it's part of the school rules that all boys must have their hair above the collar. And yours stands out more than most with those girlie curls.'

'I like it, Sir. It's modern.'

'We don't do modern at Sandalwood. A barber is visiting the school today and I've added your name to the list for a short back and sides. All you have to do is be in the medical room by three o'clock.'

'What happens if I'm not?'

'Don't test me, Granville. You've gone off the rails since you gave up your extra tutor sessions with Mr Bennett and there have been several reports of your defiance. I can only assume it's since you took up playing that guitar as well as joining the cricket team. I've therefore advised your music tutor to cease the private lessons, and the sports coach will remove you from the team.'

'What? Why? That's not fair.'

'It's more than fair. I have been far too lenient with you. Your name's been cropping up at all the staff meetings. You've become far too insolent and I can only conclude it's from a lack of discipline. Lord Granville would never have expected me to allow you to get away with such poor behaviour.' The Dean sighed, shaking his head. 'I'm sorry, Granville, this pains me to do this.' He reached under his desk and brought out the cane.

'Bend down and touch your knees, lad.' He flexed the cane in the air making it thrash.

'You've got to be fuckin' kidding.'

'I said bend down now. And there will be an extra strike for that filth out of your mouth.'

'Fuck off, no way.' I raced out of his office, across the green, and upstairs into my room. I knew what I had to do.

Robert was lying on his bed reading, *The Lord of the Flies*. I pulled Da's duffle bag from the cupboard and stuffed a few clothes into it. Robert placed his book face down. 'Hey, what's going on, pal? Are you going somewhere?'

'I'm out of here. Fuckin' Dean. He only tried to thrash me cos I won't get my hair cut. Bloody hell, I'm eighteen not

286

kindergarten. Anyway, I told him where to go so need to get out of here fast.'

'Piggin' hell, I didn't know you had it in you, pal. You must admit, your hair does need a bit of a cut. I started to wonder if I was sharing with a girl.'

'I don't consider not wanting a haircut a reason for that sadist to strike me. He just sits in his office all day looking for an excuse to cane someone.'

'So where are you going?'

'Best you don't know then you can't give me away. I'll let my aunt know once I'm settled.'

'But what about your 'A' levels?'

I shrugged. 'Who the hell cares? I've had enough of being pushed around.'

'Is that what's been bothering you?'

'What do you mean?'

'Well you've been shouting in your sleep again like you used to.'

'Oh? Why didn't you say anything?'

'I didn't want to embarrass you. So what started them up again?'

'What?'

'The nightmares. I know you used to have them as a kid, then they stopped but ever since you got back last summer, well…'

I hadn't realised he knew. Ever since the Juliette business brought back the kidnapping, the nightmares had returned but I wasn't going to tell Robert that. 'The 'A' levels, like you said.' I threw off my school uniform and quickly changed into a blue-checked Brutus shirt and Levi jeans, shoving my black Harrington into the duffle bag. I rummaged in drawers and sieved through my pockets looking for cash, but all I could find was a couple of quid and a bit of loose change. 'I don't suppose you could lend me a fiver?'

Robert hopped off the bed to get his wallet from his jacket. 'I can spare a couple of quid and fifty pence. It's all I've got until my allowance comes through.'

'That'll have to do, thanks, mate.' I stuffed the notes and change into my back pocket. I wasn't sure how long it would last but hopefully I'd make a bit of money busking with my guitar. The lads in the sixth form reckoned I was good, and my music teacher said I had potential.

'Anything else I can help with?' Robert was by my side. 'If you want to talk?'

'Nothing to talk about. Thanks for the cash though. I'll pay you back as soon as I can.' I grabbed my guitar and threw the duffle bag over my shoulder.

'Keep it. Call it a birthday present. Good luck, George. Keep in touch.' He patted me on the back.

'Thanks.' I shook his hand.

*

It was warm so I was glad that I'd slung the jacket in my bag. I made my way to the main road and stuck my thumb out. I'd never hitched before but some of the guys at school had. After thirty minutes of shuffling up and down the footpath, and almost giving up, a lorry pulled up next to me.

'Where you goin, mate?'

'Wintermore, just outside Wigan?'

'I'm not going that far but I can get you to Liverpool.'

'Thanks.' I climbed up into the cab placing my guitar carefully on the floor next to me. The driver didn't say much but just got on with his driving. He pulled the sunshade down on the side window to protect himself from sun blindness. The road was bumpy but I liked the experience of being high up. Maybe I'd become a lorry driver, I wouldn't need 'A' levels for that. Driving all over the world, never stuck in one place. I closed my eyes hoping to sleep to pass the time.

'Wake up, sleepy head,' the driver said. 'I'm pulling into this service station. We're just outside Liverpool. You'll probably get yourself another lift from one of that lot in there. Come in for a cuppa and I'll see if I can find someone going your way.'

'Thanks, that's really kind. I'll buy them. It's the least I can do.' I couldn't really afford to use my cash but felt obliged. I hoped he hadn't planned to order food too. I swaggered up to the counter and asked the young assistant. 'Two teas, please?' I handed over fifty pence.

I sat down on a wooden chair at the table with the driver, and the girl brought over two mugs of strong tea.

The driver leant over to another old bloke on the next table. 'Ernie, you're off to Wigan today, aren't you?'

'Yeah, that's right.'

'Fancy a passenger? This young lad needs a lift.'

'Oh aye, what takes you there, laddie?'

'It's my aunt's birthday,' I lied.

'Yeah, sure, I'll drop you. Leaving in five though so if you want a pee you'd best go now.'

'Thanks.' I thought I ought to use the toilet as I hadn't been for hours. When I got back Ernie was ready.

I climbed up into his cab and settled myself down on the seat. Ernie, unlike the other driver, never stopped chatting.

'You play that, mate?' He pointed to my guitar.

'Yes, a bit.'

He carried on asking me questions but I shut myself off to most of it, just nodding or saying yes or no.

It was half-past-three. I wondered if the Dean had discovered that I'd gone and how long I had before Elizabeth or Grace found out.

Chapter 19

Elizabeth

I put the telephone down. 'That was the Dean at George's school.'

Grace jumped up from the chaise longue. 'Has something happened to him?'

'Well, yes. He's gone missing but not before being insolent to the Dean. Swearing can you believe? The Dean was understandably livid. Apparently George was refusing to have his hair cut. I've no idea what's got into him lately.'

'Well it's obvious, isn't it? He's playing up because he's jealous of Vikki.'

'He loves his little cousin, he's definitely not jealous. More likely it's to do with you always spoiling him.'

'That's not fair, Elizabeth.'

'And neither is what you're saying.'

Alice clapped her hands. 'Stop arguing.' She'd come home from Greenemere for a few days because she hadn't been well. 'I waited all these years to get my family back and you two aren't going to mess it up.'

'You're quite right, darling. I'm sorry. And I'm sorry to you too, Elizabeth, we shouldn't be fighting between ourselves. Instead we need to find out what's happened to George.'

'I tried to get him to have his hair cut before he went back after Easter but he insisted he was growing it long,' I said.

'It's because he wants to be a popstar,' Alice said, 'ever since he started playing that guitar.'

'Well it's the first I've heard. I thought he was into classical music,' I said.

'Not George.' Alice folded her arms.

'Well you don't need to look so smug,' I said. 'Might have been helpful if you'd told someone. Goodness knows where's he gone, who he's with, and what he's in to. Maybe drugs?'

'Don't shout at me. I'm worried too.' Alice started crying.

'You're right, I'm sorry. I didn't mean to shout.' I put my arms around my niece to console her. I turned to Grace. 'Do you think we should drive up to Sandalwood and speak to Robert Sanders? See if he knows something?'

'That sounds like the best idea but I think we should leave it until morning. He may have just gone off for a sulk. Let's give him a chance to phone or turn up back at school.'

Chapter 20

George

As we approached a roundabout, I started to recognise places from when I'd come here with Grace to do flowers for Da. 'Anywhere here will do thanks,' I said.

'You sure? We're not in Wigan yet?'

'Yep, I'm sure. It's Wintermore I wanted.'

Ernie pulled up at the side of the road. 'Happy Birthday to your aunt.'

'Thanks.' I jumped out of the cab, grabbing my bag and guitar, and looked both ways to get my bearings trying to remember where Bamber Street was. Over to the left I could see my old school. Should I go there? No, I'd make my way to my old home first.

I ambled down a cobbled road. Some of the houses had been knocked down while others had windows boarded up. I hoped Bamber Street was still there. I turned off Union Street and spotted the coal mine but rushed past as I didn't want to think about that dreadful day. Up until then I was a normal boy, a coal miner's son, and the idea of going to fancy boarding schools and becoming an heir was a fairy story. Not one I wanted to live. I stopped at the end of the road. It looked the same. I sauntered down to my old house and stopped at number eleven. A little girl came out of the door pushing a doll's pram. Her mother stood at the entrance. 'Can I help you?'

'Sorry, I didn't mean to stare, it's just that I used to live here.'

'That must have been some time ago as we've been here for three years.'

I wondered what had happened to the family that moved in after us. 'Yes it was nine years ago. Do you know if Mrs Price still lives around here?'

'Mrs Price, at number twenty-one? Oh yeah, she's still there. I reckon she's been there forever. The woman bent down to her daughter. 'Sally, straight to the shops and back again. No talking to strangers.'

'Yes, Mam.' The little girl skipped off, talking to her doll as she went and her mother shut the door without saying anything else to me. I walked up another few doors until I got to Ben's old house. I tapped the door knocker. Of course when I lived there, we'd never have knocked on the front door. It was always the back. Within a minute the door swung open.

'What can I do you for?' A woman with a scarf wrapped around her head like a turban was puffing on a cigarette. She looked just like I remembered except a little older.

'Mrs Price, it's George Gilmore.'

'George who?'

'Gilmore, I used to live at number eleven. Ben was my best friend, remember?'

She scratched her head. 'Ah, little George, yes, yes, I remember you. You look just the same. How you doing, laddie? You look well.'

'I'm fine thank you. Is Ben at home or did he go to America?'

'America.' She laughed. 'Pipe dream. Come in and I'll stick the kettle on.' She waved me into the house. 'Sit yourself down in the parlour.' She waddled off to the kitchenette.

I glanced around the room. It looked different to what I remembered with newer pieces of furniture such as the settee. I followed her into the kitchen. The kettle whistled so she took it off the old gas stove. She hadn't upgraded to a new cooker then.

'Come through.' She shuffled back in to the parlour carrying two mugs of tea and placed them on the smoked glass coffee table. 'So tell me what you've been up to.'

'Well I've been living with my aunt in Gerrard's Cross. But what about Ben?'

'That sounds posh.'

'It is.' I laughed. 'I'd rather have stayed here with my best mate. So what's Ben up to?'

'He's down the Woodcroft at the moment. Spends most of his time there since he hit eighteen. Are you eighteen yet?'

'Yes.'

'Sit down and drink your tea and then you can go and surprise him. How about your mam? What's she up to?'

I eased myself into a comfy armchair. 'She's a fashion designer. Have you heard of House of Grace? That's her business.'

'That's your mam's shop? Really? Some lovely outfits in there. Far too expensive for the likes of me. Co-op has to do.'

'I could probably arrange a discount for you.'

'My, she's done well for herself. Of course some round here always said she didn't belong. They only accepted her cos of your Da. Bless his soul.' She made the sign of the cross against her chest. 'Your Da was well loved in these parts. Any idea what happened to Nancy? She left that day with your mam, promised to write but I never heard from her again.'

'She still lives with Mam, and Alice is at school in Brighton.'

'That sounds posh.'

I laughed.

'And what about the babby. Of course she'd be…' She started counting on her fingers.

'She died.'

She made the sign of the cross against her chest again. 'Dear Lordie, what happened?'

'Scarlet Fever when she was two.' Tears welled up in my eyes.

'She patted my arm. 'Your poor mam. You too of course, but must have been dreadful for your mam. You play that thing?' She pointed to my guitar.

'Yes. Some even say I play well.'

'Give us a tune. Go on, make an old lady's day.'

'Okay. I picked up my instrument and strummed the strings and sang, John Lennon's, *Power to the People*.

'I know that one,' she said once I'd finished, 'that's one of the Beatles. It's what's his name?'

'John Lennon.' I laughed. 'I'm going to get myself a pair of round glasses like his. Do you think they'll suit me?'

'Yes,' she said. 'Especially with those long blond curls, you'll look like a pop star then. That John Lennon, he's with that Yoyo Ona now, you know.'

'Yes.' I didn't have the heart to correct her. I picked up my mug and gulped the last of the tea. 'So the Woodcroft, you said?'

'Yes, just up the road and turn left. Thanks for the tune.'

'You're welcome and thanks for the cuppa. Maybe I'll see you later?'

'I hope so. Come back for your tea, and if you need a bed for the night, there's always the couch.'

'Thanks.' I kissed her on the cheek and opened the door to leave.

*

I traipsed down the road towards the pub, bag and guitar across my shoulder. Summer had come early but it was lucky that I'd packed the Harrington, just in case it was cold at night and I had to sleep rough. Ben's mam had offered a bed for the night but what would happen after that?

On reaching the Woodcroft I paused before opening the door. I'd never been the other side of it but spent many a day sat on the wall outside waiting for Da. He'd throw a packet of crisps or peanuts out to me and our Alice. I wondered if Ben would recognise me. Would I recognise him? Someone pushed the door open.

'Sorry, mate. Nearly gave you a right shiner. You goin in or what?'

'Yes, thanks.' I walked into the public bar looking around to see if I could spot my old friend. A couple of blokes sat on bar stools and one young chap stood up chatting to the bartender. It was Ben. I'd know him anywhere even though he'd gained a bit of weight, looking more like a rugby player.

I moved up behind him and tapped his back lightly. 'Ben Price. You haven't changed a bit.'

Ben turned around and glared at me for a few moments. 'No, it can't be. Surely.' He turned to the bartender. 'It's my old mucker, George Gilmore.' He grabbed hold of my hand, shook it briskly. 'What the hell.' He grabbed me in a bear hug. 'Is it really you? Where've you been? We'd no idea what happened to you after the flit. A pint of the same for my mate here.'

'What's that?' I asked Ben.

'John Smith's. That okay for you?'

'Yeah sure, my favourite,' I lied. I'd never drunk beer although I'd been drinking wine since I was nine. Grandfather insisted I partook at the dining table.

'You remember Jack Gilmore?' Ben said to the bartender, 'Well this is his lad.'

'Sure. I remember Jack. A great geezer.' He wiped the bar counter.

'Yes he was,' I said.

The bartender pulled back the lever, poured a pint and sat it down on the counter in front of me. 'This one's on the ouse.'

'Why, thanks.'

'Let's sit over there.' Ben picked up his pint, I did the same, and we wandered over to a table in the corner. 'You sound all posh, where've you been?'

'It's a long story. I'll tell you another time.' I sat down opposite Ben. 'How about you? What you up to? I thought you were going to America.' I took a sip of the beer and tried not to let my face show my reaction.

'Yeah, best-laid plans and all that.'

'So are you working or at college?'

'Working. Got a job filling shelves when Wiseworld's first opened.'

'What's Wiseworld's?'

'Supermarket. Even in Wintermore we've got supermarkets now. They've pushed most of the corner shops out.'

'That's progress for you.' I laughed. 'So do you see anyone from school? Ha, do you remember Smelly Susie? Good God, I wonder whether she ever outgrew wetting her pants?'

Ben's smile disappeared. 'Err yeah. I do. I married her.'

'Oh sorry, mate. I didn't mean to offend.'

'You didn't.' He patted me on the back and laughed. 'And yes, she did outgrow wetting her pants. Stopped before secondary school.'

'But married? You're only eighteen.'

'Old enough to get her preggers. Bit of a shotgun do, I'm afraid. Me hands were tied.'

'So you've got a kid? Boy? Girl?'

'Boy. He's nearly two and another one on the way. She's six months gone.'

'So how long have you been married?'

'Two years. Soon as we were sixteen, I got pushed down the aisle. Make an honest woman of er.'

'Blimey.' Ben had got a child and another on the way and I was still a virgin. 'So where do you live?'

'Still at Mam's. Got our name on the council list so hopefully we'll have a house by the time this one's born. Come back to ours for tea and you can reminisce with Susie. I think she wants to forget about those puddles though.' Ben sniggered. 'In fact, do us a favour, mate, don't bring it up.'

'No of course I won't. Your mam asked me back for tea, so yes, why not? Do you know if Miss Jones still works at the school?'

'Aye,' she does. 'Our Sandie's in her class.'

I didn't recognise the name. 'Sandie?'

'Ah, yeah, that'll be after your time. She's eight.'

We chatted for the next couple of hours but I didn't share much about myself. I wasn't ready to open up about everything that had happened in my life. A young woman with long silky auburn hair, a striking made-up face, and a huge belly entered the pub. Ben waved. My god that must be Susie. She was a cracker. No wonder Ben had got her knocked up.

'Susie meet George. George meet Susie. But of course you've met before as this is George Gilmore that used to sit next to you.'

'No…' Susie glared at me. 'You look so different, yet… you look the same.'

'Well that's a contradiction in itself.' Ben laughed.

'You look hugely different,' I said. 'You've grown into a beautiful woman.'

'I suppose I was rather plain when I was a kid.'

'Well you've made up for it now. And when's it due?' I went to touch her stomach but decided that wasn't appropriate.

'August. And if this heatwave continues, I'm not sure how long I can cope with it. Especially in the shop.'

'Shop?'

'Yeah, I work at Wiseworld's. Means I get a discount. It all helps. The staff are making a collection and asked me what pram I'd like. How groovy is that? They're going to get me one of those huge Silver Cross's. A navy blue one.'

'Wow.' I said. I'd no idea what a Silver Cross looked like.

Susie glanced at her watch. 'You comin, Ben? I promised your mam I'd get tea going as she's got Parent's evening for your Sandie and I've gotta pick up our David from me mam's first.'

'I'll just finish this.' Ben lifted his pint. 'I'll meet you there. What do you think?' he said once Susie had gone.

'She's a stunner. You're a lucky man. Although I don't envy you being tied down.'

He gulped the last of his pint. 'Best make a move, mate.'

'Listen,' I said, 'I'd really like to see Miss Jones, and I take it if your mam's gone up there for Parents Evening for your Sandie, that it will be with Miss Jones?'

'Yeah, it is.'

'Do you mind if I catch up with you later?'

'No, you go. I'd best get back to the Missus.'

We walked out of the pub. Well I walked, Ben swayed. A chip off the old block by the looks of things. He never mentioned his dad though. We went our separate ways.

Chapter 21

George

I turned right at the end of the road, followed the path across the coal mine and turned left into Union Street, stopping when I reached Silverleaf Junior. My heart pounded as I strode through the school gates. Would Miss Jones think I was silly coming to see her after all this time? Would she even remember me? I walked towards the classrooms.

A lad around ten was standing at the end of the corridor. 'Which teacher have you come to see?'

'Miss Jones.'

'Just down there on the left. She's got someone in with her. Sit on the chair outside and wait. I thought she was done. What's your name?'

'I'm an old pupil hoping to catch up with her.'

'Oh okay. Well she shouldn't be too long. I'm just packing up. Been on prefect duty.'

'You're doing a grand job, mate.' I patted the squirt playfully on his back.

I went down the corridor, sat on the small wooden chair and waited. It took me back to the last time I sat on a chair like this when Miss Jones said I should go to grammar school. I heard chairs squeak from within the classroom and could just about make out muffled voices before the door opened. Miss Jones shook the woman's hand. 'Thank you for coming, Mrs Woods.' She turned towards me. 'Are you waiting to see me?'

'Yes.' I didn't say anything else because I wanted to see if she recognised me.

'What's the name of the child? I thought I'd finished.' She glanced at the register in her hands.

'George Gilmore.'

'George Gilmore.' She tapped her lip. 'I know that name. George Gilmore.' She looked up at me and stared. 'George Gilmore. Is that really you?'

'It is.'

'How lovely to see you. And look at you all grown up. Come on in. Sit down.'

I sat down on the chair by her desk like when I was aged nine. She looked just the same except her long blonde hair was curly.

She looked me up and down. 'You haven't changed much,' she said, 'but I can see that I was right about you going far. The quality of those clothes tells me that you've not been roughing it. Where are you living?'

'I've been at Sandalwood in Westbridge.'

'That's impressive. So are you up here visiting?'

'I…' I couldn't lie to those big blue eyes. I never could. 'I'd outstayed my welcome at Sandalwood, and at home, so I've decided not to go back.'

'Why?'

'I have my reasons.'

'Look, there's a little café around the corner. Let's go and chat over a coffee. The caretaker will be waiting to lock up here.' Miss Jones picked up her bag and we departed the classroom together.

We left the school building, walked across the playground, and through the gate.

'It's just around the corner.' She slipped off her cardigan. 'It's hot, isn't it?'

'Yes.' I laughed. I remembered other years when it had been hot on my birthday and Mam would throw a tea party in the yard for Ben, me, and our Alice.

'Here it is,' Miss Jones said. It was the same café that Grace brought me to when we'd visited Da's grave.

'So why've you left home, George?' she asked once we'd sat down and had a coffee in front of us. 'That doesn't sound like the young lad I knew.'

'Let's just say that the Dean and I had a falling out.'

'In what way?'

'He wanted to give me six of the best which I didn't take too well. I'm afraid I told him where to go, and not in a gentlemanly way.'

'I'd have thought you're a bit too old to be punished that way. Did he have good reason?'

'I refused to have my hair cut.'

'I don't blame you.' She touched her hair. 'Most girls would kill for these. Mine come from a bottle. I remember your sister had a mop of curls too.'

'Not any more though. Hers is almost straight now. I like my curls and they're fashionable.'

'Quite right. I wouldn't have thought refusing to get your hair cut warranted a thrashing.'

'Not quite the birthday present I was expecting.'

'It's your birthday?'

'Yes.'

'Happy Birthday. How old does that make you now?'

'Eighteen.'

'George, you may be eighteen, but don't you think you should go home? Your mother must be frantic.'

'I don't see why. I haven't lived with her since she gave me away when I was nine. My aunt's my guardian, well was. From today I'm my own man. She won't miss me, anyway. She's got her own baby now. Gorgeous little girl, Vikki.'

'I always wondered what had happened to you. I went to your home but the neighbours told me you'd all gone to London. I assumed you were with your mother.'

'My mother, Grace, only turned back up in my life a few years ago, so I don't see why I should worry about her.'

'Because I remember you well, George Gilmore, and that's who you are. I remember how you cleared up after your classmate. Nothing was ever too much trouble for you. Consideration for others like that doesn't just slip away.' She held my hand. 'Look, my house is around the corner. Come home with me and I'll make some dinner but you must allow me to phone your aunt or mother.'

'I'm not sure. They'll try and force me to go back.'

'Not if you give them a good reason not to, and I believe from what you've told me that's reason enough. If I'm not mistaken it's illegal to cane an eighteen-year-old, and if it isn't then it certainly should be. If you were my boy…' She patted my hand. 'Never mind, let's go home.'

We walked side by side. I towered her by six inches even though she was wearing high heels. How did she manage to stand up in them all day? I suddenly remembered about Ben. I'd promised to go to tea. I shrugged. He probably wouldn't miss me anyway. I'd catch up with him tomorrow.

Miss Jones stopped when we reached a semi-detached house with a blue front door. The house had a little garden full of coloured pansies in the flower beds. Miss Jones turned the key in the lock and pushed the door open. A long-haired dog came bounding towards me.

'Down, Tassles.' Miss Jones stooped down and ruffled Tassles' coat. 'She gets a bit excited after I've been out all day. John, my hubby, does shift work so he makes sure he gives her a good run before he leaves at lunchtime and then I take her to the park in the evening. You can come with me if you like?'

'I'd like that. I always wanted a dog. What kind of dog is she?'

'She's a red setter. My favourite breed. She's so soft and affectionate. If you wouldn't mind taking your shoes off, George.'

'No of course not.'

'For the carpets, you see. We only had them fitted a couple of weeks ago.'

I slipped off my pumps and sank my feet into the brown and cream long-piled carpet before bending down to stroke Tassles. Miss Jones opened the kitchen door and the smell of cooking filled the room. 'Good old John,' she said, 'he's popped a casserole in the oven ready. We make a good team.'

'How long have you been married?'

'Three years.'

'He's a lucky man.'

'George Gilmore, you'll make me blush. You know, you made quite an impression on me when I was your teacher. I haven't come across another nine-year-old as bright as you were.'

'Now it's my turn to blush.' I laughed.

'Let's eat dinner and then I'll make that phone call to let your family know where you are. You can stay here tonight in our spare room and your mother or aunt can pick you up tomorrow. We don't want you disappearing again. John won't mind and we haven't got anything planned. And this evening we should celebrate your birthday.'

'Thank you, Miss Jones.'

'Call me Betty. And it's Pearson now although I still use Jones for school.'

Betty. Hmm, it seems I was never right when I'd imagined her as a Janet. She definitely suited Betty. I laughed to myself.

She spooned out the stew onto the plates. 'Bread?'

'Oh yes please.' I was starving. I hadn't eaten anything since breakfast.

She sliced me a couple of doorstops. 'Is that enough?'

'That's lovely, thank you. Shall I set the table?'

'Mats in there, and cutlery in that drawer.' She pointed.

I placed two table mats onto the tablecloth and laid knives and forks either side. We chatted through the meal and I found myself telling her everything that had happened to me over the years including the kidnapping which I hadn't even mentioned to Grace or Alice. Betty was so easy to talk to.

'What a rotten time you've had. I'll speak to your mother and aunt. I'm sure they'll understand.'

I smiled. After mopping up my plate with a slice of bread, I said, 'That was delicious. I needed that. Thank you.'

'My pleasure. It's wonderful to have such an unexpected guest and after all these years... George Gilmore. Right, how do you fancy washing up while I make that phone call? Can you jot down your number?' She passed me a pen and paper.

'Sure.' I scribbled the number and passed her the pad.

'Thank you. After I've made the call we'll take Tassles out before it gets dark.' She went out into the hall. I didn't try to listen in to the phone call, instead I poured a squirt of lemon washing-up liquid into the sink and ran hot water from the tap. Everyone had hot water these days, no matter where they lived. I'd just finished rinsing the last plate when she came back in.

'I've arranged with your aunt that you'll stay here tonight and she and your mother will pick you up in the morning.'

'Grace is coming?'

'Yes. There was some commotion in the background when I phoned. Your mother was there and I can tell you, they're out of their minds with worry.'

'Are they?' I felt ashamed.

Chapter 22

George

The next morning I thanked Betty's husband, John, for letting me stay over. He was very understanding. 'Anytime,' he said. 'It's great to finally meet the famous George Gilmore after Betty telling me all these years about her star student.'

'She didn't.' I laughed.

'She damn well did. It's been George Gilmore this and George Gilmore that and I wonder what happened to George Gilmore.'

Betty opened the lounge door and Tassles bounded in and straight up to me, front legs on my chest while standing on her hind legs.

'All right, girl.' I pushed her down and stroked her. 'You're such a pretty girl. How old did you say she is?'

'Eighteen months. Still a puppy. Hopefully she'll settle down a bit as she gets older. We wouldn't be without her though. Would we Bett?'

'No we wouldn't.' Betty took hold of Tassles' head and ruffled her ears. 'We love you, don't we, girl? She's our baby.'

'I'm going to get a dog just like her,' I said as the doorbell rang.

'That will be your mother,' John said. 'I'll get it.'

'Come in, come in,' I heard him say. A man's voice replied. Had Simon come too?

Elizabeth rushed over and hugged me. 'Thank God, you're all right.' Grace walked over and did the same.

'So young man, what's all this grief you're giving your mother and aunt?' I turned to see Uncle Max.

'Uncle Max. Sorry, I didn't think you'd find out so quickly. I had planned to call.'

'Well let's say the Dean wasn't happy with your behaviour. Happy belated Birthday by the way.'

'Thank you.'

'Tell your mother and aunt why you ran away,' Betty prompted.

It was a bit embarrassing. 'The Dean…'

'He wanted to give him six of the best,' interrupted Betty. 'I'm pretty damn sure that's illegal at his age. And for what…?'

'What did you do?' Grace asked.

'Nothing.'

'The Dean must have had a reason. What was it?' Elizabeth asked.

'What did you do?' Max joined in.

'Nothing. I told you. Nothing. I refused to get my hair cut, that's all. I didn't see why my hair length should make any difference to my abilities. Especially as I was due to leave after the exams. No one was going to see me.'

'He was in the wrong but then so were you. You had no right to use abusive language to him. Elizabeth will have words with the Dean before you go back. That's if they'll let you back,' Grace said.

'I'm not going back.'

'I know it's not my place but I don't think you should force him to go back.' Betty smiled at me.

'Well we'll talk about it when we're home,' Elizabeth said, 'we'll all sit down, Simon too, and see where we go from there.'

'It's my decision and if you try and force me then I'm not coming back with you.'

'Now, lad, don't get upset,' Max said, 'no one's going to force you to do anything. All your mother and Elizabeth are saying is that we need to discuss it. If you think you're old enough to make your own decisions, then you should be mature enough to sit down and have a proper discussion about it all.'

Betty looked at me and nodded.

'All right,' I said, 'but if anyone tries to make me go back there then I'm off.'

'Get your things,' Max said. 'Your Aunt needs to get back to Vikki earlier rather than later.'

I strode out of the room and upstairs to where I'd left my bag and guitar. I liked it here with Betty and John, and I loved Tassles. Betty followed me upstairs.

'It will be all right, George.'

'If they try and force me to go back to that school can I come back and stay with you for a couple of days until I sort myself out?'

'I'm quite sure that it won't come to that. I do hope you'll come and visit me though, and maybe I could visit you?'

'I'd like that.' I hugged her. 'You always were my favourite teacher.'

'You'll make me blush, George Gilmore.'

'Hurry up, George,' Max called.

Grace, Elizabeth and Max were waiting at the bottom of the stairs. Tassles was wagging her tail. I caught hold of her and pulled her to my chest. 'See you soon, Tassles.' I ruffled her ears.

'Thank you, John.' I shook his hand.

'You're welcome anytime, George. Do come back and see us again.'

Grace, Max and Elizabeth thanked John and Betty too. 'Thank you so much for alerting us,' Elizabeth said.

I climbed into the back of Max's silver Mercedes with Elizabeth. Grace sat in the front with Max. Betty and John waved us off holding Tassles in-between them.

Chapter 23

George

'Look I'm sorry to have worried you all. I just had to get away,' I said, as we congregated in the drawing room at Granville Hall.

'Before we go any further, I have a surprise for you.' Elizabeth rushed out of the room and returned carrying Vikki. She placed her down on the floor. 'Hold your arms out and call her to you.'

I knelt down on the floor holding my arms out in front. 'Vikki.' She crawled over to me, giggling as she moved at a whopping speed. I picked her up and swung her in my arms. 'Clever girl.'

'She started last week,' Elizabeth said, 'but I kept it as a surprise for your birthday.'

'What a fantastic present,' I said.

Simon scooped Vikki up. 'I'll pop her to bed and then we can sit down and discuss your future, George.'

Martha brought in coffee and biscuits. 'Happy belated birthday, Master George,' she said.

'Thank you.' I wasn't really thinking about my birthday but about what Simon had said. They were going to try and make me go back.

Simon returned to the drawing room and sat down with Grace, Elizabeth, Max and me. 'Now what seems to have been the problem at school?'

I didn't really see what it had to do with him. 'I'm not going back,' I said.

'So I've heard but why?'

'It's barbaric there for starters.'

'Well I can remember getting the cane umpteen times when I was at school but it didn't make me run away. You need to develop a backbone.'

'Please, don't talk to him like that.' Grace butted in. 'A punishment like that at his age is degrading.'

I liked the way she stuck up for me.

'Simon is quite right though, George,' Elizabeth said, 'you can't throw your future away over this.'

'You don't know what you're talking about. There are lots more reasons. I'm not going back and if you try and make me then I'll just leave. I'm eighteen now so you can't make me do anything.'

'But just go back and finish your 'A' levels, that's not a lot to ask. And what would Mother say if she gets better and finds out that we let you quit school without finishing your exams,' Elizabeth said.

'I don't give a damn what she says,' I said.

'Nor do I,' said Grace. 'If you all calm down for a minute, I think we should listen to what George has to say.'

Thank goodness someone appeared to be on my side. I thought back to when I was with Betty and she said I should tell my family everything. I had to be mature about this. 'If you're prepared to sit and listen then I'll try and explain how I'm feeling.'

Everyone nodded and all eyes focused on me.

'First of all, it wasn't just to do with the Dean. He was the last straw. For the last nine years I've felt like I've just been pushed around. Firstly, being sent to Granville Hall almost straight after Da died.'

'But…' Grace said.

I sighed. 'Listen, please.'

'Sorry.'

'Then my first day here Martha bullied me. Then Grandfather ordered my hair to be cut. Then there was that wicked governess followed by being sent to the local private school where the lads ducked my head down the bog on my first day and that day ending with me being kidnapped.' I took a deep breath.

'Kidnapped?' Grace said. 'What's this about you being kidnapped?'

'Tell her,' Elizabeth said.

I went through the story of how I was held up in the old war bunker the other side of the glade and later transferred to the cottage and how I'd finally managed to escape. Grace's mouth remained open the whole time but she didn't interrupt. 'Then I discovered that my girlfriend had cheated on me with my supposed best mate, straight after Grandfather died, and if that wasn't enough, a local girl schemed her way with her loser friends to get funds out of me. And if it wasn't for Uncle Max…'

'Why didn't we know about this?' Elizabeth and Grace turned to Max.

'Because he respected my privacy,' I said, 'shall I continue?'

They both nodded.

'And then there's the one-to-one tutoring.' I paused. They all looked closely at me, waiting. 'That was fine while Mr Higgins was my tutor but his replacement, Bennett, intimidated me. He said the work that I'd spent hours, days or even weeks on, was rubbish. He was nothing but a bully.'

'Well we can do something about that. I'll go into the school.'

'No, Aunt Elizabeth. I don't have any proof, it would be his word against mine. And then to top it all, it's my eighteenth birthday and the Dean not only orders me to get my hair cut but when I refuse wants to give me six of the best. I was

314

eighteen for God's sake and I wasn't going to be pushed around anymore. So that's why I walked out. I'd had… I've had… enough. And that's why I'm not going back.' I wiped my eyes. No one said anything, there was just the odd gasp. I took another deep breath. 'Miss Jones, Betty, said I should speak to someone and I think she's right. I don't know who I am anymore and I don't want to end up like Grandmother in a mental hospital, so I need to take action now.'

Grace broke the silence. 'I think George is right. He should speak to someone. We don't want him ending up like Mother, maybe if we'd acted earlier with her then she'd never have got to that point. We'll find you the best, George. Money is no object.'

'Thank you, Grace.' It was such a relief to get everything off my chest. The last nine years had been building up and building up.

Elizabeth wiped her hand across her forehead. 'I'll speak to my old psychiatrist, in Devon, who helped me when I had my breakdown. He'll be able to recommend someone local, I'm sure.' I hadn't realised she'd had a breakdown.

Grace asked, 'How about coming to work in Packing at House of Grace for now? Just until you know what you'd like to do. It will be better to have something to do rather than hanging around the house.'

That didn't seem like a bad idea. I could gain work experience and think where to go next.

'I hear what you're saying, George, but what about your exams?' Elizabeth said.

Grace stroked my arm. 'Once he's feeling better we can always get him a private tutor. But let's face it I never had any 'A' levels and it hasn't hindered me.'

Simon sat upright. 'Well hold on a minute, if he isn't going to be an architect, and insists on leaving school, I think he should come and work on the Estate with day release to college to conclude his exams. I mean, obviously after he's seen someone for help.'

I thumped the arm of the chair. 'I don't want to learn the bloody business.'

'Less of the insolence,' Simon said.

'Don't talk to me like that. You can't tell me what to do. Just remember, in theory, I'm your employer.'

'George.' Elizabeth glared at me.

'Taking things out on Simon isn't going to help,' Max said.

'George, you should apologise.' Grace frowned.

They were right of course. I shouldn't have spoken to Simon that way. He'd been very good to me. And I didn't want an argument. I was tired. 'I'm sorry, Simon, I don't want to fall out with you, but have you listened to a single word I just said?'

The four of them carried on chatting about what I could or shouldn't do, with Grace and Max in my corner. I stood up. 'This is what's going to happen. I'm going to take the packing job with "House of Grace." At some stage I may get a private tutor or go to night school but I need a break from the pressure of exams. And, Aunt Elizabeth, I don't want to let you down but...' I stood up and moved over to her and took her hands. 'I need this time. Do you understand?'

They all sat there stunned.

'And in time I may take over the Granville Estate like Grandfather wanted but not yet. For now I want to take a day at a time and be at home with my family. I want to forget about all the things that have happened to me and I want to get help for my nightmares.' I sat back down next to Grace.

The front door slammed and footsteps ran through the hall and into the drawing room.

'George.' Alice hugged me.

'Hello, Alice. I'm really pleased to see you.'

'Happy belated birthday.' She handed me a wrapped gift but my best present was being at home with my family around me.

Chapter 24

Elizabeth

17ᵗʰ November 1971

The front doorbell rang. It was Grace.

'Hello, my favourite little niece.' Grace scooped up Vikki and swung her around in the air making her chuckle. 'She gets more gorgeous each day. How's George getting on with the psychiatrist? What's her name?'

'Dr Spencer. Very well. He's got into a nice routine where he visits her in the evenings after work and sometimes she comes here. In fact she's asked if he can organise a group session with all the family. I wondered if you wanted to be involved.'

'Yes please. Thank you. Just let me know when.'

'How's he getting on in the packing job?'

'He's picked it up well and works hard. I don't give him any special treatment. In fact, that's kind of on the lines of what I wanted to discuss with you, but after lunch.'

'Do you think we did the right thing letting him get his own way and not returning to school?'

'Definitely. This little one isn't with her nanny today then?'

'No, I gave Nanny the day off as you were coming over.'

'Ah, thanks, Elizabeth. Come on little one, give your aunty a big kiss.' Vikki giggled. Grace spun her around. 'She looks just like Alice did at that age.' Grace lifted Vikki and carried her into the dining room and sat her inside the highchair.

'What is it you wanted to discuss?' I asked.

'Let's sit down and eat first, I'm starving as I missed breakfast this morning.'

Annie pushed in the hostess trolley laden with a green salad, tomatoes, cucumber and smoked red salmon. She set the food down on the table and poured water into crystal glass tumblers.

'So…' I asked impatiently.

'Like I mentioned, George has been working very hard at House of Grace.'

'He seems to be enjoying it too from what he's said. Although Simon and I are still hoping he'll come around to helping out in the business.'

'Maybe one day, Elizabeth, once he's older, but for now, don't get your hopes up. I've a proposition for him but thought I'd run it through with you first.'

'A proposition?'

'Yes. He loves drawing and I don't see why he can't adapt his talent of drawing buildings to fashion designs. I'm going to offer him an apprenticeship with House of Grace.'

'But he's going to take over the Granville business eventually.'

Grace shook her head. 'Isn't it better that he's happy? You've just said that he's doing well medically, let's not push him back.'

'But he won't be happy in fashion. You really don't know George at all.'

'He likes drawing, so I don't see why he can't adapt his talent to fashion.'

'I'm telling you now that George won't want to do that.'

'But you don't mind if I ask him?'

'Ask away. But when he laughs in your face, remember I told you so.'

'I hope he accepts because, well in a few months, I intend to take a step back from the business for a while.' She held her stomach.

I stared at her. 'What are you saying?'

'Vikki's going to have a little playmate. I'm expecting around the middle of March.'

'That's wonderful.' I stood up from the table to hug my sister but deep down I wanted to scream. She had everything, her fashion business, Alice, and now she was having a new baby, yet still she was trying to take George away from me.

'Pop December 12th in your diary and come around for Sunday lunch,' Grace said, 'and I'll broach the subject with George then. I'd like all his family around him.'

Chapter 25

George

They all sat around the table waiting for my answer. Grace, Adriénne, Elizabeth, Simon, Charlotte, Max, Nancy and Alice.

'So, let me get this straight. You'd like me to train as a fashion designer? Is that what you're saying?'

'That's exactly what I'm saying. It makes perfect sense. This is a family business and you have a talent in drawing and I don't see why that can't be adapted to fashion with a bit of help,' Grace said, 'I understand if you need time to think.'

'Yes I think I do.'

'Well of course,' Adriénne said, 'it's important that this is something you want.'

'But I've enjoyed being part of the team in Packing.'

'You don't want to be packing for the rest of your life,' Elizabeth said.

'So you think I should do it, Aunt Elizabeth?'

'Not at all. I'm just saying that you don't want to be packing boxes all your life,' she answered, 'and don't rule out the Granville Estate. Remember you're the heir.'

I laughed. 'Hard to forget really. How's Grandmother doing?'

'She's been a little more responsive,' Elizabeth said, 'but they don't think she'll ever come out of there.'

'It's a bit like my late wife,' Max said. 'She died in one of those places but thankfully she had no idea where she was and nor will your grandmother, I'm sure.'

Joan entered the dining room and stacked the empty plates.

'Lunch was wonderful as always, Joan.' Grace patted her hand. 'Thank you.'

'Coffee?' Joan asked.

'Alice and I will come and help.' I stood up from the table. 'Come on, Alice.'

*

I scooped coffee into the cups and Alice poured in the boiling water.

'Can you believe it?' I asked.

'Believe what?'

'Grace's proposal? It was hard for me to keep a straight face.'

'You don't fancy it then? I reckon you could do it. You could do anything you put your mind to. Even as a little boy you were always clever. I remember Mum and Dad often telling me that I should try and be more like you when I struggled with reading or arithmetic. Mum's answer was that I messed around too much. Mind you, isn't that what we're supposed to do as children?'

'I did play too, you know. I particularly liked playing footie, in fact I still do.'

'Well I think it makes sense for you to work for House of Grace because that's where I'm going to work when I leave school. Not on the design side, of course, I tried that but it wasn't for me. Charlotte's going to train me in Sales. Just think, I could be selling your designs.'

'That's not me. I'd much rather be designing new shops for House of Grace. I'm going to tell her *no*. Architecture is my dream, not fashion.'

'But I thought you said...'

'I know. But speaking to my counsellor has made me realise that I should fulfil my dream. I've decided to sit my exams and get qualified.'

'That's brilliant, George. But a shame too. We'd have made a great team you and me. And we could have carried on the company once Mum and Adriénne were too old.'

'Ha ha. Well that wouldn't have been for a while. Grace is only about thirty-seven and I don't think Adriénne is much older, or is he younger? I'm sorry, Alice, but fashion designing is definitely not for me.'

Alice laughed. 'I understand. Changing the subject but have you noticed how Mum's put on bit of weight? Maybe she's going through the change?'

'What's that?'

'Never mind. Back to you. What are you going to tell them?'

'Well *No* of course. Come on, I'd best go and break the news.' I carried the tray into the dining room and placed the coffees, and juice for Vikki, onto the table. She'd been so good sitting in the highchair for ages. I wished I'd known Beth at that age.

Once we'd sat back down, I said, 'I've made a decision.' I took a deep breath and purposely left them waiting.

'Well…' Grace said eventually.

'I'm sorry, Grace, but the answer is *no*. I can't abide fashion.'

'So you were right, after all,' Grace said to Elizabeth.

Elizabeth looked smug.

'Well it looks like I'm going to have to start recruiting for an apprentice then as I'm going to need some extra help from January.' Grace held her stomach.

'Why?' Alice and I said together.

'You're going to have a new baby brother or sister in March.'

Well that explained the weight gain Alice was talking about. I hugged Grace. 'That's wonderful news. I can't wait. We're going to be a real family again.' I turned to Elizabeth. 'It won't make any difference to us.'

'I'm pleased to hear that.' Elizabeth lifted Vikki from the highchair and placed her down on the floor. She immediately began smacking her mother's legs. 'Mama. Mama.' Elizabeth scooped Vikki up and cuddled her.

I had my family back, an expanded family and a new brother or sister on the way. 'I think you should all move into Granville Hall before the baby's born. Don't you think, Elizabeth?'

'Let's not be too hasty,' she said. 'Mother may recover, come home, and she wouldn't be happy to find Grace there.'

'We know that's not going to happen, darling.' Simon squeezed her hand.

'I'd need to think seriously about that, George. A better solution might be for you to move in here,' Grace said.

'No, I want us all to live together in Granville Hall. If I'm the heir then I should be able to make the decision and if that means Charlotte, Max and Nancy coming to live here too, then so be it.'

'I'll need to check the clauses in the will. It may well be that you only inherit Granville Hall if you stick to your grandfather's wishes,' Simon said.

'Really? And what happens to it if I don't?'

'Then I imagine it will all go to Elizabeth. I'm not saying that's the case but perhaps we should get the solicitor to look into it. You can't inherit before you're twenty-one anyway. As you know it's held in trust.'

Well I'd worry about that later. I wasn't going to let anything spoil today. Life was at last looking up. My counselling was going well and I was starting to discover who I was. I'd sit my exams and work hard to qualify as an architect. The nightmares were easing, although Dr Spencer said that I shouldn't expect things to happen overnight but talking with her had definitely helped. Everything was coming together. I'd reunited with Ben, and Miss Jones, and they were now very much part of my life. Nineteen seventy-two was going to be a year of new beginnings.

Acknowledgements

A special thank you to my friend Maureen Cullen. Not only for her perceptive and thoughtful editing but her continuous support, encouragement and faith in me throughout the *House of Grace* trilogy. And thank you to all my Beta readers.

I'd also like to thank Paul Beeley from the former 'Create Imaginations' for the cover image design and to Colin Ward for stepping up and completing the book cover and formatting.

Finally a big thank you to my husband, children, family and friends for their continued support and faith in me.

The Author

Patricia M Osborne is married with grown-up children and grandchildren. She was born in Liverpool but now lives in West Sussex. In 2019 she graduated with an MA in Creative Writing (University of Brighton).

Patricia writes novels, poetry and short fiction, and has been published in various literary magazines and anthologies. Her first poetry pamphlet 'Taxus Baccata' is to be published by Hedgehog Poetry Press during 2020.

She has a successful blog at Patriciamosbornewriter.com where she features other writers and poets. When Patricia isn't working on her own writing, she enjoys sharing her knowledge, acting as a mentor to fellow writers and working as an online poetry tutor with Writers' Bureau.

The Coal Miner's Son is the second book in the House of Grace trilogy.

Printed in Great Britain
by Amazon

24975148R00189